CASTER

ELSIE CHAPMAN

Scholastic Inc.

Copyright © 2019 by Elsie Chapman

This book was originally published in hardcover by Scholastic Press in 2019.

ISBN 978-1-338-66513-0

1 2020

Printed in the U.S.A.   23
This edition first printing 2020

Book design by Maeve Norton

FOR MY FOLKS. MOM,
HERE'S THE NEXT, LIKE YOU'RE
ALWAYS ASKING. AND DAD,
YOU WOULD HAVE ESPECIALLY
LIKED THIS ONE.

ONE

I take the coins and am compelled to remind my buyer how things can still go wrong. I thought I was over botching my last mind wipe, but apparently not.

"Like I said before, there are no guarantees," I say. The corners of the square coins dig into my hand as I riffle through them, counting the number of marks. Removing time from someone's memory is burning down a single tree in a thick forest—sometimes there's smoke damage to other trees nearby. "Mind wipes are tricky."

The last time, I didn't just wipe out a weekend as requested, but the whole week. Rudy pointed out it had more to do with the nature of the spell than my control. Mostly I believe him, if only because Rudy's not one for trying to make me feel better.

Coral nods. Her name's not really Coral—I never want to know their actual names—but it's what I call her on account of the lipstick she wore on our first meeting, the same shade she's wearing now. "Still, I'm just asking for one specific day to be gone," she says, nervously twirling the ends of her brown hair. "But if you can't do it . . ."

Annoyance flickers across her face even as her eyes stay hopeful.

The conflict comes as no surprise. It's how most of those with leftover magic feel about casters of full magic, unable to decide if they loathe us or envy us. If they need us or hate us. We're dangerous, forever having to hide who we are. Only one thing is certain—they can't do what we can. Full magic.

"Any other caster of full magic will tell you the same," I say. "No guarantees. And if they say otherwise, they're lying." I slide her a cool look, hoping nothing on my face gives away that another caster might be more confident with their magic. How they might've done more than the few mind wipes I have. How I'm actually doing this because I still need to be better.

I hold out my hand, offering back the marks. "But be my guest, if you'd like to spend the time searching for someone else."

She flushes. The network of rumored full magic casters in Lotusland is thin—holes and dead ends—and it took her months to find me, a caster willing to cast for marks. And needing marks the way I do, I let myself be found.

Still uncertain, Coral picks at her nail. She's careful to work around the material painted onto the tip. It's a trend, embedding bits of spell starters right onto your nails so you only have to curl your fingers into your palm to cast magic. The downside is that a lot of starters need to be replenished, so you're always repainting. Like most casters of any magic, I just use a basic starter bag. Blending in is good.

I do my best to hide how nervous I am as doubt continues to cloud her expression. She takes in my age—I'm sixteen, not exactly a responsible adult—my worn clothing that says I might just be trying to hustle her, and then my casting arm. Like there are signs in the limb and its palm that would give away my true control over magic.

I hope she can't tell I'm still working on perfecting that control, the consequences of which could mean disaster for me or the fragile ecosystem around us.

Finally Coral waves her hand, exasperated. "I've paid, so whatever—let's just get on with it. I have a meeting in a few minutes and need to get back to my office." She touches one of her starter-embedded nails to her palm and her hair smooths itself back, though we are indoors and there is no wind. It's leftover magic, weak enough to exact no cost on its caster.

I shove the marks into the pocket of my jeans and glance around the washroom.

We agreed to meet here secretly, this room of silver-papered walls and warm mahogany doors and ceramic-framed mirrors. We're in one of the dozens of high-rise office buildings that make up the Tower Sector of the city, and for a second my skin goes clammy.

It was not even a year ago that Shire fell from one of these buildings—maybe it was even *this* building, I don't know. It was a job gone beyond wrong—her casting full magic.

The memory of our last time speaking, the raised voices. The disagreement. I would mind wipe myself of that argument, if I wasn't too scared of losing more of Shire. She died too young, and I don't have memories to spare.

Coral clears her throat. "What's the worst that can happen again?"

I check the washroom stalls once more, though they're just as empty as they've been since I got here. "We've already covered that."

"Humor me. This isn't an easy decision."

"Fine," I say.

"I lose a lot more time than a day, right?"

"Possibly."

"It doesn't work at all?"

"Maybe."

She swallows, curls in her pinky, and hastily casts another left-over spell. The shoulders of her suit jacket neaten themselves. "I forget everything."

"Highly unlikely." Even I couldn't do that, especially not by accident. A caster would have to have zero control over their full magic for that to happen. Brand-new to their power, caught completely unaware. I think back to the day I found out I wasn't a typical caster of leftover magic, and repress a shudder.

I step into one of the stalls and she follows me. I lock the door and then lean back against it, hoping it all goes well. I'm not worried about someone interfering. Casting full magic hurts. There's always a price to pay, sometimes forever, so I'd prefer to be out of sight for this.

Leftover magic requires a starter, just like the ones embedded in Coral's nails. And it's cast by placing the starter in the palm of the casting arm.

But for *full* magic, we cast with a spell star, tracing the shape in the palm. The rule is that the more points to a star, the more magic is pulled from the earth. It's why casting real magic is illegal now. The pain that follows is a limitation, too—draw a star with too many points and you could be dead before the spell's even run out.

A mind wipe the way Coral wants it is a seven-pointed star. That's the amount of magic I'm going to need.

I *could* chance six points—I'm only wiping one day. But six usually means a nosebleed for me, and it'd be awkward to move across a crowded lunchtime lobby while bleeding from my face. Seven will give me a bad headache that I usually like to sleep off when I can. Except it's the middle of the day and my parents already think I'll be out until late, working at a job that has nothing to do with casting full magic. A job I don't actually have.

Which is why I keep a jar of healing meds in my starter bag. They're not a surefire fix, and they won't work on a bloody nose, but they should help with a casting migraine. I mean to head to Rudy's from here anyway—if I'm really still hurting, there's no better place to be than his apothecary.

If he were here, he'd remind me to be careful. To not draw any extra attention to myself. To never forget that secrecy is imperative when casting is illegal.

Shire would tell me the same. She'd remind me of Scouts and their department within the police dedicated to hunting us down. Some of those Scouts are casters just like me. But full magic never guarantees loyalty, and they've turned because of pay, or because they worry about the earth caving in while they still stand on it, or simply because they believe it's the right thing to do.

But Shire is dead. She faced the pain of casting too much magic and died.

I push back harder against the stall door, needing it to keep feeling steady. I pull out a green leaf from the starter bag I wear slung over my shoulder.

"Last chance," I say to Coral.

She's sitting on the closed lid of the toilet. Her eyes are huge. There's fear in them now, crowding out need and envy and hate. The look in them says despite her being here, it's right that my kind of magic is now banished, that casters like me no longer have a place in this world.

She exhales. "I'm in."

"Then play out the day in your head for me to find." I draw a seven-pointed star on my palm with my finger, lay down the leaf in the center, and cast.

TWO

The floor beneath me rumbles just the slightest. My feet grow hot. The heat climbs up my legs and torso until it's pooling in my hands, making them feel heavy and languid. I'd almost expect to go up in flames if I were new to how full magic works. The sensation's still odd, though, so much heat without pain.

I've learned that the pain comes later.

It's said that earth's magic doesn't have a physical form, but even so it fills my veins. Full magic glows inside, a red that's brighter and hotter than any blood, desperate for escape. A thin buzz fills my ears. My heartbeat collects in my throat, thick and pounding.

It's like stoking a fire, Shire once said to me, a conversation I go back to again and again. *The magic you draw is its fuel, but* you *control how high you want its flames, Aza. What you want the fire to burn. Where you want it to go.*

I paint a picture of my power—this strange red amorphous *thing*, real and not real, wonderful yet terrible—in my mind. At the same time, I make sure to meet Coral's eyes, the connection necessary for me to work a spell on her mind.

I drive—*stoke*—my magic forward. It enters her head as fire, red and pointed. There's a wind behind it, pushing the flames of that magic straight along its intended path. The fire seeps through the bone of her skull and then deep into her brain, where it's soft and vulnerable. Malleable. It curls into the recesses of her living mind, into its tiny hills and valleys that are full of memories and stories and *time*, all of them shaped like trees. One tree sticks out above the rest. It's *that* day, the reason why I'm casting banned magic in a bathroom stall. I will the red fire that is my power toward the tree and set it alight. A final black swirl of smoke and my job is done.

The skin of my hand burns. Full magic might have no real form, but it sits in my palm anyway, alive as a flame.

Pain shoots through my head. If not for the door I'm still leaning against, I'd be stumbling back with the intensity of it. Waves of nausea come, and I barely keep from retching. The fire that lit up my skin cools and disappears.

I drop the leaf. Used up now, it's gone all autumn on me, brown and crisp. It shatters into dust as it hits the bathroom floor.

"Did it work?" Coral licks her lips. "How do I know if it worked?"

"It worked," I whisper. Hammers are alive in my brain, and they're all going at once. I drag a shaking hand across my face. Cold sweat, nerves, deep relief, and sickness—they all wash over me.

"You can't know that for sure."

"I know because you're asking."

"How do I know if you accidentally wiped out too much?"

"It went as well as it could, trust me." I think of the last job and how it *didn't* go so well and shiver. "Anyway, does it matter? It's too late now."

I unlock the door of the stall and stagger out, not wanting any more questions, not caring if anyone else has come into the wash-room. I pull out the tiny jar of healing meds and frown when I see that there's only one left.

I found it in Shire's room, a jar clearly from Rudy's apothecary, and kept it for myself. I knew I was going to take over for Shire, and that casting magic would hurt—being able to recharge faster just meant I could fit in more jobs. I also figured out pretty quickly that Rudy must have used full magic to make the pills. Even the times they only half work, it's still better than what nonmagic medication can do.

I'll have to get more from Rudy today. I wash down the pill with water from the tap and drop the empty jar back into my bag.

"I can cast you better," Coral says. Her voice comes way too close to my ear, and I wince. "A simple skin spell for pain. I can cast those, too, just like you."

I nearly laugh, but I'm still afraid of throwing up. Her weak magic *can* cast skin spells. She can also cast bone spells, and blood, and breath ones. Just like me, but so much *less*, only able to ease a sore muscle instead of erasing someone's mind. To get rid of an ache in a bone, not clear it of disease; to form a tiny scab, not knit skin back together; to help fill a lung, not crush it.

"Won't work," I whisper. "Leftover magic isn't strong enough."

I don't tell her that pain from casting is just one way we're affected. How for some full magic casters, all their damage *comes back*. And it comes back all at once, like being stampeded over. Becoming an Ivor—the condition goes by the name of the first caster in history known for it—can happen anytime after casting full magic. Maybe weeks later, or months, or years. And for Ivors, the change is forever, their magic as good as gone, their bodies no longer able to handle even one more casting. If they're lucky, it's only on the inside that they're broken. If not, it's never too long before Scouts find them and take away their magic. Before they lock them up and display them as warnings to other full magic casters.

I used to worry about ending up an Ivor. But I don't worry about it as much anymore. I actually think most full magic casters don't. I think we worry way more about accidentally destroying a part of the world. I think we worry about the smog we're breathing in all the time, about earth being too weak to sustain the magic that we hold.

"Well, then why can't you just cast yourself better?" Coral sounds nearly as put out as she does concerned—*I have a meeting, and it's very important that I be on time.* "Wouldn't that be faster than any medication?"

I shut my eyes against the bright lighting of the room. Already the hammers are quieting down a bit. But it can't hurt to keep Coral away from wondering about such effective pills, away from wondering about who might make them and how.

"Casting another spell at this point would only mean more pain." I have to recover enough first, or the effect compounds. And then I'd be in serious trouble.

"Right. That makes sense." Then I hear her breath catch.

I open my eyes, already knowing what I'll see. The shock in that single caught breath gives it away.

A long crack splits across the tiled washroom floor, as thin as string but impossible to ignore. It's as though the opposite sides of the room are tectonic plates and there's been a shift from a quake.

This quake is because I pulled full magic from the ground.

The earth isn't too happy about it.

"So it's all true." There's disgust in Coral's voice. "It's *not* just enough that *you* hurt while casting. You have to hurt *us*, too."

"Oh, please." I manage a sneer even as the crack slowly begins to widen. "*You* came to *me*, asking for full magic. You knew the cost. You know how magic and this world work."

"But I've never seen it for myself before. It's always just been the Scouts warning us about full magic." She gazes down at the crack, then back at me, her eyes full of disdain. "How we're never going to be really safe until all casters like you are locked up or your magic is taken away. Books and the news, reminding us how it's full magic that ruined the air and oceans, so that the earth had to turn it against you."

I clench my hands over my starter bag. It was once Shire's. I struggle to think of what she might say to this weakling of magic. Shire, who was always nicer and better than me, with her discipline, her views, her ideas—even our parents think so.

But my mind stays blank even while it continues to pound. Because nothing Coral's said is untrue. I can blame her for hiring me and giving me a reason to cast—but it doesn't change that *I'm still casting*. I'm still slowly breaking apart small bits of the world, spell by spell. Shire did the same, and I guess that's why her words don't come to me, either.

I move toward the washroom door, staring at Coral as I go. "Don't forget, one word of this and Scouts will be on you just as fast as they will be on me. They might not do to you what they'll do to me, but they'll definitely haul you in anyway." It's not just the casters of full magic that are banned but full magic itself. Whether it's cast or bought is beside the point. Our power can be the end of everything.

Coral's gone pale. "I promise."

"Also, you might want to get out of here before the fire department comes to inspect. The crack's only getting wider and once Scouts get word, they'll have questions for anyone caught in the area."

I pull my smog mask from my back pocket and tug it on over my nose and mouth. With my stomach still rolling and my tongue as bitter as ash, I push the door open and step out of the washroom. I cross the lobby, and just before I step outside, I yank the lever for the fire alarm.

I hit the street running, ignoring how my head still hurts. The distant ringing of the office building's fire alarm fades behind me, and I think about what I need to do next.

Namely, bug Rudy for more about magic.

I want to be as good as Shire was. No, better, because I don't want to die casting magic for marks. And he was her instructor, teaching her to be good enough with her magic that she made the marks to keep our family's business going. Now that's on me.

Never mind that Rudy would rather be left alone, saying that he wants to focus on running his apothecary. Or that he says my personality is the very opposite of Shire's, that he actually liked having her around. Or that when I beg him to show me new magic,

I always somehow just end up helping out around the shop instead. I've stocked shelves, pestle and mortared, filled jars, plus other way more mundane chores I don't even have to do at the teahouse anymore—and I still can't figure out how Rudy gets me to work for him when it's supposed to be the other way around.

He owes *me*.

I also still haven't decided if I even like him, considering the circumstances.

He was there when Shire died. He was the one unable to save her. He was the one to make her think she could use the amount of power that killed her.

Also, I know of no other caster of full magic. There's no one else but Rudy Shen.

His apothecary is in the Tobacco Sector, which lies west of Tower, two sectors over. It's summer, but Lotusland summers are still cold and full of rain, seeing that we hug the Pacifik on the whole west side. Breezes that blow off its surface hit you in the face with damp and salt, and you remember all over again how it's the coldest ocean in the world.

Normally I walk everywhere because I like being able to choose where I go as much as I can. I like imagining I can disappear if I feel like it, for my face to blend into the myriads of shades of skin— gold like mine, but also white, black, brown—that are the people of Lotusland.

But I'm not in the mood for crowds today, or for the rain that's starting to fall. Not for the gray air that never fully leaves, either, so that half the city wears smog masks that cover their noses and mouths while outside. And my head still hurts a bit. My rider's pass still has enough marks on it for a final trip, so I decide to chance the train and hop on a westbound one.

The city can never keep up with system repairs, meaning there are usually lots of detours and stoppages around broken-up asphalt and parts of the track undergoing construction. Or the passenger cars just die on you because the city hasn't upgraded them for years, and you end up somewhere you don't want to be. Or someone has cast real magic nearby, and the earth deflates a bit more.

I only have to glance out the windows to hear Coral's words all over again.

The air and oceans and forests, ruined because of casters like me. No more blues and greens but smog and rust and dull gray concrete. All true. Lakes and rivers carry mutant fish that ate up all the normal fish, and wildfires keep burning up forests all over the world because of freak weather. Every time a caster uses full magic, we are cracking open the earth that much more.

We're considered earth's biggest threat.

Still, real magic has been dying out more and more with each generation. Five hundred years ago, every person alive could heal or mind wipe. Now we're just a fraction.

The train motors along, and we're still in the Government Sector when the engine gives out and an announcement comes on, telling us to get off and catch a different westbound train. But the rain's stopped now, as well as my headache, so I decide to walk the rest of the way over. I know this part of the city well, since it borders the Tea Sector, which is home. And the Tobacco Sector is no more than ten blocks away, then Rudy's shop another five more heading south.

I've just reached the outer edge of Tea when I spot him. Half a block away, standing on the corner. He's wearing one of his perpetual black suits and bright white sneakers, a combination I see now in my nightmares.

Jihen.

THREE

I can tell by the way he's waiting that he spotted me first.

I freeze, my heartbeat a dull thud in my ears, debating for a handful of wild, desperate seconds if I can run fast enough to escape for another day. Or if I've recovered enough yet from the effects of casting the mind wipe to safely cast more magic to escape that way.

It'd be a temporary reprieve, though—anyone who lives in the Tea Sector is never entirely free of Jihen and the rest of his gang. Jihen works for Saint Willow, and it's Saint Willow who runs the area. It's been like this since the sectors were first formed.

The only person who really owns property in Tea is Saint Willow—the rest of us just pay to stay here. The world might call it "rent," but people in the sectors know it as paying *honor* marks. If not for his protection, other gangs would move in, and then where would it all be? Saint Willow promises we don't want to know. The gangs have always had their own say about how the sectors are run, and cops who sometimes forget this end up disappearing as a reminder.

As though Jihen can read my frozen mind about trying to slip away, he moves first, closing the gap between us as quick as the oiled snake I know him to be.

"Hello, Aza," he says, smiling greasily. More than half of Tea's population is Chinese, and this includes Jihen, and so his skin is as gold as mine. He's also nearly as short as I am, but thick as a barrel through the middle.

Not that his heft matters either way. His being a distant cousin of Saint Willow's is all that's needed to give him power. It's why he got assigned the job of watching the lagging Wu family. Of dogging me to make sure we pay up as everyone else in Tea has to.

Without the marks Shire was bringing in, our honor debt is only growing, day by day.

"Jihen," I say.

"You have our marks?" He pats at his waxed black hair. The movement lifts his jacket. I can't miss his knife, tucked into his side. It's mostly for show—Saint Willow usually deals with problems more creatively—but the threat remains.

"I just paid you a bunch of marks two days ago." Jihen's what we call a squeezer, the person Saint Willow employs to chase down debts still owed to him.

"Two days ago was two days ago. Your family's debt continues to grow. Must we go through this each time we meet?"

"We wouldn't meet so much if you gave me room to work."

Jihen smiles. "Just as you must work, so must I."

"Running a teahouse is work—stealing from its profits is just robbery."

"Yet both are enterprises, and enterprises have deadlines. Your family's year is nearly up, Aza."

Stories in the sector are that Saint Willow has a principle about money owed—that a year is all he chooses to tolerate. He even has a calendar to mark down the day. One year. That's when he gets creative about getting him what is owed, if creativity means choosing between methods of torture.

"I have one more week," I say defiantly.

We managed eight months of stalling after Shire died. She was steady in paying Wu Teas's honor marks through her casting secretly for years before her death. Then it was two months of Jihen being assigned to come around the tea shop, "observing" the business until we couldn't put off paying any longer. Finally, I lied. To keep him away from my parents and the teahouse, I told him he was wasting his time because *I* was the one in charge of my family's finances.

He's been shadowing me ever since. Two months now.

"It's been awhile since I've said hello to your fou-mou." His voice goes silky over the Chinese word for parents. "Perhaps I need to pay a visit to your mama and baba at the teahouse, to stay and nem cha."

The marks I made from the mind wipe are still in my pocket. I'll have to give them over because the mention of Jihen dropping by for tea makes any other choice futile. But anger flows anyway, hot and thick in my chest. I spin on my heel, just needing a second to reclaim my own space.

His hand whips out and grasps my arm, stopping me. "Aza, *beauty*"—Jihen's still smiling and it makes my skin prickle with cold—"let's not do anything drastic. Saint Willow won't be pleased."

His calling me *beauty* is a joke. Shire was the pretty one. She and I had the same bones beneath because we're sisters, but it's like a great sculptor spent extra time polishing her face while I never got fully finished. She dressed in colorful and showy things, but it wouldn't have mattered if they'd been as drab as the sky—if they'd all been as pink as the scar on her cheek—because she looked the way she did.

I try to turn again, but Jihen's grip is still firm on my arm. "I'll pay you, all right?" I say to him. "Just . . . not right here."

"Where are we going?"

I start walking as an answer, heading deeper into Tea while still keeping away from the teahouse. I *want* to head toward the Tobacco Sector, but I don't want him to start thinking too hard about where else in the city I go. Tea is safe because it's what he expects. He already knows to look for me around home, always somewhere nearby, waiting and following and making sure I pay whatever I have on me.

This can't go on much longer.

I have to think of something to save us.

Because the truth looms, and it comes at me in stabs:

The growing shadow of Saint Willow. The jobs where my magic felt like a stranger's. Advice Rudy doles out like it hurts him to talk. The faces of my parents, miserable because our family legacy now rests entirely on me.

Jihen sighs deeply. His fingers squeeze my arm as we walk. We're still blocks from the teahouse, but the whole area smells deeply of tea anyway. Wu Teas is just one of dozens of teahouses in the sector, hence the sector's name. Housing and supply businesses and restaurants fill the spaces in between, but one sniff and there's no doubt which part of Lotusland you're in.

"This whole sector has sure gone downhill, that's for sure," Jihen says conversationally. Like we're close to friends. "This economy has gone to si, been that way for decades now. It's too bad Wu Teas has gone down right along with it."

"No other teahouse is any different. Demand's down, while supply remains."

"Good thing you are able to find work. Tea might never be needed the way you Wus would like it to be, but there's always going to be a need for teachers. Leftover magic can only do so much."

"Tutor, not teacher," I mutter, fighting a grim temptation to cast full magic on Jihen as I yank a leaf from a boxwood hedge along the sidewalk. Starters work on the things they create, so a leaf works on paper, fabric, *skin*—because just as trees are of the earth, casters are of the earth, too. And I want him to stop talking, even if it would only last for a moment, and even if most skin spells could never pass for leftover magic.

Being a tutor is the lie I had to tell Jihen to cover for my not being at the teahouse all day long and somehow still making marks. Shire was able to hide the marks she made from magic by claiming they were a part of the shop's profits. And Jihen hadn't been watching her. Saint Willow hadn't needed to send anyone then. Honor marks from Wu Teas were still coming in as scheduled.

"Tutor, not teacher, my mistake," he says. "Math?"

I drop the leaf. "A bit of everything," I lie again.

"See, I watch you, Aza. I stay in Tea because I know you'll always have to come back. But I see you come and go at all times, all over the city, in all the sectors. I know you're getting jobs. I know you're making marks. My job, on behalf of Saint Willow, is to get those marks into our hands more regularly, and in larger amounts."

"I can't control who decides to hire me."

He plucks a plum from a tree as we pass. It's unripe, as green as a lime. He casts leftover magic, huffing a warm breath into his palm.

The plum turns a deep purple.

There's another story that goes around the sector having to do with Saint Willow, and it's one about magic. How the gang leader might have marks and power and everyone's fear, but he'll never have what he wants most, which is full magic.

The whispers say that over the years he's tried to keep full magic casters under his employ, but is so overly demanding with their casting that they never last. Some have died, some quit, and some have even wiped themselves from Saint Willow's mind, if you believe the rumors.

If Saint Willow had any clue he had a caster of full magic already squirming right beneath his thumb, I bet I'd be even more chained to him than I already am.

Jihen bites into the ripened plum. "I still remember the stories our grandparents would tell us about Wu Teas. Stories their grandparents told *them*. How emperors and empresses from overseas served your ancestors' teas to their royal guests. How they would pay with bars of gold and nuggets of silver—all for your family's *tea*."

"Don't forget about castles and temples," I add, my voice stiff as I keep walking. "They stocked our blends, too."

"Now look at you Wus, with your emperors and empresses and fancy gilded palaces, castles, and temples all long gone. Swallowed up by quakes, drowned out by floods. Then other teahouses moving in, so you have to lower your prices more and more. Your family, begging for diners and shops to carry a blend or two, for handfuls of marks instead of armfuls of riches." He sighs again, a parody of sympathy for my family's troubles. "Ah, business is so mah-fung, no?"

I run my finger along a shop windowsill and sweep the small shard of broken ceramic into my palm before Jihen notices. Ceramic starter. Good for a bone spell. Rage is a hot fist in my chest as I imagine all the horrific full magic spells I could cast on him, ones I could never do without giving my secret away.

Each of his limbs twisted into the shape of a pretzel.

Bones turned to putty inside his body.

His skull turned inside out.

"The marks, Aza," Jihen says now, tucking the plum pit into his chest pocket. I've seen him keep other starters there, ones like rocks and leaves, dirt pellets and water capsules. My guess is that carrying a weapon on his side leaves little room for a starter bag. His fingers squeeze my arm until it hurts. "Hand them over."

I tell myself I'm not scared.

The truth is, Saint Willow and I have actually entered into a strange kind of partnership. Deep down, he doesn't *really* want to see Wu Teas gone—our teas might not be served to royalty anymore, but visitors to Tea still make a point of coming to his sector just for our teahouse.

Another family could take us over, but then it would not be Wu Teas.

And as for me, Saint Willow knows I would do almost anything to save my family's legacy, business, and home, and milking desperation is always more profitable than a family that has given up.

"Your boss still requiring everyone in the sector to pay honor marks isn't helping anyone's business," I say to Jihen, slowing down. We're less than three blocks from the teahouse now, from our apartment that makes up its rear, and I don't want to bring Jihen any closer to my parents.

"Saint Willow is running a business, too," he says. "A business that has even deeper roots here in Lotusland than Wu Teas. Our family's marks are why your family—why *all* the families running businesses here—got the chance to make marks of their own. Aza, beauty—"

"Don't call me that."

"—*you owe us.*"

His words are an echo of my own, the way I think about Rudy, and I tug at my arm to get away, sickened that I could have anything in common with a man like Saint Willow.

I dig out coins from my pocket and thrust out my hand. "This is all that I have."

Finally my arm is free as he lets go to take the marks. He counts, once, twice. "You really want me to go back to Saint Willow with this?" Fury turns him red. "Have you forgotten I can walk into your family's teahouse anytime I want? I don't need to ask."

I look away. "Please don't. I'll have more tomorrow."

"Any family would be happy to live in your apartment. To be given a teahouse with a nice legacy to run. It doesn't have to be yours, Aza. Not at all."

Dread's a lump in my throat as I try to stay convinced it's nothing but talk. I push the faces of my parents out of my head. "I *said* I'll pay you tomorrow."

Now he leans close, his smile overly kind, and whiffs of tea and hair wax and aftershave cloud my nose.

"You Wus were so much better at paying when your sister was alive," Jihen says softly. "On time, in full amounts. It was all so pleasant. Your sister, so much better than *you* at keeping the teahouse going. If only she were still alive, then maybe your family wouldn't be in such trouble."

I shove my hands into my pockets to find some kind of warmth, suddenly cold all over despite the midday sun. Inside the pocket where I kept the marks, my fingers hit something sharp. The corner of a mark I missed.

"Such a sad accident, falling from a balcony the way she did," Jihen says. "Twenty stories, wasn't it?"

I yank out the mark and cast. Copper coin for a copper starter. Good for a bone spell, even if it has to be a minor one. Good for painless leftover magic, because no one's supposed to know what kind of caster I really am.

I toss the mark at Jihen—I almost want to keep it; rigid starters can be used again, and it's a *mark*; but there's something about hurling it at his head that just feels so good—and run.

"Aza, I'm not done yet! Get over—!"

A yell as my magic makes his knee give out and he topples to the pavement.

FOUR

I get within sight of Shen Apothecary, keeping up running at first before letting myself slow to a half-rushed walk. My hair and clothes and even my skin smell like smoke by the time I hit the corner of his block. The Tobacco Sector is really a mix of scents—from ash to tobacco to moss—but put together the overwhelming one is simply smoke. Only having the breezy Pacifik as its west side border does anything to make a difference. And each time I leave here for home in Tea, I take the roundabout way. I head west until I hit the shore, hoping the spray from the salty ocean will wash away the smoke scent. My parents haven't forgotten where Rudy works.

I'm nearing the entrance to the apothecary when I notice the guy in a baseball cap across the street. I notice him because of two reasons.

One is, he's trying so hard to not be obvious how he's scoping out a place that he's nothing *but* obvious. He's standing near the curb, skin white beneath the cap, checking his phone every fifteen seconds or so, like he's expecting someone and they're late. But in between checking his phone, he lifts his head and stares into the front window of Rudy's shop.

This makes something in my stomach flutter, and I slow down, unsure of what to think.

The second reason I notice Baseball Cap is because he's a cop.

He thinks the silver armband is hidden beneath his sleeve, but he's oblivious about the breeze.

This makes my mouth go dry.

Why would a cop be watching Rudy's place? Sure, businesses in the Tobacco Sector have been known to be fronts, putting up a facade to sell all kinds of illegal items out their back doors.

But Rudy's legit, always sure to renew his licenses on time. And his formulas—his nonmagic ones, that is, the ones that stand in for the full magic formulas he actually sells—all meet grade. He's careful mostly because he's a full magic caster and he knows how to avoid getting noticed by suits of any kind. He knows how to get around the law.

Like with Shire—Rudy was the one who called in her death. He knew a sleazy medical examiner willing to be bribed to falsify a medical report that made sure not to include anything about her casting magic—only reporting her death as due to an accidental high fall.

Rudy still hasn't told me which spell—or spells—she'd been attempting to cast from up there. I still don't know the actual physical reason why she died. I don't know how much pain she must have been in, or if she died before it could even fully hit her.

Why were you even there, Rudy? She always sold magic alone. It was the middle of the night! Who would buy magic in the middle of the night? On top of a building?

Fresh anger builds in my throat, while a huge wave of missing my sister brings tears to the backs of my eyes. Rudy has no right to keep any of this from me. And Shire—she should have known better.

Shire, why would you try casting more magic than you could control? Why would you chance something like that when I was always right there, wanting to help?

Something else hits me then, and it twists my stomach into a huge knot.

The year anniversary of Shire's death is nearly here. If that guy is a cop and he's here to ask Rudy about Shire, how long before that cop's coming to my parents to talk to *them*? Cops hate having a case on their books for more than a year, and the pressure goes up to solve them. Many innocents have gone down just so some Scout can clear an unsolved case.

How much would my parents be forced to bend before they'd break and give away the truth about what Shire was doing? How long before they give away *me* and my full magic?

My heart's thudding hard as I force myself to walk past Baseball Cap's line of vision and into the shop.

Inside, I lean back against a wall, taking off my smog mask and folding it back into my pocket. I breathe deep to calm down so I can tell Rudy about the cop without freaking out. I glance around, searching for him.

It's the middle of the afternoon on a weekday, and the apothecary has just a few customers. Here the smoke scent of the sector lifts completely and another deep breath brings ginseng and eucalyptus to my nose, cinnamon and mint and honey. Shining amber bottles line floor-to-ceiling shelves. The air is tinged with a haze, the perpetual vapors and mists from Rudy's mixing and concocting that never seem to dissipate entirely. The place reminds of another time, an easier and mellower era in the past—maybe it's a time when full magic and casters like Rudy and me weren't quite so feared.

As a person who likes helping to heal people, he's not the greatest at separating his full magic from his store stock. Even hurting from making the good stuff doesn't stop him. His effective medications are definitely why his shop isn't wanting for customers. They're why his customers are so loyal to a lot of his remedies.

I'd tell him he should be more careful, but Rudy wouldn't listen to me. Only Shire being gone keeps him from barring me from his apothecary altogether. I've made a point to come in at random times so he can never figure out how to avoid me.

But I'll tell him about the cop outside. Because now that I'm here seeing his customers, maybe it's *not* that surprising that the cop is watching Rudy. All these years he's run this apothecary, doctoring up some of his medications with full magic and selling them as typical ones—maybe he's finally caught.

I wait for him to finish serving the last customer at the counter and then walk up.

"Rudy, there's something I have to—"

He cuts me off with a tired, heavy sigh, not looking up from a pad of paper he's scribbling on. He's older, in his forties, maybe even in his fifties. His black hair is going gray, and all his clothing always seems a size too big. His starter bag is slung around his waist, and the words START ME UP! are printed across it.

"Aza, I'm busy. Can we do this another time?"

I fight back a spurt of irritation. "No, because there's a cop outside and he's watching the shop."

Rudy stops scribbling and looks up sharply at me. "What did you say?"

He shoves his white-framed glasses higher on his nose. He's nearsighted but has never used his magic to fix the condition. Instead he likes to collect different-style frames, the way some people collect purses or shoes. From behind the glasses his gaze is startled, shaken.

I only really know Rudy as brusque, and reluctant, and borderline rude. Except for that one terrible night when he was in tears.

Closer up gives away how his eyes are bloodshot, how the bags directly underneath them are purple. His skin is more sallow than gold, and his cheeks seem more gaunt than normal. Even his hair seems grayer than the last time I saw him. I glance again at his baggy clothing—maybe I'm misremembering about it always being too big. Maybe he's been losing weight or something.

I wonder if he's having problems eating, or sleeping. I wonder if guilt can pervade even dreams so that you can be *afraid* to sleep. I wonder why I feel bad about it instead of satisfied.

I lean in. "I said, there's a cop outside and he's—"

He moves out from behind the counter and goes to peer out the window. I follow and look over his shoulder. The cop's still out there, his face turned right in our direction.

Rudy steps back, deeper into the shadows of the apothecary. "No, you're wrong. It's a cop, but he's watching the place next door."

My thoughts scramble to recall what shop is next door, but nothing comes.

I squint out the window again. "What do you mean? He's staring right over here."

"It might be hard to tell, but it's definitely next door." Rudy's voice sounds wrong—too stiff. Careful.

"What's next door?"

"It's a snuff place, but they've already been caught selling opium and pipes and stuff. The cops are probably just waiting for one more incident in order to close them down for good."

Before I can say anything to that, Rudy heads off toward one of the shop shelves and begins to rearrange tins and bottles.

I can't deny I now doubt what I saw out there, but I'm still annoyed as I follow him over. Because I'm a bit embarrassed about jumping to conclusions so fast. Because it's always so easy for him to dismiss me over nearly everything, exactly the way he just did. Because I hate how I always have to *follow* him. How even if he's using me as much as I'm using him—I'm picking his brain and he's assuaging his guilt—he never forgets to remind me just how much I still have to learn.

Sometimes I think it's worth trying to break down his defenses. How if I could make him like me the way he liked Shire, I'd learn to trust him the way she did, too.

But I never think it for long. I see him and I think of Shire dying and all the questions he hasn't actually answered. I see him and I think of my parents and how their deep grief keeps them from even really wanting to know. All that matters to them is that the daughter who's left is the one who's barely been any help at all.

"Okay, so you know why I'm here," I say to Rudy when I walk up to him.

Like before, he's too busy to look away from his work. "Thanks for telling me about the cop. I'm glad you were wrong, but it was still good to know."

I glare at him hard enough that the side of his face must be burning. "You know that's not the only reason why."

He moves glass amber bottles around on the shelf, making them clink against one another. I have no clue how he's trying to organize them. It all seems very haphazard when normally he's practically berating me to be nothing but exact whenever I'm doing some kind of chore around here. *Powder up this package of roots, will you? But make sure you use the mortar and pestle just this way with your wrist, each and every time. Otherwise the grind will be too coarse and you'll only have to do it over again.*

"Well, I think I've pretty much helped you out as much as I can, Aza," he says now, still only looking at the bottles and sliding them around and not bothering to face me. "I don't know what else I can tell you."

"You were Shire's instructor for nearly eight years!"

I can't make myself stop. Jihen, Saint Willow, my parents' despair whenever they look at me, the once-majestic legacy of a family business now needing rescue—I feel them all, breathing down my neck. And here's Rudy, trying to run away from me when he's my last hope. "Eight years! But I come here for not even one and *it's supposed to be enough*? You're not going to get rid of me that easily, okay? I—"

Rudy clamps his hand over my mouth so I can't say anything else. *You owe me you owe me you should have died instead of Shire* plays out silently in my head as he drags me behind the counter and into the shop's supply room.

He slams the door shut behind us. I'm expecting him to be furious, but instead he just looks even more tired, and much older than I know he is. A flicker of worry comes, of shame that I'm here when he just wants to be left in peace. To maybe get over Shire his own way, on his own, without her sister reminding him every day how he messed up.

But I stamp out those feelings and keep glaring at him. I'm too desperate for sympathy. Sympathy doesn't pay.

"Aza, you need to be more careful. You can't just be out there saying stuff like—"

"I wouldn't, if you'd just help me."

"I *have* helped," he snaps. He shoves his glasses up. "What else do you want from me?"

"Answers." Medicinal smells waft out from the rows of bottles and stacks of tins that fill the shelves lining the room.

"I've answered all I can."

"So how have you helped me, exactly? You've had me be your shop helper is what you've been doing. Shelving ointments, bottling tonics—how does any of that help me learn how to control magic?"

"You can cast now, can't you?"

"That's not the same thing as learning control."

He throws up his arms. "Then don't cast at all, I don't know. Make marks some other way. Go get a job at a Guz-n-Go. I know the pay is crap, but you can't be charging that much for spells yet anyway, given how recently you started."

I laugh and it's shrill. "I can't believe she liked working with you."

"No one's making you stay."

Shire makes me stay. Saint Willow and *his* family legacy make me stay. *Magic* makes me stay.

Rudy rubs his face and swears. "Look, you come here un-announced whenever you feel like it and demand advice, answers. And I'm here working, Aza, at this shop that is supposed to be just any other shop in the city. I'm doing my best to pretend I'm leftover magic because that's what we have to do."

"Then pretend. Why does that mean you can't help me?"

"Because sometimes I get *tired* of full magic, all right? Sometimes I even hate it, the way it controls you if you don't control it. And maybe I want to quit while I'm ahead of the game and not end up an Ivor, waking up with my body completely twisted up inside my skin and maybe even getting caged and put up for display by a Scout because of it."

I shake my head, surprised. "Really? You're scared of going Ivor? You're probably more likely to get struck by light—"

"So you coming here, reminding me all the time how we have to live—you're not making it any easier, that's all."

"I guess Shire being gone doesn't make it easier, either. Since casting full magic is what killed her. Since *you're* the one who taught her." Then my voice hitches and I don't know who's more surprised, Rudy or me. My eyes get hot. The rows of glass and tins all shimmer and waver. "Once I know I can beat the spell that she couldn't, I promise I'll leave you alone, all right? And you—you should *want* to teach me that, don't you think?"

Rudy's gone still. Like my words have frozen him. Finally, he rubs his face again. He cleans his glasses using the front of his shirt. His eyes are more bloodshot than ever, and I can't tell if it's him just being exhausted for whatever reason or because his eyes sting like mine still do.

He puts his glasses back on and points to a row of boxes on a low shelf. "Those need to be unpacked and sorted and then repacked."

I stiffen as he heads toward the door that takes him back into the apothecary. "Are you kidding me?"

"Aza." Rudy stops at the door. "One more thing before you start yelling."

I'm almost numb. Everything I just said and it's like he didn't hear me at all. Panic wells while a crushing kind of defeat leaves me hollow. All I can do is look at him.

"Stop overthinking it. You complaining that I'm just having you help out around the shop instead of teaching you how to control your magic? Shire used to say the same thing—before she finally understood."

FIVE

I take down all the boxes and line them up on the floor. Inside each is a jumbled mix of supplies—more bottles and tins, droppers and vials. There are packages of dried flower buds and rhubarb roots and tiny glass jars full of clear syrups.

I sit down and stare at the mess in front of me, my thoughts racing. I'm still hollow inside from the idea of defeat . . . but not so much anymore.

So Shire trained just this way, too—organizing and sorting, measuring and pouring—and I never had a clue. I always just assumed she practiced by casting real magic. How she learned to deal with the pain and then recover before doing it again.

I can blame my parents for making it part of their deal, agreeing to let Shire cast magic for marks as long as she didn't tell me anything about training with Rudy. I know they did it to discourage me from thinking I could go along, too. How they did it out of worry for me as much as for practical reasons, since I really wasn't ready at all. They only had to look at Shire's scar to remind themselves of that, to look at the scant amount of marks in the till as the teahouse went through repairs.

And after a while, I got used to not asking questions anymore. I got used to Shire heading out and coming back and the shop's honor marks getting paid on time. Just like I got used to her staying in her room for hours, quietly suffering as she healed from her last casting.

But I'm no longer willing to look the other way.

I take a deep breath and begin to empty the boxes. Something steely fills my blood, settles my racing mind—hope, determination, maybe just delusion if that's what it takes.

Shire, I'm going to figure this out. I stand bottles on the floor, stack jars and tins. *You're dead, but I'm not, and I'm going to save us from Saint Willow.*

When I finally have Rudy's boxed apothecary supplies laid out in front of me on the floor, I sit back and stare at them again, frowning and wondering what it all means when it comes to magic. The answer feels slippery, just out of grasp.

I will the panic to stay away for a bit longer. Reach again for that steeliness I need so badly to stay with me.

"C'mon, you stupid hunk of glass . . ." I whisper, reaching for one of the bottles. The coolness of its neck is soothing in my fingers. "What are you supposed to help me understand?"

I decide to start sorting, as Rudy asked. I *could* think all of this is just another chore. That nothing has changed from when I was here last time or the time before. But he's asked me to do this for a reason. I know that now.

I set the bottle down behind me where there's room on the floor, and reach for another. I start a new pile for each different kind of item, and before long, I've settled into a groove and barely think as I work. It's mindless once you get the pattern down and just follow it.

Bottles here, jars here, *green* bottles here, vials here—

I stop moving and slowly set down the vial I was holding.

My thoughts start to race again.

All those times he made me organize shelves, taking every single item off and placing them all back down. My one shoulder—the shoulder of my casting arm—was sore the next day from repeating the same motion too many times.

The dozens of bottles he had me fill with one of his formulas for treating a bad cough. So that by the time I was done, I didn't even have to think about double-checking the amount I was using because I just knew it was fine.

The rows of ingredients he had me memorize, knowing exactly where each item was just by picturing the layout in my head. A clear vision in my mind. Everything I could need, right at my fingertips.

A laugh bursts free, flooding the last of the hollowness that'd still been nestled inside me even as its echo bounces across the room. I can't miss the relief in it, the note of startled amazement.

"Really, Rudy?" I start sorting again, rushing to finish now that I understand. "Couldn't you have just *told* me?"

But I know why he didn't. I would have listened and not really believed I needed to do any of it. I would have gone out to cast full magic without worry, sure I already knew everything.

I might not have even made it to this point.

The earth might be half gone.

I slow down the sorting on purpose now, taking more care with each item as I set it in its right place. The motions of my hands move like cogs turning in a wristwatch—the kind full magic casters don't really wear anymore because each casting burns up the mechanisms inside—smooth in their repetition, from here to here and then back again.

My heartbeat runs low and gentle, an idling motor. Even the flow of my blood seems to slow. A soft, steady hum fills my ears.

But don't just sit and watch the flames dance, Aza. You have to remember to stoke the fire, too. To keep it going for as long as you need it.

It's Shire's voice in my head. It's the memory I still go back to whenever I cast full magic, from that day years ago when we were both still kids. How she talked to me about controlling magic while we built a fire in the workroom of the teahouse, a room that's hidden from the eyes of customers out front. Not just a typical fire but a *red* fire, the gentlest fire that exists. It's one of our family secrets, passed down from the ancestors who first created Wu teas centuries ago—that only a red fire be allowed to dry the delicate buds used in a Wu blend.

My mind reels back in time.

The workroom still smelled of fresh wood and paint. The new countertop around the open fireplace gleamed. Repairs had just finished days ago and the repairmen were finally gone. My parents and Shire were already back to using the room as heavily as they had before—business went on and teas still had to be blended for sale—but things had changed just the slightest.

My parents looked at me with fear. I had to tell them whenever I used a fire.

And Shire had her scar.

It was still pink and healing as I followed her into the workroom, my arms full of fragrant flower branches—chrysanthemums, wisteria, rhododendrons, jasmine—all carefully preserved as they

38

dried so that smoke from their fires would smell of their blooms. She said it didn't hurt anymore, but I wasn't sure I believed her.

"I'm supposed to tell Mom and Dad," I said to Shire, "whenever I come in here to—"

"No, it's okay," Shire said, opening up the vents along the wall. "I'm here with you. Want to start up the fire?"

I set my armful of branches down on the counter beside the fireplace. Some houses had material around to start fires without using magic. But most houses had nothing, because even leftover magic was enough to ignite tinder.

There was some on the grate already, tufts of shaved-up wood. There was also kindling on the side, ready to be added as soon as the fire began to take.

"No, you do it," I said. I hadn't lit a fire since the accident. Since the workroom had been fixed, I'd barely come in. But I still remembered how the magic had felt. Like I was sick with a bad fever.

"You're only lighting it. Use your leftover magic, like before."

I shook my head, still unsure. What if it had changed again and I didn't know it? "Will you do it? Please?"

Shire knew it wasn't leftover magic on my mind. "You can't be scared of your own magic," she said. "It's full magic. It's rare, just like mine."

"I can't control it."

"One day, you will. I just know it."

The memory of the heat I felt was so strong even then. "Not today, though."

Shire was twelve to my eight and still mostly patient with me.

She rolled her eyes and cast the fire alight with a breath on her palm.

We built up the fire slowly, keeping it gentle with the flower branches we chose as its fuel, by stoking it with the fire rod at exactly the right time, and only just so. The flames glowed a red as bright as poppies.

I asked the question I still hadn't learned not to ask. "So is Rudy a good magic teacher?"

Shire smiled. "Rudy doesn't teach 'magic'—he teaches *control*."

I picked bark free from a wisteria branch. "That's what I said."

She frowned and poked the fire with the rod. "I can't tell you anything. I promised Mom and Dad."

"A hint? I won't tell."

"Oh, Aza." I could sense her patience wavering with the flames. She huffed out a sigh and tucked her long black hair behind an ear. "How about I tell you something I got on my own? Something about controlling magic?"

I nodded, deciding it was a good swap.

"It's like stoking a fire. The magic you draw is its fuel, but you control how high you want the flames, Aza." She took the wisteria branch from my hands, dropped it in, and the fire grew. "What you want it to burn." Shire poked the bed of wood and it spilled over. The flames shot sideways. "Where you want it to go."

I backed up a step. The skin of my arms was hot, nearly as though I were casting magic again. The flames danced closer to yellow than red—too hot for drying stuff for tea now. "What do you mean?" My sister stepped back with me and grinned. The spread of the scar on her cheek went in and out of shadow. "Well, that's the part Rudy's going to teach me."

The memory ends and time is today again. The medicinal smells of Rudy's apothecary replace the floral ones—chrysanthemums, wisteria, rhododendrons, jasmine—of the teahouse's workroom of eight years ago.

Shire, now I know how, too. If only we could have talked about it together. Maybe we could have made each other stronger. Maybe you'd be alive still.

SIX

I start moving the supplies back into the boxes, careful to keep everything sorted. And just like before, soon enough the work becomes mindless, a pattern of motions I do while barely having to think about it. Green bottles in this box, amber ones here, rhubarb roots in this one . . .

When I'm done I return the now re-sorted boxes to the shelf and head out to the shop.

It's empty except for Rudy. He's doing inventory, checking his stock of medicated oils and soaps against information he's looking at in a binder. The light coming in through the main window is a gauzy dark gray, revealing it's nearly evening. Which means it's nearly dinner. I have to get home soon—as far as my parents know, I should have been done with work by now.

"Why are you still here?" I walk over and pick up a thick bar of black soap. I sniff but can't place the scent. "Doesn't the shop close around this time?"

"Pine tar," Rudy mutters as he writes something down in the binder. He sounds even more tired than he did earlier. "For rashes."

"What?"

"The soap."

I put the bar back, wondering how to say thank you. It should be easy, now that I finally have some answers. But I still have questions, ones about Shire that I'm beginning to doubt Rudy will ever tell me.

"So I figured out why you've been having me do chores around this place," I say.

No reaction. He just keeps writing, eyes planted firmly on his paper. It's like the Rudy from the supply room who gave me back a small piece of my sister never happened.

"You don't care that I know now?" My voice is stiff. The note of pleading in there surprises even me, and the skin of my neck burns.

"Only if it means you'll stop coming back." Still writing. "You can practice on your own now. There's really nothing else you need from me, Aza."

The heat around my neck climbs until my face is just as hot. I don't even mind that much—I'm used to being angry with Rudy instead of grateful. And maybe he's the same way, too. If my being here keeps being a bother, he won't have to feel bad about everything he hides from me.

"Practice on my own or not, I still need to know the spell that killed Shire. Which *you* know because you were actually there when she cast it."

Rudy shuts the binder and finally faces me. He looks like hell. Guilt slips in—I know a lot of that hell is because of me—and I drop my gaze. I can't let it matter, can't let it convince me to back off. Just a little more time is all I need, I almost want to beg him. One more week and it's over either way—Saint Willow pays the teahouse a personal visit or I'll have made enough marks from magic to clear our debt.

"I can't tell you anything else," he says quietly. He pushes up his glasses and begins to move away. "The shop's closed now, so goodbye, Aza."

He's already disappeared into the supply room before I can make myself leave. My face is still hot, and an ugly mix of fury and humiliation slicks the back of my mouth, turning it bitter.

I yank open the front door and rush outside. Smoke-scented air washes over me, immediately smothering the cleaner scents of rosemary, camphor, and ginger. It's drizzling and cold out because it's Lotusland, and I start walking as fast as I can down the sidewalk, like I'm trying to chase something down or maybe even escape from it—Rudy's secrets, Shire's, my own, I can't tell.

Baseball Cap hasn't left. At the last second, I remember to turn to check and there he is, still across the street. Except now he's inside the breakfast-all-day diner that's opposite Rudy's place. He's sitting at a window table, his head turned in the direction of the apothecary. Our eyes meet as I pass, and whatever it is I see in his, I'm suddenly sure that Rudy's wrong about the cop not keeping watch on him and his shop.

Sweat pops up on my brow as I swing my gaze forward and keep walking, pretending I haven't taken real notice of Baseball Cap in any way. And now my thoughts swivel, going from recalling all the reasons why I'm right for resenting Rudy, to breaking down why it makes sense a cop's on him and how he could be in very bad trouble.

I have to tell him.

Shire would want me to.

And the thing is, if this *is* about him lying on record about how Shire died, then I'm in trouble, too. And so are my parents.

I stop abruptly at the end of the block and make a show of searching for something in my pockets and coming up empty.

I turn right back around and keep going until I'm once again at the apothecary. I keep from looking at the cop across the street, hoping that Rudy hasn't already locked up and left. It feels too important to not tell him right away.

I pull the front door open and call out his name. "Rudy?"

At first glance, the shop seems empty. He's not even hunched over behind the counter, counting marks or gathering up the day's bills of sale.

But the door wasn't locked, so he must still be here.

The supply room.

I head over, calling out as I stuff my mask away—"It's me, Aza, where are you?"—so I don't accidentally startle him into a heart attack or something.

"Rudy, it's me," I say loudly. The echo of my voice rings off the walls, emphasizing how it's so quiet here otherwise. I go behind the counter and step into the supply room. "Hey, about that cop, I think—"

He's on the floor, lying on his back. His eyes are shut and he's as pale as porcelain. Supplies lie scattered all around him—whatever happened, it was sudden.

"Rudy!" My pulse is thudding in the back of my throat as I rush over and get down to my knees. "Are you okay? What happened?"

All I can think about is how I saw that he looked unwell, and still I pushed him. I bothered him and refused to leave him alone.

How much of this is my fault?

What if all of it is?

I'm considering patting parts of his body to see if he's injured, but I have no idea how to even tell. He's not awake to scream in pain or anything.

Panic turns my stomach icy, and I have to shake myself to focus. Where should I start? Torso? Okay, torso.

His eyes open, but just slightly. "Aza?" My name is a slow whisper.

"Rudy, what happened? Do you want me to call an ambulance? The shop must have a landline, right?" Full-time casters often have cells just because it draws attention if we don't, but most of the time, they're not working; we kill them each and every time. I've been carrying around a dead one for months. If anyone asks, I just say I'm on my way to get it repaired.

"No ambulance," Rudy says. His words are jagged, full of pain. "Knew . . . this was coming. Can't be helped."

"What are you talking about?"

"I'm sick. Been sick for years. My heart . . . is bad."

Rudy, dying? How can he—? He's always been—

"No." I clutch his shoulder with a cold hand. My blood runs colder. "No, you're going to be fine. Let me call—"

"Listen." A cough, and there's blood rushing out, and I realize that this is all real. "The cop outside, Aza. He's here for me, okay?"

"What? Why? What did you do?"

"Shire . . . the night she died . . ."

More blood, gushes of it. Panic hits me in waves. "Rudy, stop talking, I have to think. Let me try magic—"

He shakes his head. "*No.* It'll hurt you. And it's too late. I'm dying."

"*Rudy—*"

"Listen to me." He coughs again, and more blood comes. "Wanted to teach you more, but . . . scared to. Meant to enter . . . meant to finish what I started." His eyes drift shut. "Meant it as payback . . . for Shire."

Everything he's saying is a tangled mess in my brain. "Enter what? What do you mean, payback for Shire?"

"I'm sorry, Aza."

Then Rudy dies.

SEVEN

For a long time, I just sit there, unable to move because I've gone numb. From outside there's the sound of traffic, the occasional honk of a horn. One of the glass bottles on the supply room floor has shattered open and the entire room smells of rosemary, a scent I might never smell again without thinking of this moment.

Rudy's lying on his back, half-covered in blood. He's still very much dead.

I stare at him and wonder if I ever knew him at all.

Wanted to teach you more, but scared.

Meant to finish what I started.

Payback for Shire.

His words flash across my mind, leaving me more confused than ever. And then it comes: guilt, not just slipping in, but in huge washes and waves. Oceans of it, wishing it could revive a secret bad heart.

"Rudy," I whisper. "You should have told me. I would have—"

I would have done exactly the same. I would have kept coming still, choosing a ghost to avenge over the person I wanted to hold at fault for creating that ghost in the first place.

Shame makes me shiver. So how am I any better than Rudy? Who I resented so much—for all his cruel nonanswers, his cranky evasions to keep from helping me. I couldn't forgive him for letting Shire die. And now I'm the one here left with his body.

The answer is, I'm not any better. I'm worse.

I lay my hand over his heart, despite all the blood. "I'm sorry, too."

The cop outside, Aza. He's here for me, okay?

Shire, the night she died.

My stomach twists as I observe Rudy for another long, unmoving moment. I feel sick as the truth sinks in.

How this whole time, I've been right about him hiding something about Shire and the way she died.

"And so you got caught," I murmur as I stare down at his still face. "Which means it won't be long before some Scout comes around asking *me* about that night. Asking my parents."

Something contorts in my chest, making it hard to breathe. Guilt tangles with the same old anger. I might have killed Rudy, but it was from being kept in the dark—while his keeping secrets about my sister dying was absolutely on purpose.

I have to know what happened. The need for answers burns inside, just as hot as my banned magic does.

But where do I start?

"Getting away from here is one idea," I say out loud. Baseball Cap across the street saw me come in here but not leave. What if he decides to come check out the shop? And here I am with the dead body of the person he's been staking out.

I scramble to my feet, terror working like caffeine through my veins. Parts of me are shaking, turning my motions jagged and clumsy.

There's some blood on my pants, and it's not dark enough outside to hide the stains. I grab an acorn from my starter bag and cast the fabric clean. There's no pain, since leftover magic is enough for the spell.

How to leave the apothecary is another matter.

I *could* leave using the shop's back door—it's here in the supply room, between two of the shelves. Or cast myself invisible and then leave through the front.

But soon enough Rudy's body will be discovered, and Baseball Cap will know, and he'll wonder about the teenaged girl he saw go inside but not leave again.

Or I could use the front door and just let him watch me leave.

But that doesn't erase how I'd still be the girl he saw leave from a shop with a dead body inside.

So, the only option I have is to make the cop forget he ever saw me come here today, the day Rudy died. There's no escaping that I'm connected to the apothecary—my prints are all over it—but that's as a helper. I need to not be connected to his death.

My head buzzes.

To cast full magic on a cop is about the most reckless thing a caster could do. But I can't figure out another way to get out of here without ending up appearing suspicious over Rudy dying.

For a second I consider taking myself out of the cop's mind altogether. A total mind wipe, but of a person instead of a chunk of time.

But just as quickly, I drop the idea. It might save me from being questioned, but it wouldn't save my parents during his continued investigation of Shire's death. And to cast enough magic to wipe out all of us—

Cold sweat rises on my skin at the thought. That amount of magic is dangerous—to me, to the whole sector.

I leave the supply room and walk back into the shop, still unsure what spell to cast in order to escape. The light's changed again, and the inside of the apothecary is dim, nearly half-dark. I make my way over to the front window, making sure to stay off to the side to avoid being seen through the glass.

My heartbeat pounding high in my throat, I crane my head sideways and peek across the street so that the diner is in full view. A more experienced caster could do this while hidden away, but for me to do a mind wipe, I still need the person I'm casting magic on to be in clear sight.

Baseball Cap is still at the window table. I'd almost admire his doggedness if he weren't being so careless about showing it. What kind of cop is this, anyway? Maybe I'm worrying way too much about what he could possibly figure out . . .

I unzip my starter bag and dig out a small bit of bark. I draw a five-pointed star on my palm. It should be enough magic to wipe away the last few hours from the cop's memory. He'll be confused at first over the missing time. But he'll eventually forget that he can't remember how there's a small gap at all.

I place the bark in the middle of the star and envision parts of his memory being wiped clean. Like grit from a dirty windowpane, swept away with a rag.

The floor of the apothecary trembles. Heat collects in my sneakers and climbs up my legs and spreads into my hands. They grow heavy, as though I'm cradling invisible weights. My hand is on fire around the piece of bark, and the material begins to smoke just the slightest bit.

I glance up and over in the direction of the diner window to catch Baseball Cap's eye. Only once we see each other can I drive my magic into him.

But the cop's turned away now. There's a waitress at his table—he's ordering something from the menu.

Damn it.

A drawn-out casting doesn't add to the pain that comes afterward, but it *does* keep me burning up until I can finish the spell, and the building discomfort makes my head sway. Heat rolls off my skin and fills the room. Scents of apothecary supplies roll back at me, set off by the drastic temperature change—licorice, roses, beeswax, sandalwood. My vision wavers and the shop goes dreamlike, not quite real.

The waitress is laughing. Baseball Cap must have told a joke.

"C'mon," I mutter out loud. "Just finish the order and look over here."

My veins are flooded with full magic, this vast nebula of glowing red fire that only my mind's eye can see. It dances off my skin in swarms, circles me in a blood-tinged hug, looking for somewhere to land. The inside of my mouth is hot. My eyeballs feel singed, gone raw and red. My pulse is a thousand drums inside my ears, beating out a mad rhythm.

The waitress finally leaves and the cop turns and peers out the diner's window.

His eyes meet mine.

Magic surges.

EIGHT

I pull away, breathing raggedly. Out of Baseball Cap's head and back into mine. Immediately my skin grows cold, and where my veins were filled with magic, now they fill with pain.

Bruises bloom across my arms. They crawl out from beneath the sleeves of my shirt, patches of purple as dark as midnight, blotches of maroon as red as wine. I don't need to check beneath my jeans to know my legs are just as bad. There's a dull ache inside my limbs that feels close to a fever. I press my fingers all over my face. I'm lucky; only my left cheek and jaw hurt—my smog mask will cover most of that.

Five points—bruises until tomorrow, at the very earliest.

But it's done. I stagger back from the window, steadying my breath, and go back into the supply room.

The scent of blood wars with that of rosemary, and bile rises.

I go to check Rudy's body for signs that might give me away, grabbing a pair of safety gloves Rudy used when handling some of his more volatile ingredients. First, his wallet for any cards or whatever else might tie him to Wu Teas. But there's nothing. I'm about to put it back when I decide to take the marks that are inside. Rudy would want me to.

I check the rest of his pockets, and they're all empty except for his chest one.

A note. It's written in Rudy's handwriting, which I recognize from all over the apothecary.

Midnight
July 15th
987 Scalding Way
FC

That's it. Four lines. Midnight tonight. An address in the Meat Sector. Nothing more to explain what it means. The *FC* is even more mysterious. Someone's initials? A password of some kind?

I flip over the note and there's a small black coin taped to it. I take off the tape so the coin falls into my hand. Its shape and weight and thinness are about right for a mark, and it has the same center hole, but everything else is different. Black metal instead of copper or nickel, perfectly blank on both sides.

I have no clue what it is or what it could be for.

"You couldn't have elaborated on this a bit?" I gesture toward Rudy with the note and the coin. I tell myself he looks at peace. At least not sick anymore, anyway.

The note could mean something as simple as Rudy having plans tonight. Maybe it's the address of a friend? Maybe there's a party and Rudy had a date? Maybe it means nothing at all.

But his last words are again in my head.

Wanted to teach you more, but scared.

Meant to finish what I started.

Payback for Shire.

They're still cryptic. I can't tell what Rudy might have meant by them. The note doesn't help at all.

But to have an address, and a time, for something Rudy might have meant to be at. It eats at me—him dying with all his secrets about my sister, leaving new questions behind.

I fold up the note and tuck it and the strange black coin into my starter bag.

Tonight at midnight. Scalding Way. I'll figure out the FC part when I get there.

I touch Rudy's cold shoulder once more. *I wanted to trust you because Shire did, Rudy. But maybe she never really knew you, either.*

I get to my feet, tear off the gloves, make sure my sleeves are still hiding my arms, and pull on my smog mask to cover the bruises on my face. I slip out through the back door.

Outside, there are the sounds of an approaching fire truck, but I don't make the connection until I turn the corner.

It's an eruption of a stretch of asphalt. Cars are spiraled across the still-flat part of the road like toys, while pedestrians ogle from the sidewalks.

I walk along, trying to blend into the crowd, convinced at least some of them must realize they're seeing the result of full magic being cast somewhere. I'm careful to avoid meeting the eyes of any of them.

Of casters of leftover magic because they might detect my guilt.

Of casters of full because they might nod in understanding, giving us both away.

NINE

It hurts to walk—each step is like a slap on my bruises—so I take the short way home for once, cutting through the sector instead of going along the salty shore. I figure seeing the bruises will be enough to distract my parents from asking me why I smell like Tobacco instead of Tea.

My parents think I work for Saint Willow. On account of falling so behind on paying our honor marks, they think he hired me two months ago as a courier for his gang. That the marks I make doing this go toward paying our debt.

This is another lie I've told. And so while they think I'm going around to other businesses in the Tea Sector picking up and dropping off packages, I'm actually either at Rudy's apothecary or somewhere else, casting full magic for marks.

My parents believing I work for Saint Willow explains Jihen's sudden disappearance from their lives, his threatening presence no longer darkening the teahouse. That lie, in turn, rests on my lie to Jihen about being a tutor so he will stay away from my parents. Between my two fake jobs, nobody knows where I actually get my marks from—selling spells as a caster of banned full magic. Magic that if Saint Willow knew I could cast, he would make me cast for him, regardless of how I would suffer for it.

Sometimes I lie so much that I think I'll stop knowing what's real anymore. Or maybe it's just being surrounded by the lies of so many others that they change what truth even means.

Even my parents have lied to me. About what they let Shire do for them. For us. A lie by omission. *Don't tell Aza.* The thick scents of smoke and moss soon swirl away and the lighter ones of tea take over—images of green fields and orchards full of lushly leaved plants float across my mind. The sky's gone a clouded, deep charcoal by the time I reach the teahouse, and cold drizzle continues. The front window of the teahouse glows gold against the rain, so warm and cheery that it seems almost impossible people like Saint Willow and Jihen and a hungry cop looking for answers that will destroy us can also exist.

For a second, my throat goes tight at how everything's going wrong. Rudy's dead, his body probably still on the floor in his apothecary. I can't decide if I should warn my parents about Baseball Cap possibly showing up or just leave it in case I'm wrong and he was never on a trail leading right to our door. My desperation for marks is real, but no matter how many I might make, they won't bring Shire back. Nothing is the same.

One week.

A breeze comes right then, and I imagine it's Jihen, breathing close.

My mother pushes open the front door of the teahouse while I'm still climbing the steps. Her long black hair sweeps across her shoulders, and she places her hands at her hips. You have to really study her black silk trousers to notice how old the fabric's gotten. That same golden light from the now-closed-for-the-day teahouse flows out from behind her.

"You're very late, Aza."

As always, her tone is both soft and sharp, both concerned and irritated.

And your dead daughter's old instructor is dead, Mom. I'd tell you, but you'd ask how I know. I'd tell you, but you'd probably be glad, and I don't think I want to see you glad over something like that.

"Sorry," I say, taking off my smog mask and folding it back into my pocket.

"Dinner is . . ."

Her voice falls away as I reach the top step, and she glimpses the two bruises on my face. Her gaze immediately goes to my arms and she tugs up a sleeve, checking for more because she knows how pain from full magic works. Beneath the dimness of the sky, the blotches on my skin seem even darker. She blinks fast, as though she can't believe what she's seeing. Then she rushes me inside and slams the door shut.

"Casting full magic out in the open? *Why?* What were you thinking?"

I swipe rain off my forehead. I tug at the zipper of my starter bag, making sure it's still secure. Forcing my thoughts away from the mysterious note, I let go of the bag and take a deep breath. The inside of the teahouse always smells like a mix of tea and forests and dried flowers—it's the scent of legacy, of the ghosts of emperors and empresses and *security*. Sometimes it's comforting, and sometimes it's smothering.

"I'm okay, by the way," I say as I walk through the tidy retail area with its display cabinets and tall shelves. "They'll fade by tomorrow."

"I'm glad you're okay, of course," my mother insists as she walks alongside me. Her eyes flicker to my jaw and then flicker away. "It's just—"

"You worry."

"Every day."

On my other side is the teahouse's small dining area, with its main window that faces the sidewalk. During the day, customers sit here and order tea and pastries and buns.

Once it was a lot busier, not just with customers but also with family. We used to eat out here every night, after the teahouse closed and the space was ours again. But that was before Shire died, and now it's a rare thing for my parents and me to bother bringing dinner out here. Now we just sit around the beat-up wooden island in the cramped back kitchen and pretend we're really talking.

My father is already seated at the island in the kitchen, hunched over paperwork, a plate at one elbow and tea at his other. His face falls when he peers up at me. "Aza, what—?"

"Nothing happened," I lie. "I cast magic and the price is some bruises. A car was about to run a light and I had to help it slow down, so don't freak out." I pull out a stool, sit down, and start piling food on my plate. It's Thursday, so it's pork dumplings and broccoli salad and lemon rice. The stool beside me still feels huge in its emptiness.

He pours tea into a cup and pushes it toward me. "Is this why you're so late? Maybe we should finally get you a new cell so we can at least reach you while it's working."

I shake my head and take a sip of tea. It's our Conversation blend, which I think is ironic. "My last delivery was on the other side of the sector. It just took me a bit to walk back."

"You could have taken the train."

"Pass is used up, and I didn't want to spend any marks."

My mother sits down beside my father and picks up her chopsticks. But instead of eating, she just holds them over her plate. "That doesn't explain why you're casting. Why did they need your help so badly? That car would have likely stopped in time on its own."

I shrug. "Some people were slow to finish crossing."

My parents exchange a look.

"You're not ready," my mother says.

The food in my mouth turns dry, and I take a minute to wash it down with tea, wondering why I'm suddenly bothered. My mother *always* says I'm not ready. She says it as often as she says she just worries about me.

"I'm not eight anymore," I finally say. "I don't actually hurt someone each time I cast."

"And your surroundings? Did you check to see what you broke or just not bother?"

"Some asphalt fell apart. I might have done the city a favor—I'm pretty sure that road needed an upgrade anyway."

"No one was hurt?"

I shake my head again. There were no ambulances.

My mother slowly stirs her food, while my father just watches me. He's still holding the paperwork. I can see now it's the teahouse's files on our suppliers and distribution systems that we have in place in the city.

He points at my arms. "So maybe not hurt someone else, but what about *you* getting hurt?"

"This is—" I nearly laugh. "This is just part of it. You know there's a cost. It's nothing new."

"And your sister is dead from casting full magic. Have you thought about that?"

"It's pretty much all I think about, okay?" I stab apart a dumpling with my chopsticks. "Just like it's all you guys think about," I add under my breath.

"Aza," my mother starts, "we just—"

"Worry, I know. You worry because you don't want the same thing to happen to me, and that's why you won't let me cast to help out with all the bills." I break open another dumpling, hoping my face doesn't show how my stomach's gone tight.

"We *don't* want you getting hurt, and we're thankful you want to help. It just means we shouldn't ever forget how lucky we are that you get to work for Saint Willow."

"So you really sleep easier knowing I'm spending each day as a courier for the sector's gang leader instead of casting full magic?" The moment I say it, it hits me how furious I am with my parents for feeling this way. It's like they're okay if something bad happens to me, even if it's because of someone as evil as Saint Willow, as long as it's not because of full magic.

How much do they care about me staying safe, then?

My parents exchange another look.

"We know you're angry with us for not letting you go to Rudy," my father says, "but we just think you need a bit more time."

"Time for what? Saint Willow says we're nearly out of it."

"How can you learn how to control magic if you don't understand that magic in the first place? Can you ever be sure you're using magic and it's not using you?"

I eat salad to hide how my eyes are prickling. *I'm not eight anymore*, I want to scream again.

My mother clears her throat and casts to turn on the television we keep mounted to the front of the fridge. One of her favorite dramas starts playing. It's a Pearl of the Orient production, the kind she watches the most because she likes their tropes. *Liar's Lair* first came out when I was a kid, so I've seen it a bunch of times already. It's about two casters from rival gangs who each go undercover to infiltrate the other's in order to find secret intel.

It's always reminded me a bit of Lotusland just because of the gang thing, but my mother says Lotusland isn't nearly so brutal. We'd argue about it, about the rumors that spread throughout the city the way poisonous fungi pop up in the dark.

I heard that Earl Kingston demoted one of his own cousins the other day for trying to conspire against him. And you know what "demoted" means.

I've heard the stories, Aza. Just because a businessman operates with a firm hand doesn't mean he's a monster.

Well, the stories are true, Mom. A nice little drowning for poor Milo Kingston in the good ol' Sturgeon River.

That is not what "demoted" means. And Earl Kingston would never do that. He takes care of families in the Tobacco Sector as though they are his own. Just like Saint Willow takes care of all of us here in Tea.

It was only Earl Kingston's third cousin, twice removed, if that means anything.

Oh, Aza.

Paperwork rustles as my father looks away and starts once more to read the file, as my mother turns to watch her show.

So many ways they don't see me. How I'm not a kid who can't control her magic anymore. How, in the end, it still wasn't me who killed Shire.

I keep eating and drinking more tea, trying so hard not to think back to that day. But I fail, and soon my mind is no longer in the kitchen but instead in the workroom.

I'm eight again. And I remember it all.

TEN

I was holding fragrant branches in my arms—chrysanthemums, jasmine, rhododendrons, wisteria—each carefully dried under very specific conditions so their fires wouldn't smoke too much. Shire and I had been put in charge of drying the buds for our mother, who would be mixing up new teas that day.

It was also the first time my parents trusted us to build the red fire for the drying. To do it all on our own, without their supervision.

Watch for signs of yellow in the flames, girls. You must cool the fire a bit if it turns close to yellow. And if there is any blue at all, suppress the fire and start over again. Blue is too hot and will destroy anything.

Shire went around the workroom and opened the vents in the wall. Sunlight filtered in and danced off the smooth, unmarked skin of her face.

"Aza, want to check on the fireplace? Do we have enough of everything?"

I set the branches down on the counter and peered down. "Yes, there's lots of kindling *and* tinder."

My sister came over and moved some of the tufts of shaved-up wood around. "Okay, I'm going to start the fire now."

I nodded, stepping back to give her room to cast.

Shire cupped her hand and blew into it.

The kindling caught, and I reached for the fire rod to pass to Shire for her to poke in some of the tinder.

She shook her head and smiled. "Let's not use that today."

Full magic.

I grinned back, excited. I wanted to see Shire cast full magic more than anything. It wasn't often that our parents let her since the world said it wasn't allowed, and because it hurt her, too.

My excitement died down a bit. I didn't want her to hurt, either. And I didn't want her to get into trouble.

"Mom and Dad will get mad," I said. "Plus casting hurts you, remember?"

"Not very much. I'll use a spell that will just leave my bones sore for a bit. It's not permanent. And Mom and Dad won't even be able to tell."

I hesitated, torn. I trusted Shire because somehow she always knew how to keep our parents from getting mad, while I never did a very good job with that. And to feed a fire with full magic—it would be like making rain with a wish, like growing snow from your fingertips . . .

I tried once more to be obedient. "They don't like it when you use your magic for no good reason."

"There's never a good reason, then."

I grinned again and leaned the rod back against the wall. "Okay."

Shire picked up a stray shaving from the side of the fireplace. She drew a five-pointed star on her palm and placed the shaving in the middle of it. Then she stared hard at the pieces of tinder that lay on the hot grate. The tiny strands of red that were our fire had already raced themselves through the rest of the kindling.

The tinder slowly lifted up into the air. There, the thin pieces of wood hovered for a second before each slowly flipped once, twice. Then they flopped back down onto the strands of red. The edges of the tinder caught, began to glow.

"Shire," I whispered in awe—we wouldn't find out until later that day how earth had paid for our moment of fun, the wild blackberry bushes that lined the ditch behind the teahouse bent low to the ground as though a giant foot had come down from above and stomped on them. "All of that was you?"

My sister laughed, then winced. The pain had hit her bones. She slowly opened her hand, and the tiny bit of charred wood that was all that was left of her starter floated downward. "Of course it was me—who else?"

Sometimes my heart ached with how much I wanted full magic, too. I cast leftover magic all the time, but now it was no longer special. It felt dull, second best. I wanted to be like Shire, who was older, prettier, and better at so many things. It almost seemed unfair that she had full magic on top of all that, but I knew it wasn't up to her. She was just really lucky. I hoped I would be as lucky one day, too. And if I was, I would never become one of those casters who Scouts had to hunt down, the ones who destroyed bits of the earth at a time. I would never be terrible with my magic.

"That first time." I was staring at the fire, watching it grow. "Did you know the instant your leftover magic turned into full magic?"

I had no memory of Shire's discovery since I'd only been two when it happened. But I knew the story. How it'd been at breakfast, and how Shire had heated up a cup of water for tea—still a caster of leftover magic. But that's all such a caster can do with a breath spell—heating a single cup at most. So when she went on to heat a whole teapot, everyone knew.

"Well, you don't really lose your leftover magic," Shire said. She rubbed at her arms, checking the pain. "It's more like full magic comes and . . . swarms it up."

"That's what I meant."

"I told you how it gets hot while casting, right? Your whole body does. That's really the only difference, since you don't feel anything when you cast leftover magic."

"But that first time, could you tell *before* you cast that your magic had changed?"

She shook her head. "I can't really remember. I was only six. Mom and Dad would remember better if I told them anything then."

"There had to be something."

"I really can't remember, Aza. One day it was just there."

I frowned, wanting to believe her. But it seemed too simple. If it was so simple, why was full magic so powerful, then? I began to add some of the dried branches to the fire, wondering if I could help her remember, trying to come up with ideas. "Was it maybe like getting a burst of energy?"

"Sure, a burst of energy, just like that."

Shire didn't sound convinced. It sounded more like something she was saying because she knew I wanted to hear it.

"Maybe I should go look it up," I said. "Someone must have talked about it before, since every single caster on earth once used full magic. Right?"

"Really, Aza, it just happened all on its own." One day it was just there. And then as I got older, it grew stronger. Now she sounded nearly bored. It reminded me of how she was already twelve and I was only eight and how sometimes she seemed tired of me always being there. "You can't make it come or anything. It just means not everyone is meant to cast full magic—not anymore." She passed me another branch. "Here, one more. Last one, though—the fire's pretty much ready right now, and if it gets any hotter, we'll have to bank it back before we can dry anything. I'll be right back—we left the box of buds behind the front counter."

She left the workroom, and I stared at the red flames, feeling their gentle heat. Restlessness stirred.

I dropped the branch onto the flames and decided I had to at least *try* casting full magic. Shire hadn't had any warning before she found out, after all. What if I'd had full magic for *ages* and had just never known because I'd never tried it?

Then there was just *how much* magic I wanted to pull from the earth. Just how strong of a spell did I want to try casting? Shire's five-pointed star had pulled enough to make pieces of wood dance in the air.

Which meant ten might lift up the larger flower branches and make *them* dance.

Fifteen might make the *whole entire fire* dance.

My heart was beating fast, a pattern of notes of anticipation and hope, of dread and fear. I had to be fast. I knew if Shire got back and saw me trying that I would feel stupid. She wouldn't mean for me to, but I would anyway. Maybe if only I was better at *something* than Shire, or had something she didn't. But no.

I reached over and picked up a piece of fresh kindling that we'd missed.

I drew a star of fifteen points on my palm.

I laid the kindling in the middle of the star.

I looked up and stared at the red fire and imagined all those flames dancing in midair. I tried to imagine feeling suddenly energized. I told myself that I *was* energized. How I had all the energy of all the casters who ever existed, right there in my blood.

But nothing happened.

My palm stayed cool, the starter on it unburned. The red fire on the grate didn't dance.

I felt no differently than if I'd been trying to cast leftover magic.

Disappointment surged, surprising me with its force. I blinked back tears. So Shire wasn't lying. You really couldn't wish for it to happen. The earth was so different now, and not all casters were allowed to—

The red fire turned yellow.

My shoes, tingling with heat, the way kindling must as it ignites. My legs, crackling and snapping and smelling of char—they were tinder, feeding a fire. My hands were tangled bunches of fragrant branches that smelled of sweet blooms as they burned.

Aza!

Shire's voice came from somewhere far away, a wave of sound in my heated ears.

Aza!

My vision turned thick and blurry. I was jerked backward. It took forever for me to fall to the ground.

Shire's hazy outline as she faced the fireplace. The shimmer of her profile as she turned away.

I was eight, and on the grate in the workroom, blue fire exploded.

And then I am sixteen again, and on the television in the kitchen, rival gangs are hurling threats at one another.

I blink to shake myself out of the memory. The scent of fire is gone and smells of dinner come back. My plate still has food on it, and with numb hands, I begin to eat again. My parents are now looking at paperwork together, the teahouse's file opened up and some of its pages spread out on the wooden island.

"Maybe you can speak to them just once more?"

My mother, sounding worried again. But this time, it's not for me. Her expression is clouded as she reads something on one of the pages.

The tone in her voice forces the past from my mind.

"I've spoken to them over the phone a few times now," my father says. There are creases on the sides of his mouth I haven't noticed before. "I even offered to go over to the office so we could speak face-to-face. But Leafton said no, it wouldn't change anything."

Leafton is one of our longest-running suppliers. We've been getting a bunch of our tea ingredients from them for years. Without them, a handful of our most popular blends wouldn't be the same. Saint Willow owns them, too.

Back to reality, I ask, "What's going on?"

"Leafton is terminating its contract with us." My father's expression is as clouded as my mother's. "They're 'refocusing their customer base,' is the line we're being fed. Which doesn't say much, as it never does in business."

"We didn't get much warning," my mother says quietly. "Twenty-five years of working together, and they end it with a phone call. I'm actually a bit surprised with how they've handled this."

"Well, we'll just have to find a new supplier." My father shuffles papers together. "We need those ingredients."

A new suspicion comes, and suddenly I'm uneasy. The bruises on my arms and legs and face pound along with my pulse. "Doesn't Leafton have contracts with a few other teahouses here in the sector? Have you talked to them to see if they know what's going on?"

"We have." My mother pours more tea. "They're not affected. It's just us. You'd almost think it was intentional, but we've never had problems with Leafton before."

But we're having problems with Saint Willow now, aren't we?

My stomach churns, and I push my plate away. On the television screen, a gang member is screaming as he dies a painful death.

I wonder how much clout Jihen has with his boss. Did my casting him to trip hurt his ego so badly that he went to his cousin and told him to up the pressure?

Or maybe it's really all just Saint Willow. Maybe he got Leafton to cut ties with us so we wouldn't be able to pay. Maybe he likes to use his power in petty ways.

Maybe he's so angry with the pathetic amount of marks I paid him today that he's snapped.

"Let me guess," I say quietly. "Leafton is giving you one week before the process is finalized."

My father finishes shuffling papers and tucks them into the file. "How'd you know?"

"Like I said, just a guess." I start to get up to begin clearing dishes. Rudy's note and the strange black coin are still in my starter bag, their presence like live bugs contained in a jar, waiting to be released. I want to get to my room to look up directions for the address. Midnight can't come fast enough.

One week.

The ticking bomb grows louder each day.

"Aza, hold on a second." My father rips off a small piece of his napkin. He casts around it.

The pounding deep within my bruises recedes a tiny bit. I peek beneath one of my sleeves; blotches that were as dark as violets have gone a muted lavender.

"It might not be full magic," my father says, smiling, "but we still do what we can, don't we?"

ELEVEN

I leave the teahouse at eleven, sneaking out my window and trying not to wince as my bruises knock against the sill. My feet sink into the grass of our backyard, and I shut the window as quietly as I can. It can't be locked from the outside, and it's not worth the pain to cast it locked (and then unlocked when I get back), so I leave it as is.

Once, my mother locked it on me, exasperated to wake up in the middle of the night to find me gone and the apartment vulnerable. *You have a key to the door of the teahouse, Aza; simply leave that way instead of like a criminal.*

But I still sneak out, because of Jihen, who's been ordered to keep an eye on me, Jihen who my parents think is my coworker.

Slipping on my smog mask, I step over to the row of snowball bushes that grow so tightly together they act as our back fence, and peer through a tangle of branches.

No sign of Jihen.

I squeeze through the bushes and out into the alley, then turn and head toward the street.

The Tea Sector isn't really the section of the city most people aim to be late night—that's mostly Culture because of all its theaters and shows, and Electronics because of the arcades and opens-at-dusk shops—but pockets of it stay busy long after typical business hours. I take a more thorough look around, checking for the contrast of white sneakers against a dark suit on the sidewalk patios of the late-night tea cafés and teatini bars that don't close until dawn. Jihen's like me, never sticking to a schedule or route to keep me guessing when I might run into him.

I also remember to check for signs of a cop wearing a baseball cap. Chances are that he's still in the Tobacco Sector and nowhere near here. If he's staking out the apothecary, it makes sense that he's checked into a motel near to it. Or if Rudy's body has been discovered, then he'd be there for that, too.

But still.

It's a waiting game now. If he's going to come looking for us, I just need him to find me before he finds my parents.

I walk, sweeping petals of snowball bush blooms from my hair and shoulders. I might be sneaking out now to hunt down this place on Rudy's note, but it used to be Rudy himself I'd sneak out for. I would leave home at dawn to make sure I got to the apothecary before it opened, cast full magic to let myself inside, and wait there for Rudy to arrive. So he could never forget I was always around with my questions. So one day he would have to give me the answers I needed. Because he failed in teaching Shire how to stay alive, so he owed it to both her and me to become *my* teacher.

I was Rudy's Jihen. His Saint Willow. His weak heart's worst enemy.

My own heart goes tight with this fact as I finish crossing the street. A chilly drizzle is coming down so finely that it hangs in the air like a mist, unsure of where to go. I turn the corner, that cold mist having nothing on the way I'm already like ice inside.

I know Rudy's dead because of me.

For all that I swore as a kid to never become terrible with my magic, here I am.

Rudy, whatever I'm going to find at this address—if it's anything to do with what you said about finishing something, I'll do it for you.

The Meat Sector makes up the northeast corner of the city, and is about as distant from Tea as you can get and still be within Lotusland limits. So I take the most direct route, cutting my way through the sectors that stand between us.

I leave behind Tea and I step into Government, where all the buildings look the same and the streets run neatly square to each other. I gradually angle my way north even as I keep east. Every few blocks or so I double-check for the dim glow of white sneakers, the curve of a baseball cap, wanting to see them before they see me.

The ring of aged marble statues in the middle of a courtyard lets me know I'm crossing the literal center of the sector. The statues are of the greats, the first seven casters the earth ever created. Together they once made up the Guild of Then. Each of them contributed something to the original magic system—skin spells, bone spells, blood spells, breath spells, the casting arm, the starter, the pointed star—and the statues were once considered the figurative center of the city. Casters came here to celebrate full magic and honor the Guild.

But then casters couldn't stop using all that magic. Over centuries they abused it, leaving the earth on the verge of collapse. So earth adapted to save itself before it fell apart by turning full magic back on its own casters. It made them bear the burden of their greedy powers. Over time, the number of casters of full magic dwindled, while that of leftover grew.

It's only half working.

Earth waited too long to get rid of full magic, so each time it's cast, more of the world still breaks. And its casters are still here, even if we're mostly pretending and hiding, and dying out.

I step around the garbage that's strewn across the ground and finish crossing the courtyard. It's all wrinkled flyers and torn posters—another protest must have just ended. The protests are always over the same issue—how the Guild of Then monument should be taken down. Or at the very least, amended. Why honor a magic system that's become a threat and is no longer the gift it once was?

I leave the Government Sector and walk along the street that divides Spice from Tower, keeping straight east for a bit. As with a lot of the city's sectors, Spice has its own distinctive scent, and the smells of bright peppers and tongue-stinging salts fill my nose. On my other side, lights from the high-rises that make up most of Tower's buildings wink against the dark. Then the road curves south, so I leave it and go north again, cutting into Spice proper and zigzagging my way through its streets. I'm twenty minutes away from 987 Scalding Way.

"Magic? Got magic for me? Who's got magic to spare?"

The faint call comes from the intersection just up ahead, through the thin sounds of late-night traffic.

It's a display caster. An Ivor. Road lights gleam off the steel bars of the human-sized cage that hangs from the tall lamppost on the corner.

"Magic, anyone? Cast me some magic to get me something to eat?"

It's a busy area, and gawkers loiter on the sidewalk nearby, standing outside twenty-four-hour pancake houses and all-night inhalant bars. One catcalls. Another asks if the display caster would take some marks instead. Someone else yells how all full magic casters should be locked away.

I look up as I near the cage to get a glimpse inside. The city keeps a display cage for every sector, and Scouts save them to display the worst of the Ivors they catch. Mostly repeat offenders, like casters who get recaptured after escaping lockup or those unlucky few who get on the bad side of a cop in a mood.

The Ivor leans toward the bars, pressing her forehead into them so she can peer down at me as I go by. She smiles, and there's too much fury in her expression for me to believe she's actually insane.

"Hello, little one," she croons. "I smell magic off you. Won't you share, since mine's all gone?"

I keep walking, stiff with discomfort at being noticed, at the risk I'm taking. I don't know if I could stay as furious and alive as that Ivor if I lost everything. What if I just faded away, nothing without full magic? What if all these risks I'm taking *is* magic using me instead of me using it, and there's no winning this game?

What if it's *right* that casters like me disappear?

I walk faster and push away the questions. More answers I might never find.

Smells of blood and grilling meat greet me as I enter the Meat Sector. I find a street that's more steakhouses, fish markets, and delis instead of processing plants and butchers, not wanting to see for myself if what they say about this part of the city is true—that from dusk until dawn, curbs from certain places turn red with runoff as they clean.

987 Scalding Way turns out to be an underground mall at the edge of a small retail area. Everything around it is closed except for a twenty-four-hour gas station a block down; the large clock on its display says it's five until midnight. I'm standing across the street, and the only parts of the mall that are visible from here are the length of its top floor and a cone of a roof that's like a small hat perched on an oversized head. The top floor is banded with wide windows that are covered up with paper from the inside.

After double-checking the address that's painted on the roof against the one that Rudy wrote down, I fold up the note, return it to my starter bag, and cross the street. I go down the mall's sunken front steps and walk up to the glass-fronted entrance. The glass is boarded up, covered over with plywood. The sign taped over it says the entire mall is set to be demolished in two weeks.

I'm not sure what's more surprising—that the address on Rudy's note is for a mall or that he might have actually meant to be here at midnight.

Midnight and malls don't mix.

I'm pretty sure *Rudy* and malls don't mix.

I tug at the handle of the door, feeling both ridiculous and annoyed. And of course the door's locked, so I let go of the handle and stand there for a moment, considering. Then I peer closer at the lock to see how much full magic it would take to open it.

Everything logical says I should turn around and just go home, but there's no way I can leave this place without going inside. Rudy died while speaking of meaning to finish things, while having this note on his body—to leave this place now would be doing the very opposite of what I promised him while coming here tonight.

The lock is a typical one for an outer door. Meaning, as with all locks in public places, that leftover magic can't touch it. You either need its key or to cast full magic.

I take a small rock from my starter bag, draw a six-pointed star, and cast.

Nothing happens.

The ground stays asleep instead of sending the full magic I just called for. My feet aren't even remotely hot. The rock starter sitting in my palm is just as cold.

For a second, the world goes off-kilter: My full magic is gone. I'm transported back in time to a workroom and a red fire that wouldn't dance, to those few seconds when I was sure I would only ever cast leftover magic. Failure turns my mouth ashy.

My ears are roaring as I numbly open my starter bag and begin to riffle through it with unfeeling fingers: *Something else in here will work, something* must. As if ancient rules about how starters work have suddenly changed. Or a cure for lost magic can be found inside my *bag.*

The strange black coin clinks against my nails.

My heart pounds inside my chest as I pick up the coin. So much like a mark but not one at all—useless, then, unless you happen to know its real purpose. The world stays off-kilter as I hold the coin tightly enough for its edges to dig into my fingertips, a near kind of vertigo that still leaves me dizzy. Nothing seems real.

Oh, Rudy—what were you up to?

I draw a six-pointed star on my palm once more. I drop the coin into the middle of it.

There's a clicking sound as the lock of the door twists open.

I wait for the pain to come like it always does, a thrumming ache that starts behind the eyes and ends up a sting in my nose. Sometimes nosebleeds from casting gush and sometimes they don't—a six-pointed star for unlocking a door has a different effect than six points for a mind wipe—but their arrival is always the same.

The pain, when it comes, is a fraction of what I'm expecting. Here and then gone, a spark that doesn't catch fire.

I keep waiting for it, sure it's only delayed, not understanding. Full magic without pain is as disorienting as the sky without its robe of smog—it's impossible.

I look at the starter still in my palm. The black coin had been an oddity from the start, but only because I'd never seen anything like it before. Its strangeness feels different now. Like I'm about to encroach on something much bigger than I am. Something meant for someone stronger, more experienced.

What am I getting into here?

I drop the coin back into my bag with shaking fingers.

"Last chance," I mutter out loud. Just as I said to Coral this morning, which feels like an eternity ago. *So are you in or out?*

I release a shaky breath. "Guess I'm in."

I pull open the door and go inside.

The dark wavers but stays mostly solid—the paper covering the band of windows is thin, but so is the light from outside. It takes my eyes a minute to adjust to this part of the mall. The only sound in here is my breathing. I take off my mask and fold it away.

There's an elevator in the middle of the floor. A mall directory juts out from the floor beside it. A blur of deep shadow farther down is likely the escalator. That's all. There's nothing else.

I go to the directory, half-convinced someone's going to pop up from somewhere and know I'm not Rudy. Know I'm trespassing—a fake—and make me leave.

But no one does, and I squint in the half dark, reading for something to explain this weird night.

There are three more levels below this one—two of retail and a food court floor on the bottom. A typical setup.

Then my pulse speeds up.

Food court.

FC.

Everything I see says the power to the whole place has already been cut—the covered-up windows, boarded-up door, and a demolition date just two weeks away. The idea of walking down the escalator in the dark, step by step, feels like a terrible one. So I move over to the elevator to see if it's working.

I blow a breath into a cupped palm and cast leftover magic to call the elevator.

The motor stays silent.

Just as the lock outside did not twist open.

But now I know about the strange black coin.

The vertigo from earlier—that sense of things not being quite real—swims back. I fumble open my starter bag and fish out the coin. I cast.

The motor hums to life and the cab climbs. The elevator doors open with a ping.

I step inside before I can change my mind. I jab the button for the food court and cast around the coin again. The doors shut, the floor drops, and my stomach drops along with it.

Cold sweat films my skin. I shove the coin back into my bag and clutch it to me like it's some kind of lifeline.

"Yep," I mutter out loud. "I guess I'm definitely in."

TWELVE

I curse Rudy for dying with a cryptic note. Curse myself for finding it, for not being able to let things go.

Third floor.

Aza, what are you doing?

My own voice in my head, sounding panicked.

You're in a building you got into using magic that makes no sense. Go back.

The black coin's peculiarity, still on the skin of my palm like something alive. "I can't. I have to finish this."

Second floor.

Rudy didn't write that note for you.

"I know."

How is this going to help you with Saint Willow? Help you with the cop?

"I have no clue."

FC.

The ping sounds again, the elevator doors open, and I step into the food court.

Everything comes at me at once. I don't know where to look first as an already off-kilter world tilts even more.

You and parties at midnight, Rudy—I never would have guessed.

However this place appears during daylight hours, I'm willing to bet magic that it's far different.

People are everywhere—two hundred, maybe even three. Groups of them fill the middle of the floor, which has been cleared of the eating stations, having conversations and calling out names to those who pass by. Others are busy looking for empty spots at the tables and chairs pushed to the sides of the room.

There's a sense of anticipation here. The noise of a crowd that's waiting for something to happen. My own nerves buzz, wanting to understand what's going on. The room's setup reminds me of a show and its audience. Was Rudy coming to watch something?

I peer upward at the lights that float just beneath the ceiling, dozens of oversized bulbs, running on magic because the power to the mall has already been cut.

My mind struggles with the impossible, with the *possibility* of the impossible. What if there is a third kind of magic in this world? One that works when the others fail, and only with certain starters like the strange black coins? What if there's a kind of magic that's as powerful as full magic can be, but is kinder to its casters? Pain that is a brief eclipse instead of a long blackout?

Or maybe it's magic that works only at this address. Or only after midnight. Or according to rules I've yet to understand.

Rudy, did you know? Or would you have been here, just as stunned as I am? I think you'd agree with me that if either of us had to pull enough magic to keep all these light bulbs lit, we'd already be dead and the city burning.

". . . want to enter, make sure you're registered!"

I swivel at the raised voice, my pulse speeding up at the word *enter*. I hear Rudy again as he bled on the floor: *Meant to enter . . . meant to finish what I started . . .*

"Fighters, come get registered! You've got to register if you want to fight!"

Fighters? There's a *fight* tonight?

I *really* didn't know Rudy.

I follow the sound of the voice, weaving through the crowd, and soon I've crossed the floor and am at the restaurants lining the back of the food court.

The voice belongs to the guy who's standing behind the counter of a burger place. The word REGISTRATION is scrawled across the front menu in thick white chalk.

"Fighters," he calls out, "if you mean to enter, come get registered! As always, first fight opens as soon as we register fighter number fifty!"

I hesitate, unsure, wishing there were someone to ask. I'm only here because I'm supposed to know—will they kick me out if they realize it's Rudy's note, not mine? That would end my search for answers before it's begun.

A caster—a girl, White, younger than me—moves up to the counter.

"Fighter, here to enter," she calls out, her tone completely confident.

I move a step closer, listening as closely as I can without being obvious about it. Less obvious than Rudy's cop, anyway, I would hope.

"Ring name for the books?" The guy drags over a clipboard.

Ring name.

The name a boxer or wrestler uses for matches to keep their real name a secret.

Dread threatens. Boxing and wrestling—what do I know about either? And yet, Rudy was definitely neither, so why did he mean to come? And the girl doesn't seem to be any closer to being a boxer or wrestler than I do, but she's here entering without seeming scared at all.

What am I missing?

Maybe this isn't about boxing or wrestling at all. Maybe there's still magic somehow, if floating light bulbs and mysterious black coins mean anything . . .

"Kylin," the girl tells the guy behind the counter.

He nods and scrawls her name down on the clipboard. He uncaps a white pen and holds it out.

Kylin leans forward, her braid a stream of bright chestnut down her back, and the guy writes something on her face.

"Don't forget to get over to the starter counter as soon as you can," he tells her. "It's the pizza place tonight. And listen for the bell—if you're late, you're out. Winnings and cuts can be picked up at the bets counter after the fight. Good luck."

Starters. Relief swamps me.

"Thanks." She turns to leave. The name KYLIN glows from one cheek as she slips into the crowd.

I move up to the counter before I can chicken out. If it ends up that there are actually no answers to be found here, or if it's impossible for me to keep my promise to Rudy—I'm no boxer *or* wrestler— I'll just leave. No one will ever know.

"Ring name for the books?"

"Rudy."

I watch him write it down on a lined piece of paper. He puts the number thirty-eight in front of it.

Then he writes on my cheek.

I feel better with my ring name on it. No one seeing it would guess I don't know what I'm doing. A deception is as good as casting magic, and I don't even have to be in pain for it.

But now to get to the starter counter. *Don't forget*, the registration guy made a point of saying not just to Kylin but also to me. Which means it's probably important.

I find the bets counter before the starters one. As much because I see it—the word BETS is written over the main menu of the noodle bar—as I hear it. Just as the guy at registration was calling loudly for fighters, *two* more men from the bets counter shout out for wagers. They're standing in front of the restaurant, their voices rising above the crowd. Behind the counter, three people are frantically taking bets.

"Spectators, get your bets in now for tonight's match!"

"Place your win here! Fifty fighters going tonight, so c'mon and get your picks in!"

"Minimum bet is five marks, and you got your choice of status- or technique-style wagers!"

Gamblers press close at the counter, hurrying to place their bets and calling them out over one another.

"Ten marks on Cheddar to be a bow-out!"

"Seventy-mark technique on Paddy to cast two skins!"

"Fifty marks on returning champion Finch to survive, and five on Clayton to be a knockout!"

"Twenty on Lil to survive, then twenty on Aimee to cast a blood!"

Cast two skins.

My ears pick up on the phrase the way speakers listening to a foreign language strain to catch words like their own. It's more proof there's magic involved in some way tonight. And while I don't understand any of the betting terms I just heard, something the registration guy said comes back:

Winnings and cuts can be picked up at the bets counter after the fight.

Winnings must mean fighters can place bets, too, maybe even on themselves. And cuts must mean if anyone bets on you, you get a portion of whatever they win.

Maybe tonight isn't just going to be about Shire and Rudy and uncovering secrets, I think as I leave the bets counter and continue searching for the starters one. Maybe I'll make some marks along the way. If I can figure out what I'm doing and make others believe it enough to lay bets on me.

One week before Saint Willow snaps.

My already-buzzing nerves wind up even tighter.

I spot a few other fighters in the crowd as I keep walking along the food court's restaurants. The white writing on their cheeks flickers and winks as I walk by, like stars do in a dark sky.

A guy in his twenties whose ring name is Wilson.

A balding Asian guy in his forties, and his ring name is Crawl.

A tall blonde, fair-skinned woman in her thirties—Aimee.

Who are you? How did you come to be here? Why do you fight? Did the ghosts of those you've failed chase you here? Promises you mean to keep? Marks? Cops and gangsters and families who don't see you?

I get to the pizza place a few minutes later. The word STARTERS is scribbled across the menu in white chalk. It's a woman behind the counter, looking bored. I keep a few steps back, remembering to be cautious again.

Instead of pizza slices, there are baskets of coins behind the glass of the display case. Square holed coins just like the black one I found with Rudy's note, but in shades of red, white, silver, and gold.

I peer around for Kylin, hoping she listened to the registration guy just like I did and is here. But there's no sign of her, and no else has gone up to the counter yet, either. I hesitate, not wanting to wait so long that it becomes too late to do whatever I'm supposed to be doing.

I glance up at the guy who's come up beside me—tall, dark hair, hazel eyes. He's around seventeen or eighteen and White, like Kylin.

"Are you in line to buy, or . . . ?" he asks me, trailing off.

The seriousness of his navy button-up shirt is saved by the perfect way it fits. His tone is friendly enough, but his expression says he's in a hurry. His cheeks are bare. So either he hasn't registered to enter yet or he's not a fighter.

"No, go ahead," I say. In my head I'm already calling him Navy. "Sorry, I'm still . . . deciding."

Navy's eyes slide to my cheek, and he nods and moves up to the counter. I can hear him from where I'm standing, so I just wait, listening.

"Hey, seven of each," he tells the woman. He sets marks down on the counter. "You need a ring name from me before selling or anything?"

"It's fine, I still remember you from last year's tournament," she says. "Need another key just in case?"

Tournament.

The word and all its implications echo loudly in my head—so much for simply showing up at midnight and somehow getting all my answers. I should know it's never that simple. If it were, then I wouldn't be casting illegal magic while lying to my parents, avoiding a gangster's henchman, and running from a suspicious cop, all because I'm trying to save the family legacy.

And Navy was around last year. Had he been a fighter? I wonder how much I can get him to share about the whole thing while pretending I know exactly what he's talking about.

"Nope, no more keys needed, just the ring ones," he says to her now.

She takes out seven coins of each color—all but the black—and sets them down on the counter. "That's two hundred and eighty marks."

Navy nods, places his marks on the counter, and slides the colored coins into his hand. "Should all be there, thanks."

So the black starters are *key* starters, while the colored starters are *ring* ones. And while the key starters are reusable—I cast on both the mall door and the elevator using the same black coin—the ring starters aren't, considering how many Navy bought.

I get the black ones being called keys, since they got me into this place. But as for ring starters, I'm still lost. I wonder if it's connected to us choosing ring *names*. If it is, then us being fighters explains a lot—we must have to use the starters in a ring of some kind. But in a ring for . . . a match? A match consisting of . . . what, exactly?

I guess I'll find out soon enough. The registration guy said that the fight starts once fifty fighters are registered—I'm number thirty-eight, so that means there are twelve more fighters to go.

It hits me then—I don't have any marks. After Jihen found me this afternoon, I had to pay him what I made casting magic for Coral's mind wipe. I haven't had another buyer since.

My heart sinks, and I start to dig my hand into my jeans pocket to check anyway. Now I do regret chucking that last mark at Jihen's head, no matter how pettily satisfying it felt in its childishness.

Navy pauses slightly as he passes me.

Uncertainty flashes across his face as he takes in whatever he sees on mine. His eyes flicker toward the crowd before coming back, and he slows down to an actual stop. I can practically hear him stifle his impatience as he forces himself to be polite.

Don't bother, I almost feel like saying out loud. *Seems like we're only going to be fighting each other anyway—I bet it's better for us to not even meet.*

"You lose something? You seem kind of distracted."

I shake my head. "No, it's okay."

"I could help you look if you think it might be nearby or something . . ."

His hope that I turn him down is so obvious I bite back my own impatience, then a wave of embarrassment comes. It makes me think of Rudy and how he was always so reluctant with whatever I asked of him.

"I didn't lose anything, I just—"

I break off when my fingers hit the bulk of a folded-up wad in my pocket. Marks. But where did I—?

Rudy's wallet, that's where. Now it comes back to me. Checking his wallet for accidental paper trails, then taking his marks because he would have wanted me to . . .

I take them out and count—two hundred. Not too far off from Navy, who just spent two hundred and eighty and seems to know what he's doing.

I smile to let him know he can leave. "I thought I left all my marks at home, that's all. Thanks for offering to help, though."

His return smile is tentative. "Well, good thing you didn't actually leave them, then. Probably wouldn't get too far tonight without any ring starters."

"Definitely lucky. I don't think this is the kind of place that would let me buy on credit, either."

He laughs, and the sound of it is genuine, with a hint of rust in it that tells me he doesn't laugh like this a lot, and I'm not sure what it means that I don't feel very bad that I'm keeping him. I like how he doesn't seem like he's dying to get away anymore.

Since he really doesn't seem like the tattling type, I decide to take the risk and hint at how little I know. "Now I guess I need to decide what ring starters to buy."

"Oh." He drops his gaze to his new ring starters, still loose in his hand. He gives me a look that says he'd almost forgotten why he was here in the first place, and wariness slides into his eyes. And I can tell the second where he might have considered saying more slips away, if it was ever there at all. His expression goes tight, like I've secretly pulled magic on him to make him talk.

"You'll get your strategy down soon," he says. "All fighters do."

"You're right, they do. I'm sure I'll figure it out, too."

Navy nods and moves away, stuffing colored coins into his pocket. "See you."

I almost call out "Good luck!" as he disappears into the crowd, but think about how that might sound sarcastic when presumably we're going to be fighting each other.

Unless we're not. He had no ring name on his face. And I don't know the rules for this tournament yet. I assumed only fighters could buy ring starters here, but maybe that's not true. And the woman saying she recognized him from last year could mean almost anything.

I approach the starter counter, even though I'm still unsure of what to buy. But I can't wait any longer—what if I run out of time?

The woman behind the counter is still bored-looking. "What would you like?"

"Do you . . . have recommendations?" I know how inane the question is as soon as I ask it. Like I'm asking about a dinner special. I could just do as Navy did and buy some of each.

But if he's not a fighter here—or maybe not one any longer—maybe there's a reason for that.

The woman slowly lifts both eyebrows. "Say again?"

I sense the red climbing up my neck. "I mean, do fighters usually buy one kind of starter more than the other?"

She shakes her head. "Fighters buy what they buy. I really can't say much more about ring starters than that."

"Okay, thanks." It does make sense that she has to stay impartial and not have any suggestions. It wouldn't be fair if she had favorites and still had to work with every single fighter.

I stare at the baskets of coins, thinking fast, knowing I'm

supposed to *know* how ring starters work. The woman's gaze is unmoving from my face, and I wonder what she sees. I'm worried about being kicked out for sneaking in, but what if I'm not thinking dark enough? I could be a spy. Or working for a Scout. Something happening to me would send a definite message to cops hunting down certain kinds of magic.

One of the spectators I overheard placing a bet put marks on whether a fighter would cast skin spells. Which means it's reasonable to assume that each coin is just a different kind of starter. And that they work with this third kind of magic that I don't yet understand, the same kind of magic that worked with the black key.

Four colors—red, white, gold, and silver—for four different kinds of spells—skin, bone, blood, and breath. I'm afraid to ask which color coin stands for which spell, so I'm just going to have to guess.

"Five of each kind, please," I say, hoping my voice doesn't shake. Her eyes are still probing, and I want to get away. I'm buying some of each as Navy did anyway, despite doubts about mimicking his strategy if he's not a fighter. If Rudy would have had a different method, I'll never know.

"Need another key?" the woman asks.

Navy didn't buy another ring key, so I'm assuming I won't need another one, either. "No, just the ring starters, thanks."

She sets the pile of coins down on the counter. "Five of each, for a total of twenty ring starters. That'll be two hundred marks even."

I hand over every single mark of Rudy's, and the gesture feels very final somehow. It lands somewhere in my stomach and sits there like a cramp. The gravity of the moment presses hard—passing over this last thing of Rudy's is like losing my last tangible grasp on Shire's secret life.

I slide the starters off the counter and stuff them into the pocket of my jeans, not wanting to mix them up with my usual ones in my starter bag. I know the rules of full magic and of leftover magic, but not the ones of this magic and its specific starters. A quick escape in an emergency wouldn't be so quick if I grab a starter that doesn't work.

I'm sure that they must be getting pretty close to fifty fighters by now. So I duck inside the food court's washroom, remembering to listen for the bell that says the fight's starting—*if you're late, you're out.* Only one of the five stalls is occupied, and I hop into a free one.

I'm about to flush when the sound of quiet retching comes from the other stall.

I wait, holding my breath, unsure of what to do. Ignore? Ask?

"Um, you okay?" I finally call out.

There's a long pause. "Yeah, I must just be nervous."

Another fighter. She does sound nervous, her voice thin. And young. I peek down to see her shoes from beneath the stall.

Rose-gold sneakers, their canvas properly scuffed up. They're cute, even if they're not my style. But she's definitely more a kid than a grown-up.

"I'm nervous, too," I tell her, trying to make her feel better. It's the truth anyway.

"You're also fighting tonight?"

"Yes, and I have no real clue what I'm doing," I let myself admit. I probably should be more careful. But since Shire died, there's been a lot I can't talk about with anyone—using full magic might be the biggest thing—but there's also all the stuff I keep from my parents. I can add killing Rudy to that list, too. And now, in this bathroom stall where no one can see me, I sense some of those secrets coming way too close to the surface, the ways they make me feel wanting to come out. "I'm still trying to figure out what I signed up for."

"Maybe I'll just cast a shield spell so I don't die, and wait everyone else out." Her laugh is tinged with hysteria. "Exciting, right?"

Die.

A chill washes over me.

The tile floor swims, and I brace my shoulder against the side of the stall. *Rudy, you couldn't have known, right? Couldn't you have just made plans for a midnight date?*

"I'd do a shield spell, too," I finally manage just for something to say. Though I'm not sure what she means.

"Well, right now I don't even care about winning," the other fighter says. "I just want to make it to the next round."

Her secrets are just like mine, threatening to bubble over. Would she be saying any of this if she could see me? It'd be like her handing me her fighter's psyche on a silver platter with the permission to take it apart.

Want to exchange secrets? I'm nearly tempted to call out. *You tell me what kind of fight this is supposed to be, and I'll tell you I don't belong here. Deal?*

But all I say is "Good luck." I don't really know how I mean it—not sarcastically, just as I wouldn't have meant it that way when I nearly said it earlier to Navy. Maybe I do want her to stick around during this tournament. Or maybe it's her secrets I'm wishing her luck with. I understand secrets right now more than I do this whole fighter thing, that's for sure.

"Thanks," she says. "You, too."

She flushes and the stall door opens.

I let her go without trying to see who she is. Which likely says something about *my* fighter's psyche, too.

Out in the food court, a loud bell rings.

THIRTEEN

I rush out of the washroom, my heart drumming high into my throat. My nerves are raw, too close to the surface of my skin. I wind my way into the crowd, heading toward the center of the food court. The expectancy in the air from just moments ago has gone sharp, vibrant, and my blood runs faster along with it. Excitement, fear, a kind of thrill that I don't fully understand but that's formed anyway—I feel everything.

The crowd is splitting up. Spectators go to line the walls and edges of the food court, cheering and clapping exactly the way crowds at events always end up doing. The tables and chairs being pushed to the sides make sense now, with people standing on them to see us.

I stand with the rest of the fighters in the middle of the floor, being seen, waiting for whatever's supposed to come next. I look at them, and terms like *bow-out* and *knockout* and *shield spell* run wild in my brain.

Some of them are alone, like I am.

And some of them aren't. A red-haired woman in a bright yellow silk dress fusses over a fighter whose ring name is Luan. He's taller than anyone else on the floor and has an artist's well-muscled hands, and I have no idea if either is an advantage or disadvantage here—you can't judge magic by its caster. The smallest person can cast the most powerful full magic, just like a physically clumsy person can have the most spell control.

I watch them and think that they are lovers. But then the woman ties a pink silk ribbon around his upper arm, shakes his hand, and leaves, and I realize it's something different. Boxers and wrestlers sometimes have managers, investors who make sure they get the right training and support—I guess fighters here have backers, too. Maybe Rudy was coming here to be someone else's.

The floor continues to thin. Soon there will only be fifty of us here in the middle.

There's Wilson, and Crawl, and Aimee. There's a fighter named Doll who's either got a condition that curves her back, or she's an Ivor who's managed to hide from the Scouts so far, her condition not dire enough that she needs to stop casting altogether. There's Robson, whose smirk doesn't hide the anxiety in his eyes. And more names, all flashing bright and white until they form a jumble in my head.

I spot Kylin, the fighter I listened to entering the tournament. She sounded so sure of herself and her expression says she still is. Her eyes are the same chestnut as her hair, and their gaze cool as she stares straight ahead, uncaring of everyone else still streaming away. I size her up, going from head to toe, and freeze.

She's wearing rose-gold sneakers.

Oh.

By the time I'm able to meet her eyes, she's already watching me. Her face says she peeked in the washroom to see my shoes, too. Another *oh.*

I'm debating if I should go over and say something—though what, I'm not sure, and she looks stunned enough that I can't predict what might happen. Then I see Navy.

His cheek is still blank. Not a fighter. But he's with a guy who *is*. He's about my age, blond to Navy's dark hair, green eyes instead of hazel. His gaze is flat and unfeeling, while Navy's has only been careful, wary. But they look enough alike anyway that I bet they're related—brothers, half brothers, maybe cousins. Shire and I were so different, but beneath everything our bones were the same. We shared the same kind of magic, if not its control.

The fighter's ring name is Finch.

I struggle to think back to where I heard that name tonight.

Fifty marks on returning champion Finch to survive . . .

So *he's* why Navy was around last year, and why Navy's back again. Not for himself. The woman at the counter remembering him being around last year's tournament also makes sense now—Navy wasn't memorable as a fighter, he was the champion's backer.

Navy ties a blue-striped ribbon around Finch's upper arm, gives him a light punch on the shoulder, and leaves. Finch doesn't bother to watch him go but instead turns to take in the crowd, like he's expecting a reaction. Demanding it.

They remember him. There are cheers of his name, a rise in the level of applause. I wonder how many people have bet on him tonight, how many marks are riding on him.

Beneath the coldness, his eyes are empty, and a chill runs along my skin.

Ghosts or promises or marks—but what if a fighter chooses to be here for no reason at all? Would they be the kindest because they have nothing to lose? Or the cruelest because of the same?

Soon the trickling away from the middle of the floor ceases and there's no one left but us.

Fifty fighters.

The food court slowly falls silent, the final throat clearing and bit of applause fading into echoes.

In one far corner of the crowd, a man stands up and begins to make his way toward us.

His suit is a dark slate-gray, sharp and classy. As he nears, I see the black plum blossom print on his tie, a paler gray handkerchief in the jacket breast pocket. He's in his forties, and he wears his dark hair slicked back from high cheekbones. Bright teal eyes take the time to meet each of ours in turn. It's a single glance that tells me everything I need to know: Whoever he is, he's the most powerful person in the room.

He reaches the middle of the floor and comes to a stop.

"Once, before the world banished full magic, it was full magic that helped create legends." His voice is a low rumble, too soft to reach everyone's ears. But somehow it does anyway, and his words hold the entire room rapt.

"Fifty competitors and a contest of skills," he continues. "Who would be the last caster standing? Who would be the strongest, fastest, most cunning? Who could fight honorably more than not? The ancient Tournament of Casters is why we still know legends such as Amani the Strong, Horvath the Fast, and Kelton the Clever. It's why we know Etana the Cruel, who *chose* dishonor in killing in order to win."

The power I saw in his eyes—it's the same kind that lines his words, threads through his voice.

"When the age of full magic came to an end, so did the tournament. For hundreds of years, no more contests of full magic were held. No more legends were created. Only leftover magic was permitted." Teal sweeps the crowd. "My name is Embry Rush, and as the Speaker of the Guild of Now, I'm here to welcome you to this year's Tournament of Casters."

Loud applause breaks out, but I remain unmoving, stiff with disbelief.

Nothing about this makes sense.

There's no such thing as the Guild of Now. There was only ever the Guild of Then. After the last of the original seven casters died, the Guild as it was died with them.

As for a Tournament of Casters, yes, once it *did* exist, and during the years that it did, legends *were* made of some of its champions. The Guild of Then created the tournament as a challenge and celebration of full magic, and every year casters from all over the world would gather together and battle one another to test their skills.

The first tournament took place nearly two thousand years ago, halfway across the world in the now-flooded Kan Desert of Barra. Some years saw the entry of less than honorable casters—every kid in school learned about Etana the Cruel—but whoever the champion and wherever the chosen location, the theme of showcasing full magic remained the same.

Just as Embry said, the Tournament of Casters hasn't taken place for a long time. After full magic was banned, the age of leftover magic took over and anything to do with full magic came to an end. And there's a very good reason for that. Fifty casters casting magic against one another over the course of a single tournament would shatter the earth into about a million pieces.

I watch Embry with narrowed eyes, not sure what to think at all. I'd thought him powerful, but I might have just mistaken it for madness.

He waits for the crowd to quiet. He hasn't smiled despite the applause. The directness in his gaze nearly convinces me he's sane.

"The rules of the tournament are still simple. Survive, and you move on to the next round. Don't get knocked out, and you move on. Don't request a bow-out, and you move on.

"And though full magic has changed so the tournament can't run as it once did, we've made it as close as possible. We'll be casting full magic—a diversion spell—around the fighting rings so no Scouts will be able to find us. The Guild's magic will help contain your magic to within the ring—damage to the earth will be minimized. Our magic will also strengthen your bodies as you fight, so pain and injury will be slowed.

"There will be a fight every night, for a total of four, including the championship. The last caster standing will be crowned champion, the winner of two hundred thousand marks, and eligible for membership in the Guild of Now. To become a modern great."

Now Embry does smile, and it turns him from powerful to charming, from frightening to merely intimidating. The change is disarming for how sincere it seems. I almost wonder if I'm wrong about him being dangerous.

I look for Kylin to see her reaction, but I can't see her. I *do* catch sight of Finch, and the raw hunger on his face is startling, almost hard to look at.

So now I know what he's fighting for anyway—not just for two hundred thousand marks but to also become a member of the Guild of Now. To become a modern great.

"Of course, while every member must be a champion, not every champion will become a member," Embry continues. "We use the tournament to help us determine who might be a fit for the Guild—who will be great, as it were. It's not just about how much magic you can draw, but how you control it, how you use it, how you *don't* use it. New membership is determined by a majority vote, and because we maintain a strict seven-member standing, only when a current member chooses to leave is a new one considered and put to the vote.

"It doesn't need to be said, but as Speaker of the Guild, I will say it anyway: Outside of fights, the tournament doesn't exist. If you decide to reveal us, you will experience the full magic of seven very powerful casters turned against you. And I can guarantee it will not be a particularly pleasurable experience."

I very nearly glance around, wondering where the rest of the Guild *is*. If Embry is just one of its seven members, shouldn't there be six more of him around, all of them casting all their magic to keep the tournament running?

But then I realize how they *are* here, even if I can't see them. The Guild is the *tournament* itself, its own nebulous cloud of the very magic that has put it together. The Guild is in the floating light bulbs, in every single ring starter, in the air, maybe even as parts of

Embry himself. They are everywhere here. To be a fighter in the tournament is for the Guild to always be close.

I shuffle a bit on my feet, not sure if I'm more creeped out or impressed.

Now Embry's smile does disappear, and his teal eyes go back to reminding me of his power. What is he when he's not a member of a secret and powerful guild of casters? A lawyer? A con man? A gangster like Saint Willow?

"The original Kan Desert is long gone now, flooded over," he says. "But as the original greats once brought their tournament there, then so will we."

FOURTEEN

The world changes and I'm standing in sand.

The floor of the food court is now an endless stretch of dunes, of swirls of dusty clay. The ceiling's turned into a sky of blue that no longer happens over Lotusland. There's already grit in my mouth, coating my teeth. The air is dry and hot.

The Kan Desert.

It hasn't existed for over a thousand years.

I bend down and touch the sand, letting it run over my fingers and get stuck beneath my nails. It covers my sneakers, the trickle of it brown and dusty through the laces. A sudden thirst prickles my tongue, and I'm parched, desperate for water. My throat hurts for real.

Embry's power is a palpable thing—I felt it myself. But each of the seven members of the Guild of Now must be just as powerful, their full magic working together to convince not just one mind of a lie but hundreds of minds, all at once. How else to explain full magic that doesn't hurt its creators? Magic held together with a level of control that doesn't split the earth but turns it into its toy?

If my own full magic is a red fire, then that of this tournament is like all fires put together. It is magic of another time. When we didn't have to pretend.

I stand up on trembling legs and peer out at the cheering crowd. A chill passes through me despite the desert heat. Reality wavers, and I know I'm slipping—who am I? A caster pretending to be someone else, sneaking around the back alleys of this city to keep surviving? Or a caster who really believes she can become a new great, about to measure her magic against that of others?

The food court tables and chairs are gone, the outer ring of them now upswept piles of sand. Spectators sit on their tops the same way crows perch on power lines. They're shouting down at us from above, cheering and calling out our names. I don't have to see their eyes to know they want to see full magic. To see us fight with it. It's in the air like an electric charge, a storm about to break. What had been anticipation in the food court has become a thirst out here in the desert.

I suddenly feel very small within the vastness of the Guild's magic, inside this tournament that is beyond a contest. In reality, this building should be hanging in tatters. This ancient part of earth should never again exist before anyone's eyes.

But I rub sand from my fingers.

Rudy, you should be the one seeing this. I'm sorry to have taken it away.

"The tournament's full magic is a closed system," Embry says. "Only the Guild's key starters will give you access to the fighting locations. Only our ring starters—red for blood, white for bone, gold for skin, silver for breath—and the elements taken directly from within the fighting rings will work as starters. As the world once was, you can cast full magic here and not die, just as the world won't die."

Embry turns and heads out toward the crowd. Desert kicks up at his feet.

Five seconds later he stops and looks back, like he's forgotten to say something. Everyone goes quiet, waiting.

"The opening round will be a ten-minute free-for-all—whoever remains standing at its end will move on to the next round." He squints teal eyes against the bright sun as he moves away. "Those ten minutes start now. Good luck."

In the blazing hot desert, time freezes. Fighters around me go absolutely still. I don't even breathe because I forget how to.

Just . . . fight?

Just . . . start?

It's the caster whose ring name is Aimee who wakes up first.

She bends down and scrapes sand into her palm. She turns to the fighter next to her—his cheek is emblazoned with his ring name of Morton—and casts, her finger a blur.

An eight-pointed star and a bone spell. Full magic.

Morton lifts off upward and back. Like his entire rib cage is taking off and dragging him along. Three long airborne seconds later and fifteen feet away he lands with a dull thud. Sand flies up in a cloud around him. His groan of pain comes through it.

We all stare at Aimee. She stares back, just as shocked. She drags her hand to her nose.

There's a single long smear of blood on her finger. No more comes.

No one speaks as we all wait for a sound, a sign. What part of the landscape is going to crack?

But the desert remains unchanged.

Then someone shouts, another fighter casts, and Aimee doubles over as though she's been kicked. Two seconds later everything is chaos as fighters turn on one another. Through all the frenzy, I'm vaguely aware of searching for Finch. To keep track of his bright blond hair and unfeeling eyes and the danger he is as the reigning champion. For a second, Navy and his perfectly fitted shirt appear in my mind, and I think of how he's somewhere up in the sand, watching.

Whoever Finch is to you, you'd understand why I'm going to have to try beating him, right?

The chaos deepens. Casters are yelling, falling, throwing magic at one another to prove their own is the best. Someone is pinned to the ground by some spell I can't see, and he slams his hand down on the ground three times.

"Bow out!" his lips bellow. "Bow out!" A second later he turns into a statue, a marble form still lying on the ground.

No, something else has turned him into a statue, I realize. He's been turned by the Guild of Now that is all around us in its nowhere-yet-everywhere form, watching for fighters who are eliminated and putting them on hold until the end of the match.

I can't seem to move. Everything around me unfolds, and it's like I'm watching a movie. This isn't happening right here, it only appears to be.

Sort these, Aza. Rudy in my head, saying what he always said to me when he set me to work in his apothecary. *Think of a good system. First things first, then work outward from there.*

I drop to a crouch, mind whirring as I peer low across the sand. The same way I peered low in a washroom stall to see rose-gold sneakers, to hear another competitor's secret to survival.

Maybe I'll just cast a shield spell so I don't die, and wait everyone else out.

Shield spell.

Because first things first.

I dig at the ring starters in my pants pocket. My fingers are clumsy, already sweating, and I swear out loud. I'm still glad I kept the starters out of my starter bag, but I'm not so sure about being able to get to them fast while they're in my pocket.

And I swear out loud once more for Embry and his Guild of Now—if anything from a fighting ring can be used as a starter, why build a ring that is nothing but an endless field of sand?

Finally I'm able to yank my hand free.

In my palm, flashes of white and silver.

I stuff the white coin back into my pocket.

How many points to cast a shield spell and keep it going? Too many, and it'll weaken any other spells I cast; too few, and someone else's magic will break through.

Everything's a jumble, so I let caution win. I draw a seven-pointed star, drop the silver coin into my palm, and puff a breath onto it. I imagine an impenetrable layer of red fire wrapping itself around my body, as cool and safe as flowers, jasmine and wisteria.

The air around me bends, goes wavy, like a just-invisible cocoon—an invisible suit of armor. The bodies of other casters blur the way hot pavement blurs. I'm standing on sand that appears half-liquid. The sound of the desert goes muffled and gauzy.

I let the spent silver starter slip from my hand and brace myself for the pain of casting to smash into my bones. Only when the wave of it comes, goes, and then doesn't come back, do I remember: Casting here won't hurt as badly.

But then a *different* pain comes. A dozen punches all coming at once.

I let out a strangled half scream.

The image of red fire slips away as I slam forward onto my stomach. Pain drives down on my arms and legs and back, and my mouth kisses the desert.

Shock reverberates as I struggle to turn my head, spitting out sand and trying to absorb the truth:

I'm going to have to get way better at holding on to a shield spell.

The desert around me is a swelling tide of noise, cheers and applause and heckling from the crowd, fighters yelling and screaming.

I move my eyes and there's a guy two feet away—thin, pale, watching me. His cheek says his ring name is Teller. His hand is still in a fist, clutching the starter for the spell he just cast on me.

I don't have to see the starter to know that it's a gold coin. Good for a skin spell, an impact one on my muscles to break my concentration so I'd drop my protection spell.

Teller grimaces as his hand lifts to his temple.

Headache.

The price he has to pay for having cast that nine-point spell.

The invisible hammers of my own pain start to pull back, and my thoughts rush together as I slowly lurch off the ground. My fingers grapple at sand.

Casting nine points would normally take me half a day to sleep off. I'm guessing it'd be about the same for Teller. These are the most general rules of full magic, of the spells we cast and how much they cost.

But not here. And not for this headache, which will only be a glimmer, the pain of it just as brief.

Before I can waste time deciding how long I actually have, I pick up the sand I've scrabbled together with my fingers. Different skin spells I can choose to cast flash across my brain.

I can make his muscles go numb or knot them up. I can turn his headache blinding.

Or I can simply cast to kill. Only here in this fighting ring, with its made-up rules that don't punish me for knowing full magic, is this chance possible. And I want to win this tournament, don't I? What do I care about being dishonorable and not getting voted into the Guild, when all I want is the two hundred thousand marks? How would honor help me figure out things about Rudy and Shire and payback?

Can you ever be sure you're using magic and it's not using you?

My father's words as we sat at the table in the teahouse earlier tonight, the kindest ones he knows for telling me he doesn't trust me.

I cast before Teller has recovered, while still a bit breathless, with sweat dripping down my face.

A palmful of sand, and he's clutching at his eyes. A thin shard of agony ripples down my spine.

Another palmful, and the desert around Teller rises in a cloud. It circles his head, a mass of swirling sand.

I dig out a second silver ring starter from my pocket. I cast, and my shield spell comes back. I draw six points this time, paint up cool red fire and rhododendrons and chrysanthemums in my mind.

I stagger, unsteady; blood drips from my nose, once, twice, three times. The desert pales, turns gray, before righting itself.

The sound of the crowd changes, a surge of cheers and applause the way an incoming tide surges. I wipe my face and turn to see what's happening. Bright blond hair glints beneath the sun, the wave of a blue-striped ribbon. It's Finch, being impressive. I catch a glimpse of his face, and it's back to the way it was before he gave away his longing for the Guild, stony and unreadable. He cuts his way through fighters, and I look elsewhere around the desert.

Casters have fallen.

There are thirty of us left, maybe thirty-five. Eliminated fighters are sprawled all over, marble statues tipped on their sides. Spilled blood lies in dark, coppery swaths across the sand. The air smells of fire and smoke as earth is drained more of its magic, a well visited by too many buckets. I taste salt and metal on my lips.

It's too easy to imagine this fake world being on fire for real. A single fighter here could do it with one spell, if the Guild's magic wasn't so protective. No wonder the earth took back our magic when we couldn't learn limits. It must have been able to see itself being set on fire, too.

Teller's tripped out of that swirl of sand I cast around him and is stumbling in my direction.

My hand's still in my pocket as he goes flying through the air.

The fighter who cast the punch on him is a woman with the ring name of Nola. She's in sand up to her ankles, having snuck up on him while he was still coiled up and more than half-blind.

He crashes to the ground.

Nola pushes up her glasses with a light brown finger, draws another star on her palm, and begins to cast. She casts over and over again, her hands a blur as she draws, blows on her palm, repeats. Each punch of air pushes Teller deeper into the desert, until he's nearly entirely buried.

Finally she stops. She's gone ashen beneath her complexion, breathing hard. She leans over and retches.

Teller doesn't move at all. Knockout.

A second later, he is a marble statue, held in the invisible arms of the Guild until it's over.

I jerk a starter out of my pocket. It's red, good for a blood spell. I'm about to cast on Nola when another fighter finds me first.

I know this because I can't breathe.

A ringing sound fills my ears and time shrinks. My eye sockets start to burn. It could be a skin spell on my lungs so they don't work, on the part of my brain that tells those lungs how to work, manipulation of my air itself with a breath spell, but what does it matter when I can't breathe, *I can't breathe*—

It's Kylin.

Her eyes stay locked on my face as I strangle. They shimmer like they're damp, like she's sorry. Gray fog swims across mine, turning the desert into stormy sea. My heart is bursting.

You know my secret, her gaze says. She swipes at her eyes. *I have to do this.*

And because I still can't breathe, I picture the blood spell I know will save me. I picture my hand on a spigot, turning it to full blast, and cast.

Kylin begins to bleed—from her mouth, nose, eyes, ears. Breath whooshes back into my lungs, and I'm gasping, coughing, crying as the pain pounds at me like a dozen fists.

The desert sand begins to turn black at her feet. She begins to gurgle, the sound too much like my own still-jagged breathing.

The crowd is louder than ever. The sound smashes into the roar of the casters around us, still fighting. My mind is at war.

I should save her. A counterspell will do it.

I should eliminate her. Because only one of us is going to win in the end, and she knows one of my secrets, too.

The smell of the air has turned salty. Kylin's clutching at her neck, and her bloody eyes bulge. Her rose-gold shoes have turned maroon. Shoes for a kid.

I swear to myself, drag out a new red starter, and cast.

She falls to her knees, heaving in huge breaths.

I drop the red coin, and the desert swallows it up.

The blow comes without warning. A slam to the side of my head so that I see a blur of colors and taste blood. Before I can fall, I'm twisting through the air. My back smashes hard into the desert floor so that sand arcs up in sheets.

I can't even gasp for breath. Overhead, the sky is such a bright crystalline blue, it almost hurts to look at it. Sand floats back down, and for a second, it's like being buried.

He appears through the clouds of tan and gray, the fighter taller than anyone else in the desert, with the perfect hands of an artist. Luan's skin has gone as pale as milk where it's not covered in bruises or blood. There's enough desperation in his eyes that I know he's completely dangerous. His silk ribbon hangs from his arm, sodden with blood.

He's holding a starter in his fist. I can't see the color, can't predict the spell.

He opens up his palm, about to draw.

I roll over before I feel how much my body hurts. I scratch at dirt as I go and drag myself to my feet, finally able to gasp now. I draw and my mind reaches for red fire. I draw and imagine it filling my veins and making me more than I am, powering up muscles until they are simply power contained. I draw until my arm is lightning and its cracking is in my mind, stinking and smoking and alive.

Rudy, controlling magic is like sorting, putting everything in its place.

But sometimes it's also just like another way you said it might be.

About not overthinking it, about just letting go.

I stagger to my feet and face Luan. I start running at him, and surprise widens his eyes when I don't stop—magic has never needed contact.

I cast right as I slam my fist directly into his face.

Full magic meets bone and surges through. He soars through the air and lands twenty feet away. Sand halos up around him. He doesn't move.

Knockout.

The crowd shouts. It's a waterfall of noise, crashing down. Faces go in and out of focus.

It finally sinks in that they're cheering for *me*.

I turn in a jagged circle in the middle of the desert. Pain is a knife that cuts through my middle, and I half hunch over as I keep turning. I'm searching for the next caster to fight, the next fighter I have to knock out. I'll let it happen without thought, let it be borne on nothing but impulse. I won't fight what just wants to be. *What I am.*

I want to say dread fills me at the idea of having to cast, and it does. But there's a sick anticipation, too, because casting full magic is what we do.

The taste of the blood that coats my teeth makes my stomach roll; it makes me thirsty.

Can you ever be sure you're using magic and it's not using you?

What if I don't care to tell the difference anymore?

Then a bell rings across the desert.

The first round of the tournament is over.

FIFTEEN

There are twenty-one of us left.

I observe the others without trying to be obvious.

I bet they're all doing the same thing.

Beneath a fake desert sun, while standing in sand turned black with our blood, we're shy again with one another.

There's Nola, wiping her glasses on her shirt and squinting at nothing in particular.

The twenty-something-year-old guy named Wilson, his grin huge and delighted.

Kylin, still covered in blood. Who won't meet my eyes. Who stares down at her ruined rose-gold sneakers.

Only Finch doesn't hide how he's observing. I sense his green eyes on the side of my face and wonder what he saw, if anything, of my fighting tonight. I wonder if Navy saw me fight and if he'll tell his fighter about it. And I wonder what Navy's real name might be, something that should be weird to think about right now if I weren't so desperate for normal things to think about.

Twenty-one.

I feel like a giant bruise. The pain from casting that last spell has already begun to fade, but I still hurt all over, from fighting and falling and being thrown. Adrenaline that kept me pumped during the fight is leaving me as quickly as it came, and now it all hits me at once—how it's long past midnight, how I just hurt a bunch of strangers with magic, how I'm still alive despite everything.

The crowd is still perched high on the sand above us. They won't stop cheering and clapping and the sounds of both hurt my ears.

I make out one chant:

Rudy the First!

It's not Rudy the Amazing, but it's also not Rudy the Dishonorable. I'd hate to be Rudy the Killer.

And then the Kan Desert is gone and we're standing in the middle of the mall food court again. The room is all floating light bulbs instead of a blazing yellow sun, a ceiling instead of the kind of blue sky the world hasn't seen for decades. The dunes are once more just tables and chairs. The sand's gone and the tile floor is back; used-up ring starters lie all over it the way coins do in the bottom of a wishing fountain.

Eliminated fighters are waking up, no longer marble. They get to their feet and head into the crowd, mere spectators now. Teller, Aimee, Crawl, Luan, others with ring names I can't remember. No caster was killed in the desert tonight.

One fight down, three more to go.

Embry is crossing the food court floor and heading toward us.

"Congratulations, everyone," he says. "And now we have twenty-one."

Wilson lifts an arm and hollers. His eyes flash with triumph, sweat glistening on his brown skin. "And soon it'll just be me."

The crowd whoops and whistles.

Embry's teal eyes glint. "You're confident."

"I'm a programmer. Built to always be thinking outside the box. It'll be easy." Wilson taps his temple with a finger.

The corner of Embry's mouth twitches. The reveal reminds me how he can easily be as charming as frightening, a desert made real with magic in order to fool.

"I beat a programmer one year to become champion," he says.

There's another whoop from the crowd. Wilson slowly lowers his arm.

Embry faces us, expression already back to veiled and cool. I bet that's how he looked when he fought, before his days in the Guild. I wonder why he stopped. If the memories of his fights are good memories or ones he dodges.

"The second round of the tournament will take place tomorrow at midnight, 1212 Thorn Avenue. Third floor. The third round the night after, and then the final the night after that. The Tournament of Casters *is* a test, and tests that are easy test nothing at all, so feel free to withdraw now if you think you're only going to withdraw later.

"If you move on but then miss a fight, you will unfortunately be eliminated from this year's tournament. A final thought for you to consider in the meantime: However well you think you fought tonight in the Kan Desert, you'll have to find a way to be even better, each and every night. On the night of the final, the fighter who wins will be the one who didn't only get better, but figured out the way to become the best."

Then he leaves, slipping away as smoothly as oil moves over heat. The crowd cheers some more before dispersing throughout the food court like bees leaving a hive. Most of the spectators head toward the bets counter, picking up whatever they've made tonight before leaving. Some linger close by, as if they're getting something by staying near those of us who cast as we did without dying.

When one of them pulls out a notebook and a pen for autographs, I turn and head toward the bets counter. Chances are small that anyone would have placed any bets on me. But it can't hurt to check. I have no marks left, and if Jihen finds me while I'm still empty-handed, Leafton might only be the first of our suppliers to mysteriously stop working with my parents.

But hoping for others to bet on me so I can eke out marks is one thing—winning the two hundred thousand marks as champion is another. Only one of them is under my control, so that's what I'll focus on.

The floor is still really crowded, but there's a sense of the night being over, and exhaustion tells me I need to get home and sleep. Just as before, the crowd in front of the bets counter is the thickest and loudest. Behind the counter, the three clerks who were taking those bets earlier are now checking spectators' bet receipts against the fight results.

I stay at the far side of the group, unsure. I don't have a receipt because I'm not a spectator and I didn't place any bets, but didn't the guy at registration say fighters got a cut of whatever winnings they brought in?

Soon I've shuffled my way to the counter. "Anything for Rudy?" I gesture toward my cheek. "Fighter number thirty-eight if you need to check the register."

The clerk has about half a dozen binders open in front of her. She pulls one over and flips through its papers.

"Oh, here you are. It's your first tournament."

I nod. Something like hope rises, though I know it's stupid. Maybe if the tournament allows betting *during* a fight, I have a chance of earning some marks. I started off okay with Teller, and then there was me not killing Kylin, and finally Luan at the very end.

The woman checks even more binders, and just when I'm sure there's nothing, she nods and checks off some columns. She reaches for an envelope from a box set below the counter and holds it out. "Fighter thirty-eight."

Stunned, I take the envelope from her. Inside are fifty marks. It's not much, but it's also not nothing. And someone—maybe *someones*—actually bet on me.

She reads my continued shock as disappointment. "I saw you fight, dear. I'll be shocked if dozens more bets aren't placed on you next round."

I smile and stuff the envelope into my starter bag. "Thanks."

I turn to go, weaving through the still-clustered crowd to get to the elevator, when I spot her.

The red-haired woman in the yellow silk dress, the one who was Luan's backer. Luan's tree height and strong hands meant little when it came to casting magic. My fist still stings from the punch, a tenderness in the knuckles that has less to do with the pain of having cast the magic for it than just smashing bone against bone.

Seeing the woman makes me think of another backer, and for a second I glance around for signs of Navy. Finch is last year's champion—it means a lot of spectators are betting on him. Navy, as his backer, would be here, picking up his winnings.

But he's nowhere to be seen. And it's just as well because neither is Finch, and the memory of Finch's delving eyes is something I can do without.

The woman in silk nears the bets counter, stopping to talk to one of the men who are calling out for spectators and their receipts.

I slip back toward the edge of the crowd and watch.

"Hello, Hugo," she says. "I'm here for my fighter's winnings."

He nods. "Just give me and Jack a few minutes, Piper, and we'll get you your marks. Not sure if it'll make you feel better that only a few spectators wagered on him getting knocked out tonight."

She arches a brow. "It doesn't."

"Sorry for the tough night."

"Yes, well, there will be other fighters." She opens up her evening bag, but instead of taking out a starter, she's checking her hair in a compact. "At least I'm saved from having to fund ring starters now—until I find someone new, anyway. Maybe next time I'll choose a fighter with a bit more flair. Luan was just so *conservative*."

I wait until Hugo's turned back to the crowd before approaching her. I'm too tired to be timid. I want to stop worrying about having marks for ring starters. And I don't think I'll get another chance as good as this.

"I'm the fighter who eliminated yours," I blurt out. There's no real good way of saying it. "And I'm looking for a backer."

SIXTEEN

Piper slowly drops her compact back into her purse. Her gray-eyed gaze goes to my cheek. The letters of Rudy's name must still be legible because I watch her eyes scan them.

"Ah, yes, the fighter who knocked out Luan from the tournament." Her tone is practically breezy. "Rudy the First for a physical punch, something the tournament's never seen before."

"I'm—"

"If you're about to say you're sorry, then you don't need a backer, as you won't last long enough to make it worth their marks."

The back of my neck gets hot. I don't regret beating Luan, but it's true I was about to say it.

"It seemed like the right thing to say," I mutter.

"Maybe anywhere else, but not at a tournament where you have to beat forty-nine others." Piper smooths a painted nail, oozing cool aggression much like the way Embry oozes power. "Backers can't have their fighters be sorry about winning. Poor investments, if so."

Her tone is still light, but it doesn't hide how she's grown annoyed. With Luan leaving her without a fighter, yes, but just as much with me for talking to her about it.

"I'll be your new fighter," I say. "Since Luan's been knocked out."

"Unfortunately, I'm not looking to back another fighter yet. I'll need at least one more round to watch and decide. You'll have to ask someone else."

I have no one else to ask. And one more round is one more round where I can't be sure I'll have marks to buy more starters.

"You'll be spending the tournament just watching other backers get rich," I say. "Not the greatest business tactic."

Piper's gaze sharpens. Her smile is nearly amused. "And I'll want to back you, since you're the one who knocked out Luan."

"I need a backer and you need a fighter."

"Backers only *need* fighters as long as they enjoy having a stake in the tournament," she says. "Now, why do you *need* a backer? You did well enough tonight. A lot of fighters never even consider it."

"I want to win those two hundred thousand marks. But first I need marks to buy starters."

"Piper," Hugo calls out, "got your fighter's winnings sorted here at the counter. Ready for you whenever you want to grab them."

Piper ignores him and keeps her eyes on me. Beneath them I feel like an insect pinned to a board. I can sense her coming to a decision the way I sense pain comes for magic.

"That's also unfortunate, but it doesn't change how I'll want to watch you fight once more before deciding. Come find me after the next round—*if* you survive it."

She steps away and heads toward the bets counter.

"You saw me fight tonight," I call out after her. My voice is thin and hoarse. The desperation in there hurts my throat. "I thought you wanted flair."

Piper slows down but keeps going.

"You *know* why I'm Rudy the First," I say.

I'm thinking it's too late when Piper stops. She speaks over her shoulder.

"The Mothery, Textile Sector, tomorrow. We'll talk."

"Wait—I—what?" But Piper ignores me and keeps moving. I swear she's laughing at my being so shocked. My pulse is fast and jittery, like I've been running. Or maybe it's real hope and it's just that I'm no longer used to it.

I want to wait for her to finish so I can talk to her again. What if I heard wrong? What if she's just kidding? What if—?

"Hey. Rudy."

I spin on my heel, nearly crashing into her, she's standing so close behind me.

Kylin.

"Sorry," I say to her when my mind goes blank for something more meaningful. *I'm sorry I nearly killed you, but I only did it because you tried first.* "I didn't see you there."

She frowns, but it's a thoughtful one, as though she's measuring me up. There's no sign of the confident caster I watched register as a fighter, but she's also not the one who couldn't meet my eyes afterward.

"Can we talk really quick somewhere?" She glances around. Her shirtfront is stiff with drying blood, and her rose-gold sneakers have been ruined forever. "Not here."

Suspicion comes. I make myself see the kid she is—thirteen, maybe fourteen—beneath the blood still on her face, the white ink of her ring name clinging to her cheek.

I wait for a group of casters to walk by before saying, "I think it's against the rules for fighters to talk." I'm making it up, but I don't want to say any more to her than I already have. Casting battle magic at someone is easier if you don't know them.

"There's no rule about not talking or Embry would have said it," Kylin argues.

"It's still not a good idea." I start to move away. So much for thinking I might wait for Piper.

"Just two minutes. I promise I won't try to kill you again."

I wish I could hate her or something, when really I just wish I'd been as gutsy a few years ago. Maybe I would have been able to convince my parents to let me help out earlier. Maybe then Saint Willow wouldn't be the problem he is now. Maybe Shire would still be alive, still here being my older sister.

"Two minutes," I mutter. "And if you try anything—"

"Why would I, now that you'd expect it?"

"Is that your fighting strategy, then? Just catching casters off guard?"

She shrugs with both shoulders. The gesture makes her seem even younger. "So can we go somewhere, then?"

"Where?"

She half smiles. "The washroom?"

Kylin twists shut the main lock using full magic. The pain from casting leaves her pale and trembling, tired-looking. The Guild's protection spell must have ended with the match. She should be saving her magic for tomorrow, but if she hasn't figured this out yet, she's not going to hear it from me. I'll be fighting her tomorrow, and I need all the advantages I can get.

I've already figured out I won't be able to cast myself clean before getting home, just as I won't be able to cast myself to heal, either. Casting more full magic now would just add even more pain.

More than that, I know casting full magic outside the fighting ring over the next three days isn't going to be a smart move at all. Not only would I be using up full magic when I should be saving it for fighting, but any pain from casting that magic will then come with me to the ring.

I'll have to turn away buyers, something I've never done before.

Saint Willow, Jihen, my family's debt—their shadows loom that much larger in my mind.

"Okay," Kylin starts, taking a deep breath, "I just wanted to talk to you about what I said before. About not caring about winning. You kind of said something like that, too, remember?"

"I didn't, I only said I was nervous. But okay, what about it?"

"I didn't mean it. Obviously. That's why I tried so hard to knock you out of the tournament."

I lift a brow. "That's an interesting way of saying you tried to kill me."

"I was trying to make you pass out."

Kylin does her best to look sorry when we both know she's lying. I know it because I've pulled the same trick before on Shire. My stomach clenches—I don't want to see myself in Kylin, to be that age again. It makes me think of Shire, being a big sister.

"You could have done it a dozen other ways," I say, trying to sound as cold as possible, "ways that wouldn't involve trying to kill me."

"I could have. I didn't. I'll choose better next time."

"What's the point of this conversation again?"

"See, what I said was stupid, and I really regret it now. So can we make a pact? For us to both forget what each of us said and not use it against each other during the tournament?"

"You know we might still end up having to fight each other, right? If we're the last two left, I'll still try to beat you."

Kylin nods. "But for now, let's pretend we never said that stuff. I kind of need to if I want to believe I can do this."

I'm pretty sure this moment might never happen again in the history of the tournament. How this might even be the very first—two fighters agreeing together to pretend to be brave.

Of course, I could always just say no.

I glance up at my reflection. My eyes are lined with purple, and a sheen of dried blood covers most of my skin—my clothes are unrecognizable. No, *I'm* unrecognizable.

Is this what being a fighter instead of just a caster means? To have to become someone else entirely? I drop my eyes, not liking this face of full magic that feels like a stranger's.

I use my finger and some spit to wipe the blood off my face and neck, then turn back to Kylin.

"Fine, we're making a pact. This doesn't mean we're friends or anything." *Don't make me care about having to save you again.* "We're both still going after the same thing."

"Thank you. For stopping out there, by the way." She attempts a smirk. "I guess it was the least you could do after ruining my lucky shoes."

"How lucky can they be, then?"

Kylin snorts and casts the door unlocked. The thick metal of the lock twists back into its original shape.

I move to leave, deciding to make a point of avoiding her over the rest of the tournament. I can't make friends while at this tournament. Not when enemies are easier to cast magic on.

"I'm going to need more than luck to beat Finch, anyway," Kylin says as I take another step. She sounds tired *and* miserable now. "Maybe it was beginner's luck—I still don't like how he won last year. But he must really want to be in the Guild, and unless you win, you won't even be considered."

Impatience ebbs and flows. I want to remind her, *You said two minutes, time's up, this conversation is over.*

Is this how Shire felt each time I pushed her? When I clung a little too hard, or for a little too long? And her eyes couldn't hide her frustration—the way I wanted too much?

"Still, he won," I say. "He must have been the strongest."

Kylin does that double-shoulder shrug again. "I was just a spectator last year, so maybe it's different when you're only watching. But he wasn't the favorite. When he won, I was really shocked. I think he cheated somehow."

I glance over at the washroom door and half wish for someone to come in. Then I could leave and not feel bad.

"I think a lot of people were shocked. This fighter named Shire was the favorite and—"

My head swivels. My heart begins to pound hard enough that it hurts. "Shire?"

Kylin nods. "She was the favorite all the way to the final round. But then Finch killed her during their final battle. That's how he won."

SEVENTEEN

There's a roar in my ears. It wants to drown out Kylin's words, but they're in my head all the same. I can't unhear them.

Shire didn't die casting banished magic for marks. She died while fighting in this tournament.

No.

She didn't *die*. Finch *killed* her.

This is the payback that Rudy was talking about. To do this one last thing for Shire and enter the tournament so he could fight Finch for killing her. He was dying and didn't tell me, maybe hating the idea of taking me down with him as much as my possibly ruining his chances.

Maybe he even meant to kill Finch in return.

I'll never be sure how far he meant to go. You have to really know someone to make that kind of guess, and that wasn't Rudy and me. I don't think we were even really friends. Not the way he and Shire had been.

And of the three, who is left now?

I shut my eyes as the room spins. The past presses close, full of all the moments that kept me in the dark. Rudy and Shire spun them to keep me safe, and yet—

How far can *I* go?

"What's the matter?"

I peek out and Kylin's face is close, searching mine. "You look like you're going to be sick."

"I— Do you remember if Shire had a backer?"

"Yeah. A guy. But I can't remember his name."

"Was it—?"

Kylin freezes. It's almost comical watching the realization hit as her eyes land on the letters on my cheek and get huge. But only almost, because nothing about this is exactly funny. "Rudy," she whispers.

I shudder. So it's all really true. I guess it's never easy having ghosts change on you, when there's already too little of them left behind. "Shire was my sister."

Kylin's eyes might pop out of her head soon. *"What?"*

"We knew she died casting full magic, but just not how."

"Wow. Wow. *Wow.*"

I silently will her to not say another wow. If I hear another *wow*, I might just scream.

"She deserved to win, you know."

My pulse trips as I stare at Kylin, a sharper, even uglier dread now swirling in my stomach.

I think he cheated somehow.

"She was better than he was," Kylin continues. "But then—"

"You said you think Finch cheated?" Shire losing fairly is one thing. She would have known the risks of the tournament, going back for each round the way she did. Even Finch going all Etana the Cruel on her and killing just to win is completely fair— dishonorable, but fair—because Shire would have known that that was a possibility, too.

But Etana never cheated when she fought. During the years she was champion, she at least killed her opponents in clean combat.

Something in my tone must scare Kylin, because she pales and rears back a bit on the counter.

"I don't really know if he cheated or not," she says. "Killing isn't cheating according to the rules, but it's just—I was so shocked when he actually won and—"

"But that's what you said. *You said he cheated.* And I don't mean killing, but cheating in some other way, then. Is that possible?"

Kylin just stares at me. She's still pale, still backed away from me, but now something on her face says she feels sorry for me.

"The thing is," Kylin says, "even if Finch *had* used a gathered spell—which aren't against the rules, either, just like killing isn't— what can you do about it now?" The door opens and two women come in and Kylin snaps her mouth shut.

I run from the washroom, needing to escape.

A gathered spell?

The food court is much emptier now—a clock on the wall says it's two in the morning—as I dart across. The registration area and starter counter are deserted, and even the bets counter has calmed down.

Is all of the Guild of Now needed to run the magic for this part? It's a question for Embry I'll never be able to ask, because who am I but one more fighter in a long string of them? *Or is it only during the actual fights that all of you have to work together so the whole place doesn't snap in half? How strong are each of you on your own? Did any of you do as Etana the Cruel did to become champion? Do any of you remember my sister?*

I nearly fumble my key starter to the ground as I cast for the elevator to take me back to street level.

Gathered spells.

What was Kylin talking about? It's like trying to catch the wind, the way I'm having to learn about the tournament even as I'm in it.

The elevator comes and soon I'm outside. I take all the wrong streets and the Meat Sector smells raw and bloody as I head toward Tea. Or maybe it's just the tournament I'm still smelling, carrying it home with me on my skin. I'm wide awake now, the late hour meaningless as bits and pieces of the night swirl in my head, trying to form themselves into something I understand.

If Shire had won a year ago, everything would be different now.

Two hundred thousand marks would have paid off all of Wu Teas's debts. Saint Willow would have left us alone. Jihen would be off shaking down someone else. The cop who's probably already moved on from watching the apothecary to watching me—he would have no reason to be around at all.

Shire would be alive.

My parents would be happy.

Something in my chest wrenches.

Even if Finch did *cheat and used a gathered spell or something, what can you do about it now?*

The question keeps me moving fast despite still hurting from the fight. My bruises ache with each stop, and the soreness of my bones is a feverish hum within my skin. The idea of fighting tomorrow while feeling anything like this fills me with dread. Because what if everyone else won't have to? How do I know they're not all better at healing, even?

I shove my smog mask on and head west, cutting through the sectors of the city—Spice, Tower, Government. The streets glisten from a recent rain, as wet as the Kan Desert was dry, such that it burns. My lungs burn, my sore body shouts, and my mind continues to race as I run.

Time winds back.

It was nearly a year ago, an hour before midnight.

I checked the time again on my bedside table and listened. The sounds in the kitchen were soft enough that I knew it would be Shire, being careful to not wake up our parents. They agreed a long time ago to let Shire cast in order to keep Wu Teas alive, but it existed for them as an unhealing sore, a thorn they could never fully extract. Shire always did her best to help them forget. She did what she could so that her marks entered the teahouse without notice and then left nearly the same way—silent payments for the banks, the suppliers, to Saint Willow and the dark web of his business.

There was the sound of a drawer being shut, then the bang of a cupboard door. I heard Shire saying something to herself, over what she was doing as she prepared to leave for a job.

Too restless to lie still anymore, I climbed out of bed. Not bothering to change out of my old T-shirt that I wore for pajamas, I slipped on jeans and grabbed a light jacket from the floor. I looked at my starter bag that I'd placed on my desk, hesitating, then picked it up and slung it over my shoulder. I left my bedroom and headed down the hall.

Maybe tonight would finally be it. I would be able to convince my sister to let me go along and watch her cast full magic. I would

135

watch and learn and then I could help, too. I was more than old enough, and not getting to learn with Rudy wouldn't matter so much if it just meant getting to learn from Shire.

Hope brimmed in me like hunger as I turned into the kitchen.

My sister was at the island. She was concentrating hard enough that she didn't hear me come in. Only half the lamps were turned on, and the light of them skimmed off her face.

"What are you doing?" I asked in a loud whisper, going over to see. Whatever it was, it must have been something beyond leftover magic, something important that needed full. Shire had learned to be careful about casting anyway, but on days she had a job, she was especially so—never do more than needed. This was something special.

She swept away the tangle of metal before I could see. The lot of it fell into her starter bag that she held on her lap. "Nothing much, just fixing something," she whispered back. "What are you doing up, Aza?"

"I couldn't sleep. And I heard you in here, getting ready to go."

Shire's gaze fell to my jeans, the jacket I held, the starter bag at my shoulder I would leave behind if promising just to watch made any difference.

Her dark eyes flashed with irritation. Over the years her patience with me had slowly faded, worn thin by my unchanging insistence, the little sister who kept asking for the one thing she couldn't have.

"You know you can't come," Shire said. "How many times do you have to keep trying?"

"If I stop asking, it's always going to be a no."

"Stop asking because it's always going to be a no."

"C'mon, I'll stay out of your way." I slung my starter bag around so it hung from my back, out of easy reach. "Your buyer won't even see me."

"And what if it was a Scout who saw? Then it'd be the both of us in trouble."

"You've never been caught all these years. And Mom and Dad would never know, either—why would I say anything?"

"It's more than Mom and Dad, it's—" Shire zipped shut her starter bag. "I have to go. I'll be back soon."

It was true that our parents hadn't been Shire's main argument for a long time. Now that I was fifteen, I could keep a secret as well as anyone. And though I wasn't nearly as good at controlling my full magic as Shire was with hers, I was definitely better than I had been at the beginning—so how would I get even better unless I practiced when I could?

A part of me was also sure that *Shire* herself could help convince my parents to let me help. How with the two of us making marks together, Wu Teas would never have to be in trouble again. Shire would stop being in danger from casting. The honor of our family's legacy would be safe.

But then, I couldn't tell *what* it was exactly that kept Shire from letting me go. It seemed like she didn't want me to go for her *own* reasons. Not because she was worried about me getting hurt or accidentally killing off a species or a forest somewhere, or because of our parents and all their forever worrying, but because she wanted to keep being the one who did it all. The one who could be trusted.

Resentment swelled until there wasn't room for anything else.

"There's always going to be buyers in Lotusland looking to buy real magic, you know," I said. "Maybe one day they'll be able to come to me. And you and Mom and Dad won't be able to stop me from casting."

"Oh, Aza." Shire got to her feet, telling me she was done.

"I'm serious. I only need one buyer, and then it's word of mouth. Just how you did it. It can't be that hard."

She looked at me, her expression exasperated. "I trained with Rudy for years, and then there were more months where I cast for almost nothing because I messed up more than I didn't. It *can* be that hard."

"I'm not stupid." I clutched my jacket close even though we were still indoors.

"I'm not saying you are. I'm saying that learning how to control your magic by casting on those who think you already know is reckless." Shire walked past me as she left our cramped kitchen and headed toward the front of the teahouse.

I hated hearing her call me that. *Reckless.* It was one of the words our parents often used to describe me. She knew I would argue with them over it. She'd always taken my side.

My throat was tight, my eyes gone all hot and stinging as I stared at her. It was like she was someone new, not the sister who'd always said she had faith in me.

You can't be scared of your own magic. It's full magic. It's rare, just like mine.

I can't control it.

One day, you will.

"You're just like Mom and Dad, you know," I said. "Not trusting me."

Shire's expression went hard. The low lamplight of the teahouse at night deepened her scar and turned it full of shadow.

"I *do* trust you," she said. "But you have to trust me, too. And you can't come with me for this, okay?"

Then she left, going off to save us the way she'd been doing for years. But she never came back. She died that night, and now I know how.

EIGHTEEN

The loud rush of a train thundering overhead on steel tracks brings me back to the present, and I'm in the Tea Sector again, just a few blocks from home. The same late-night tea cafés and teatini bars I passed earlier are still open, even with dawn not too far off. Nothing looks any different, only hours have passed since then, but the world stays tilted on its axis, knocked over that way by my discoveries of the tournament and how Shire really died.

I tug my starter bag closer to my chest, the one that was once hers.

After she died, my parents let me take whatever I wanted of hers. And I knew Shire would have wanted me to, because she'd shared everything with me when she'd been alive, so why would that change after she was gone? A week after her funeral, I'd stepped into her room and stood there in the doorway, looking around with a heart turned into fire in my chest. I felt a grief that was too huge to escape, so it became a part of me, burrowing into my bones and knitting itself into my muscles, coloring every single word I might ever speak from then on.

I was sure that nothing was real.

The last conversation I had with Shire couldn't have been an argument. Rudy couldn't have called the teahouse at dawn to say she'd cast too much full magic and had lost control of it. My parents couldn't have spoken about full magic with such poison in their voices that they almost made me feel like poison, too. They couldn't have spent the next days whispering together at night over the state of the teahouse, never asking me if I was willing to help in any way.

It wasn't until I touched her starter bag left on her bed that I finally accepted she was really gone, her absence final. I felt it like someone had sucked all the air out of the room, out of my lungs so that I was just a dried-up shell—now that the person I used to follow behind was gone, the wind would just blow me away, wouldn't it?

This bag held the items that started Shire's magic, and it'd just been *left on her bed*. Discarded there like any unimportant shirt or pair of socks. *The starter bag was Shire's connection to her magic and she would never need it again.*

My eyes stung as I picked it up, knowing instantly I wanted nothing else of hers, needed nothing. My own starter bag was stained dark gray canvas, nothing special. I bought it because it went with everything in my wardrobe. But Shire's was the yellow of chrysanthemums, of emperors and empresses, and the shiny silk moved like liquid gold. It suited my sister, who always dressed like she had better things to do than pay off a gangster.

But now, walking this last part home, I wonder if I missed something in her room. Something I wouldn't have guessed about because how could I have known? Tonight, fighting and using ring starters, I found out for myself how impractical it would be to use a starter bag in battle, my pockets not much better.

Kylin said Shire had been the best. Shire, who never jumped into anything the way I did, who spent months training and then practicing in order to be exceptional.

That last night had been the final fight, the one for the champion-ship. She'd been fixing something on the table. Something she'd rushed to hide to keep me safe. All her life, Shire had only ever hidden one big thing from me, and that was how she was really using her magic.

My nerves prickle with the lightness of discovery.

It's all a guess, but it also feels very right. Like *I'm* making a new connection to Shire, even if she's gone. She had to keep everything about being a fighter a secret when she was alive, but now that I'm a fighter, too, she's finally able to share. Distant laughter from the teatini bar I pass drifts over but I don't entirely hear it, and it's starting to drizzle again but I barely notice. Shire's never coming back, but I have these pieces of her now that I never had before, pieces I think she's giving me herself.

Shire, maybe I was wrong to think I didn't need anything else of yours. Maybe I'll see if I can find a tangle of metal in your room.

When I reach the block of the teahouse, I duck into the alley that runs behind it and squeeze my way through our fence of snowball bushes. I fold my mask back into my pocket, walk up to my bedroom window, and yank.

It doesn't open.

My mother, exasperated, locking it from the inside.

"Damn it," I whisper before yawning hugely. I dig out my key to the teahouse from my back pocket. Exhausted, I half walk, half limp my way around the side of the building, every part of me crav-ing sleep.

Golden light flows out from the front window of the teahouse.

I slow down, then climb the steps to the door.

Confusion dances with the murkiness of my brain as I work the lock with clumsy fingers. Could my parents be waiting up for me, discovering me gone and thinking I'm coming back from handling a late-night package for Saint Willow? Even so, why would they be waiting in the dining room instead of our regular kitchen? The kitchen is where my mother has her television and *Liar's Lair* for her to disappear into, where my father chooses to drown in paperwork.

I open the door, and there's a man sitting at the back table. He has a cup of tea in front of him. For a second I see my father, with his parental intuition somehow knowing that I'm hurt from fighting and wanting to cast leftover magic to help.

But then my father lifts his head and it's Jihen.

NINETEEN

My blood runs cold. My heartbeat pounds in my fingertips, wrists, behind my eyes, as I struggle to make sense of Jihen being here, in this place that's too good for him. The scents of too many gentle things like red fire–dried leaves and smoky green fields aren't supposed to make room for anything else.

I shouldn't be surprised, though. I of all people understand the reasons for staying unpredictable. And hadn't I done this same thing to Rudy? Breaking into the apothecary and waiting for him to arrive? If he felt as I do now, invaded and vulnerable, no wonder he was always particularly livid those days. Shame flows now, and I let it.

"A late night for you, Aza," Jihen says, "and a rough one by the looks of it." His gaze crawls over my face and the bruises and the blood on my clothes. He makes a sound of disapproval. "You teenagers, always so confusing with the things you do. Like wild animals, like gnau neng. Dare I ask for details?"

"It's none of your business." There is no explanation that would work. Not that I owe him one anyway. Anger begins to boil up.

"Delicious tea." Jihen sniffs from his cup. "I can see why you're so determined to keep the family business alive."

"How did you get in here?" Jihen's leftover magic can't have broken open the lock. And now an absurd sense of betrayal begins to creep in—he *agreed* to never show at the teahouse again. I've been paying each time he finds me, haven't I?

"The simplest way, Aza." He holds up a key. "Saint Willow doesn't like it when things get unnecessarily complicated."

They have a key. Of course they do. I forgot that Saint Willow and his family technically own nearly every piece of land in the sector, so it makes sense that they also maintain access. It's a given so obvious that no one actually talks about it anymore—if you are here, it's because Saint Willow allows you to be. Our home isn't really ours because it's really his. It's Jihen's. It's any of his henchmen's.

This place being off-limits is just one more illusion I've let myself be fooled by.

"We had a deal," I say. "I pay you directly, and you stay away from the teahouse. How is that complicated?"

Jihen sips at his tea. Seeing his thick fingers gripped around one of our most delicately designed cups makes my stomach roll. He was in our kitchen. He was in my *room*, locking the window to make sure I came in through the front. My stomach rolls harder.

"Well, beauty, here's the problem. You're *not* paying—not the way you promised you would and definitely not the way Saint Willow needs you to."

His voice is louder than it needs to be, and I think he's doing it on purpose. I force myself to keep from glancing down the hallway that leads to my family's apartment, willing my parents to stay asleep.

"I *did* pay you today, and I'm sorry it wasn't enough. I told you that. But I can't just cast more marks into my pocket."

While it's not impossible to cast an object into something else, it *is* nearly so to keep it from changing back. Same for casting objects into reality and making them stay that way. It took the

145

Guild combining all its power together to re-create the Kan Desert, and even then, all that sand had still been more illusion than real. I don't have that type of spell, and neither did Shire. Of course, a thief like Jihen would want to take full advantage of being able to pull marks from the air.

"Now wouldn't that be nice? Full magic my way and everything's fixed." Jihen's smile is mocking. "Know anyone I can tell the boss about?"

My throat goes dry—why did I have to mention full magic to Jihen of all people? His boss would collect full magic casters the way a child collects toys if he could. I hope my face gives away nothing. "Would we be having this conversation if I knew someone who had real magic?"

"Perhaps one day, then." Jihen slurps from his cup. "We can always dream, can't we?"

"So just tell Saint Willow exactly what I told you—that I can't pay what I don't have. I'll have more the next time I see you."

"Beauty—"

A bitter helplessness surges, coats the back of my mouth. "Don't call me that, remember?"

"—you don't think the first thing I told the boss was that you just didn't have it? I was walking in there with a pathetic amount of marks—of course I had to explain how it wasn't me doing a bad job, a job Saint Willow says even a beebee could do." He lifts his palm and casts, picking up his cup. "I hate cold tea."

A waft of the freshly heated tea tickles my nose. It's our Content blend. I've never liked it.

"What do you want, Jihen?"

"Where is the teahouse's till money?" Now his voice has softened, and it stirs the hair on the back of my neck. "The day's sales. Boss sent me here for them. Consider it interest on your frequently late payments."

Panic is a vise around my ribs, squeezing. I picture where my parents always keep the day's sales, in the safe in the family kitchen.

"I— You can't. That's for everything else we have to pay—bills, suppliers, insurance, rent to the company that *Saint Willow owns*."

"Ah, but there's one less supplier to worry about now, yes? If you like, we can look into getting rid of more contracts for you. Anything to help remind you to pay your debt of honor marks as soon as possible."

The vise tightens. I can barely breathe as the name *Leafton* floats across my mind. "Saint Willow can't do that."

But of course he can. Saint Willow can cut Wu Teas off from companies one by one in Lotusland just to see how hard he can push, how far we'll bend. How I'll do almost anything to save us.

"The day's sales, Aza."

I make Jihen wait outside the teahouse, just in case my parents wake up. I walk over to the safe inside the deep cupboard in the kitchen and open it with shaking fingers and a heart full of hate. The number of marks I take from it fills my stomach with a real nausea as I step outside and shove the envelope at him.

Jihen takes it from me with a small, smug grin. "Much appreciated, beauty."

I go back inside, lock the door. Exhausted or not, it takes me until morning before I can fall asleep.

TWENTY

I'm still stiff when I wake up the next afternoon—sleep didn't do as much as I hoped. Worry nags at me as I get dressed. How will I feel by the time I get inside tonight's fighting ring? How will the *other* fighters be feeling?

When I open up my starter bag to see what needs replenishing, I go still. My thoughts race as I dig the tiny glass jar out from the pebbles and leaves and other starters I always keep in my bag.

Having Rudy's healing meds would change everything. I wouldn't be walking into each fight still hurting from having to use my magic. Shire must have used the same method, since the pills were hers.

But the bottle is empty. I took the last pill after casting for Coral's mind wipe. I meant to get more from Rudy yesterday when I visited the apothecary, but given that he died during my visit, asking for a refill slipped from my mind.

I decide I'll have to break into the apothecary. I'll have to use full magic to do it, but then I'll at least have medicine afterward to help with the pain from casting. I'll go today, before heading for the Mothery to convince Piper I'm worthy of being her fighter.

I cross the hall to Shire's room.

It's been a year and my parents have left it mostly untouched. Other than using it to store the odd bit of supplies, they rarely come in. Shire's room is just like family meals out in the teahouse dining room—too painful still for them to consider.

Maybe it doesn't help that I've let them forget. Maybe I should remind them that Shire wasn't the only one who liked those family dinners.

I check her bookshelf first, then her trunk, before finding it in the pull-out drawer of her desk.

The tangle of metal isn't as random as my glimpse of it that final night made me think. It's actually a lot like one of those octopus-style key holders, with a flat disk as its main body and then half a dozen small loops coming out from along its edges where you would attach your keys. There's a sturdy clip at the top of the disk for attaching it to something, which I think is what Shire might have been adjusting when I caught her with it in the kitchen.

The small loops are spring-ring ones. A single hard tug and—

Then I get it. How it works and why Shire must have made this to give herself an advantage in the ring.

I take out the ring starters from my pocket—I transferred them there from last night's still-ruined jeans—and lay them out on Shire's desk. A smattering of square coins—red, white, silver, gold.

I pick up a red coin and slide it onto one of the small loops through its center hole. After a second of debate I attach the clip to one of the belt loops on my pants. I test my theory, giving the red coin a single hard tug as though I'm in a fighting ring right now, needing a starter without wasting even a second.

The red coin drops smoothly into my palm.

Shire, you really were the best, weren't you? The favorite, there in the ring and here at home, too. But now I think it's my turn to try, and I think you're helping me try. I feel the ghost of you and I hope it'll be enough.

I detach the holder and slip on the rest of the ring starters, making sure I know where each different color rests on my hip. I spend the rest of the afternoon practicing reaching for starters and yanking them free until the motion is mindless, until I grab whatever I need entirely by feel, and in a fraction of a second. It's the repetition of Rudy's sorting exercises in his apothecary all over again. Then I unclip the whole thing and place it securely in my starter bag. Slinging the bag across my shoulder, I head for the kitchen, starving because it's long past lunch.

The kitchen is empty, the island top wiped clean. My parents are in the tea shop, and their voices as they serve customers float back down the hall, along with the scents of fresh tea and pastries.

There's a covered plate on the island, though—wedges of scallion pancake, sides of fruit recently ripened courtesy of leftover magic, a teacup with water and a selection of tea bags next to it. Like they know I haven't slept enough and food is still one of the ways they can speak to me.

My eyes go to the deep cupboard beside the fridge. The safe inside hasn't been touched since I opened it for Jihen in the middle of the night. My parents won't open it until closing tonight, which is when they'll add today's sales to it. At the end of the week, they'll use the saved-up marks to pay off our family's long-running suppliers, business partnerships as old as the sector we live in.

I take the fifty marks from last night out of my starter bag and slip them into the safe. The amount isn't nearly enough to cover what I took to pay Jihen, but I just have to hope my parents won't notice anything is missing until the end of the week. That's when they'll take it all out to make their payments. By then, I'll have hopefully replaced everything with more winnings from bets getting put on me during the tournament. Getting Piper to agree to back me is a huge part of replacing the marks. Of course, winning two hundred thousand marks is also another part of the solution.

Pressure swells in my chest as I lock up the safe. I can't let my parents notice anything at all. It's not my having to pay Jihen that will throw them, but my doing it the way I did. Why would I need to give him marks from the safe when they believe I'm working down our debt as Saint Willow's courier?

My head spins over my own web of lies. The shadows between its spirals are like traps—one wrong move and I'll be falling. The family legacy will tumble down behind me.

I cast leftover magic and the water in my cup heats. I cast the television on so I can stop thinking for a few moments about all the ways I can mess up.

It's just the news, recaps of the city since early this morning. I'm only half paying attention as I tear open a bag of our Energizing blend to steep and start in on the food.

I nearly choke on a bite of pancake when I actually start listening to the news report.

At dawn, a huge sinkhole opened up in the Meat Sector. Measuring fifty feet across in both directions and nearly forty deep, it took out an entire intersection between major streets. No one was injured when it happened because all the adjacent businesses were still closed for the night. Though there's some structural damage to some of the nearby buildings that will take weeks to fix, the one that suffered the most damage—a nearby underground mall that was completely crushed—was already set to be demolished in two weeks, luckily enough.

I could try believing it's just a coincidence. Every day, somewhere in the world, something falls apart or is destroyed or dies out. Not because someone's currently casting full magic, but because too many someones did so a long time ago, and the earth's still paying for it. A quake. A freak wildfire. A tsunami. Lotusland isn't saved from any of that.

But the underground mall—I can still feel the sand of the Kan Desert between my fingers—is too much to ignore.

A knot of dread sits in my stomach.

I helped do this. The Guild of Now's magic is powerful, but it can't turn earth back to being unbroken. Last night's fight, fifty of us, just casting full magic as though we'd been reborn into casters of old, as though no consequences existed. No price for magic.

And just like that, I realize I should have known.

Because just about a year ago, didn't the same thing happen? A series of disasters, memorable because they were all located within the borders of the city, each one the breakthrough damage from the battles of last year's tournament.

First, a minor quake in the Paper Sector. Then a landslide in the High Shore Mountains that wiped out a bunch of houses in the north end of Spice. The unexplained overnight death of hundreds of crows in Culture, their raven corpses scattered throughout the streets like spilled coal.

Then finally another quake, this one in the Tower Sector. It leveled an apartment building. People died.

They were the cost of Shire and Finch fighting on the roof of that building in the final tournament battle—those people, that wedge of earth. They paid for the Guild of Now insisting on casting full magic just as the Guild of Then once got to. *Shire* paid.

But how has Finch paid? How has Embry paid, or any of the other members of the new guild? I thought entering the tournament—winning it—would fix all my problems. And maybe it will, still. But who's going to pay *my* cost?

I put on my smog mask and leave the kitchen. I slip out of the teahouse, glad that my father is serving a customer at the till and that my mother is putting together a tray of tea and cakes for one of the tables. So that they're too busy to see me leave, guilt ablaze all over me like I'm fire itself.

TWENTY-ONE

It's late afternoon as I head toward the Tobacco Sector, half looking out for Jihen as I make my way out of Tea. Going to Rudy's apothecary means more healing meds and getting to fight unhurt, while Piper's in Textile means getting to fight in the first place. But Tobacco is closer, with no backtracking, and midnight isn't that far away.

I wish it were the other way around. It shouldn't make sense to have to go back to the place where Rudy died. Where I left him lying on the floor, cold and alone.

The scents of fire and ash thicken the deeper I get into the sector, and soon there are the barest hints of camphor and mint in the air—the apothecary is close. I wait at the corner for the light to change, shifting on my legs, unable to keep still. It's starting to rain and I wipe my wet face. The need to hurry presses, an ache of its own kind. A mantra plays itself over and over in my head: *healing meds—Piper's shop—tonight's location, healing meds—Piper's shop—tonight's location, healing meds—Piper's—*

"Aza Wu?"

My heart trips in my chest, and it's like the world slows down as I look up and see the cop standing in front of me.

Rudy's cop. Baseball Cap.

I haven't thought about him all day. In between the loss of the till money and getting ready for round two, the possibility of the cop finally showing up to ask about Shire slipped through.

My own foolishness keeps me speechless as he waits for me to respond.

Baseball Cap is younger than I first thought, late twenties max. He must be new to being a cop, which explains the doggedness *and* the carelessness. Maybe I should have called him Puppy instead of Baseball Cap.

"Are you Aza Wu?"

I don't want to be, not to you. "Why?"

He gestures to his silver armband, now in full view, to show he's a cop. "My name is Cormac." Then he smiles, blue eyes crinkling at the corners, and the smile is so earnest and proud that in some bizarre parallel world I might even *want* to help him. "Well, not just police, but a Scout, actually."

The world slows down even more. My stomach crawls into my throat and sits there, a fist. "Oh?"

He nods. His intent to help the city—no, the *world*—beams from him. He shines like a little kid who's just cast his first leftover magic.

I shiver and it's not from the cold rain. A Scout. Right here, within arm's reach. A destroyer of full magic casters, someone who makes his living hunting down people like me.

"So, you're Aza Wu, aren't you?" He gestures to his chin. "Mind taking off your mask for a second? I have your picture on file."

I slowly slip off my smog mask. "File?" I'm only capable of useless answers because the word *Scout* is blaring too loudly in my head and swallowing everything else up.

"Yes, the file on your sister, Shire. I've been meaning to come and talk to you and your parents, actually. About Shire's death last year and some discrepancies . . ."

His voice fades, becomes a hollow rush.

Parents. Questions about Shire. *Discrepancies.*

I've been worried about this scenario ever since seeing Baseball Cap, ever since Rudy mentioned it with his dying breath.

But hearing the cop say it now fills me with fresh dread.

He *can't* question my parents about Shire and the details of how she died. He can't question my parents, *period*. They loved Shire and they love me, but they also hate full magic, and that conflict would spill from their faces like tea from a cracked pot.

The secret of my magic suddenly feels newly raw, a fresh wound.

"What do you mean by discrepancies?" I finally manage. "We saw the medical report. It explained everything."

Cormac shakes his head. The rain's coming down harder and the shoulders of his jacket are starting to darken. "As it turns out, the medical report *is* the problem. The medical examiner who signed off on it had been under investigation for falsifying reports. After he disappeared two weeks ago, investigators looked closely at all the reports he's *ever* signed off on; your sister's is just one of them that has turned up with issues that need to be resolved. Now I'm just following procedure and trying to reach those who can tell me more about how Shire died. I've already spoken to a Rudy Shen—him being the one to find her—but he was surprisingly unhelpful. Unfortunately he's also just passed away, so . . ."

For a second I can't decide if I should already know that Rudy's dead. I don't think I should because it was just yesterday and his ties to us on record should look thin. But I also know I'm no actor. "I . . . heard. He had a weak heart. He—it was just a matter of time."

"Oh, so you already know?"

I nod.

"I'm sorry. I wasn't sure how well your family knew him, or if he'd been friends with just Shire . . ."

His voice trails off, waiting for me to add more, but I just nod again. He doesn't need more than what's already in the file—Rudy was there that night, present when Shire fell. The rain pours.

"Well, I'd like to come speak to you and your parents together as soon as possible," he says. "Perhaps tonight?"

"Why you?" I hope my voice isn't as shaky as I feel. "Why a Scout on this? A medical report with holes—shouldn't that just be reviewed by Lotusland's coroner system or something like that?"

"Typically, yes. But certain wounds don't match up with how she died, and *how* they don't match up—well, it was decided the file should be passed on to a different depart—" Cormac's gaze seems to sharpen as he watches my face and he frowns. "I'm sorry, but I really do need to speak to your parents about this, so if tonight sounds—"

"Wait. There's—" My hands clench. If only I could cast full magic right now. Just rip from his mind the existence of Shire's report, Shire herself. Rip from his mind who *he* even is—I've already cast into his mind once before, why not again?

But he's a *Scout*. If I tried anything in front of him, he would stop me before I could even grab a starter from my bag. And then there's the tournament tonight—casting a mind wipe so close to starting time would leave me useless. Goodbye, chance at two hundred thousand marks.

"There's something I think you need to know about Shire that might change your mind about this investigation," I tell him.

I have no clue what I'm saying. The words are meaningless as they spill from my mouth. All I know is I have to say *something* to stop him from going to see my parents. My mind whirls even as it goes blank, telling me I'm making a mistake.

Cormac's face lights up. Boyish eagerness flows even as his eyes stay sharp. "Tell me over coffee? I know a good breakfast-all-day diner just down the street."

TWENTY-TWO

We get seated at the same window table I saw Cormac at last time. Through the rain, Rudy's apothecary across the street is a blur of glass and stone. The blinds of the windows of the shop are pulled, probably by whoever discovered Rudy's body. There's no sign on the door to say why the shop's closed and I wonder what's going to happen to it. Rudy never talked about family, and I never felt like asking, and maybe that's another difference between Shire and me. Because I bet she would have asked.

The healing meds that I still need inside seem very far away.

"So you have information about Shire you think I should know?"

I watch Cormac stir sugar into his coffee and my own stomach churns. The smells wafting from his loaded plate aren't helping. I pick at my dry toast, needing something to keep me from throwing up.

"I have information," I say, starting my act now. "But I need a guarantee before I tell you."

"A guarantee?" His brows pull together slightly. "I don't know if I can do that. Not if it keeps me from doing my job."

"This information will *help* you do your job. The guarantee is actually for me—so I can do mine."

You *have a job to do with this?* I read the question in his puzzled gaze. "What's the guarantee you need?"

"This stays between us for now. So you can't go to your bosses and you can't talk to my parents. You asking about Shire is just going to upset them, and they won't be able to help you anyway because they don't know anything else but what they were told last year by the medical examiner."

"I'm listening. I can't promise anything, but—"

"No, it's the guarantee or nothing. Go to your higher-ups and my whole setup's collapsed. Talk to my parents, who won't be able to help you, and I won't help after that, either. So I won't talk without the guarantee. It's the only way."

Cormac smiles. That there's as much sympathy in it as condescension reminds me how new he is to this job—Scouts are supposed to be ruthless in their casework.

"Look, I know this is your sister we're talking about and that you're only trying to help, but this is now official Scout business."

"And you're a new Scout, trying to make an impression," I say. "Trying to clear up an old case before the full year hits and it gets filed against your department's annual performance. How is it going to look later when it ends up you just ignored someone who offered to practically spoon-feed you your answers?"

He takes a sip of coffee. "Tell me how working with you is going to get me what I want."

"This obviously goes deeper than clearing up some discrepancies on a medical report, doesn't it?"

"Yes. The discrepancies are just the symptoms of a bigger problem. We think the medical examiner has connections to full magic, whether he was getting paid to cover for casters of full magic or was a caster of it himself."

Goose bumps lift. His suspicions fill the air between us at the table, as strongly as if he'd said them out loud anyway.

That Rudy and Shire had something to do with full magic, too.

"Rudy and Shire had nothing to do with full magic." My fingers spin my glass of orange juice, over and over again. Nerves prickle in my throat so that I have to clear it. "But if you're looking to take down some full magic casters, the information I have might be the lead you need."

Cormac leans forward, waiting. All around us diners are eating, the sound of cutlery on plates almost surreally normal.

"First the guarantee," I say.

He exhales. Ten seconds later: "Fine. This stays between us, for now. So talk."

I take a small bite of toast and chew slowly, working myself up to being able to meet his eyes. My web of lies trembles with me struggling to stay balanced on top of it, as I begin to weave it more tightly.

"Rudy and Shire were both undercover cops," I begin, lowering my voice. "*Undercover* undercover—only Rudy's immediate boss knew. Rudy had been undercover for years, secretly working on growing intel about the gangs that run Lotusland."

Cormac's mouth twists the slightest at this. A single glance at his face and I get the skepticism. He's new to being a cop, still full of bravado, still learning how things really work around the city. He's likely based in a sector where its gang keeps a lower-key profile than Saint Willow does in Tea, than Earl Kingston does in Tobacco. A sector like Tower or Culture, one that's filled with more people who look like him than people who look like me.

And it's people who look like me who first formed the city's dozen sectors into empires to run as their own. Which means families like mine are the ones who best understand how the city's gangs work, the sectors that are still mostly ours where a certain kind of culture is unspoken truth. My parents and I have never disputed the payment of honor marks, but people like Cormac probably half doubt they actually exist.

"Two years ago, information started going the wrong way," I continue, "with one of the gangs gathering *cop* intel. Rudy figured out the gang must have planted a mole in the cops. So Rudy enlisted Shire to be *his* mole, planting her as a member to uncover from the inside who the gang's mole was."

Cormac is rapt. "Which gang?"

"Saint Willow's."

He barely reacts to the name, which is what I'd been more or less expecting. To someone like Cormac, it's just another easy stereotype, the idea of what a gang is. A faceless entity he doesn't understand should scare him, but he's too cocky for his own good.

"Okay, go on," he says.

"Then last year, Shire was killed. Rudy got the medical examiner to sign off on the altered medical report to hide how she died, to make it seem like she'd just fallen off that building. And not mention what had happened before that, so it wouldn't break her cover. But he believed it was the gang's mole in the cops who had her killed up there. That it was only a matter of time before he was also found out."

"And so he was."

I nod. "Yesterday."

The Scout sits back in the booth and looks at me for a long minute. "So let's say I believe that Rudy and Shire had nothing to do with full magic. How they just had the bad luck of choosing a medical examiner sloppy enough to give away his own corruption, whether it's through magic or not. How is this information going to lead me to casters I can *take down*?"

"I've been secretly working as an informant with Rudy since Shire died, trying to figure out who the mole is in Saint Willow's gang. Now that they've killed Rudy, too, I can't just leave it. It means they knew he was close, which makes me close. People with information about the gangs—they aren't as tight-lipped around someone who looks like me as they are with someone who looks like *you*. I still have my leads, good ones that aren't just about the mole, but about potentially much more."

"Casters of full magic."

"Yes. We think the gang may have been using one to clean up their messes."

"A full-magic *hitman*?" Cormac sounds alarmed.

I nod. "But you can't get involved now or everything I've worked on is going to fall apart. Try to get to Saint Willow on your own and they'll make sure you never see light again. So I need more time before you can move in. After I get the mole, then you can have your casters. Deal?"

Cormac's eyes glow with the need to do what's right, to do his best as a Scout. Whatever he might see in mine, I hope it's not the truth.

He asks, "How much time do you need?"

"A month." I'll know in a week if I've saved Wu Teas from Saint

Willow or sunk us. If I've saved us, then this ridiculous lie I've just laid out to get rid of Cormac might actually work out for me. Our debt to Saint Willow will be paid. A cop poking around Saint Willow's gang won't be enough for them to kill him; even Saint Willow will think twice about starting a war with the Scouts, but his influence will be able to scare Cormac off for good.

And if I *can't* pull this off, I might still have enough time afterward to figure out another way to get rid of him.

"No way," he says, frowning. "I can't buy a month's time from the department. I can try pushing for . . . let's say a week. But that's all I can do. After that, I'll have to go back to procedure, talk to your parents, see if they can come up with leads of their own once they know what Shire had really been up to."

A week. Of course it has to be a week.

"Fine," I say, while my head screams that it's not enough.

"I'll find a motel close to the teahouse—the department will expect that."

"You can't let my parents see you," I remind him in a rush, hating the panic that leaks into my voice. *Just stay away from them, you damn Scout.* "Your guarantee, remember?"

"They won't see me. But I'll have to make a show of tracking you, even if actually I'm giving you room to work."

I nod, though the idea leaves me cold all over. Two people tailing me, one of them a gangster and the other a Scout—and somehow I'm supposed to make it to a secret tournament where I'll be fighting with illegal magic without tipping anyone off.

I chug some of my orange juice, feeling light-headed.

"Can I admit to being a bit blindsided by Shire and Rudy

working undercover this whole time?" Cormac shakes his head, thoughtful. "All of that just comes from nowhere—I really had no clue."

Maybe if you'd ever seen a Pearl of the Orient drama called Liar's Lair, I think, *you would have recognized the plot.*

But I was counting on Cormac's not knowing a story full of people as Chinese as the city's gangs, a story as Chinese as the person who's telling it to him.

"One week, Aza." He holds up his coffee mug in some kind of toast. "Here's to taking down some casters."

I lift up my glass, smile weakly, and will myself to not throw up.

TWENTY-THREE

I escape a minute later with the excuse of having to help out at the teahouse. I pull my mask back on and take off at a run once I'm out of sight of the diner, trying not to think about the healing meds I can't get to, how I feel like my web has me more trapped now than anything else.

The rain has stopped by the time I get to Textile. Some sectors in the city are noted for their smells, but some leave their mark on the eyes, and Textile is one of these. Windows of shops grow colorful and lustrous with their bolts of fabric on display, posed mannequins dressed in suits and gowns. My mother has to come here whenever the shop needs new napkins or place mats. But before, she would send Shire, who would then take me, and the two of us would study the windows for hours.

Today, though, I see none of this. The Mothery is in the middle of the sector, and as I weave my way through the streets to get there, all that's on my mind is convincing Piper to be my backer. It helps that the sun is already low, so that it flashes off the windows and hurts my eyes if I'm not careful. Midnight, getting closer.

Piper is beginning to feel essential. One, I need a steady flow of marks for ring starters, to get to fight. Two, I need the answers to the secrets that haunt me, and Piper could be a key. Did she back a fighter last year? Did she see Finch kill Shire? Could she know if he cheated? And three—well, it'd be nice to have one person on my side. Everyone else in the tournament I've spoken to is off-limits. Kylin's just a kid and a part of me is drawn to protecting her, but she's also a competitor. Navy is the champion's backer. Embry is Embry.

The Mothery's window display is beautiful—wide spools of silk in different shades of blue are stacked in the back to imitate a sky of old, while spools of silk in shades of brown and green line the floor to create a healthy earth. Tinier spools of gold and silver are inserted randomly in between all the blue of the sky, for stars.

I head inside and a bell over the door dings. The shop is basically the window display, only bigger. More bolts of silk along the walls, cabinets here and there with shelves stuffed with panels of color. The place smells how it looks, like roses and perfume and dust.

Piper is helping two customers choose between patterns, and I wait for them to leave, doing my best to not run my hands over every single inch of silk I see.

Then it's just Piper and me. She shuts the door, casts leftover magic to flip over the sign on the window to say CLOSED. She makes no move to lock the door, and I wonder why she's assuming no one's going to try to come in anyway.

Maybe it's because no one trying to uncover secrets would ever guess they could be in a place full of silk. Or maybe the customers around here really would stop at the sign. But mostly I think it's just Piper. How if someone came in, she'd only have to give them a single pointed look to make them leave again. Piper is someone you cross at your own risk.

I take in her sleek pantsuit and perfect makeup as she approaches and barely keep from pushing back my still-wet-from-rain hair in response. The look in her eyes as she scans me is a reminder that I'm just business, a potential investment. How I need her more than she needs me. How neither of us is in this for friends.

"Rudy the First," she says. Her gaze goes to my casting arm, the palm of my hand. I think of how Coral did the same thing, as if potential can be judged by sight. "I've been thinking all day about that move you pulled on Luan."

"Because you want flair."

She smiles. "If you're going to fight, you might as well do it in style."

"You invited me here so we could talk about you maybe being my backer."

"Do you know what it means to have a backer?"

I nod. "You give me marks for ring starters, and if I become champion, you get a percent of the pot."

"Wrong."

I peer up at her, surprised. "What do you mean?"

"Having a backer means you're representing that backer and yourself." She circles me, all gloss and hair and silk, just as intimidating as Embry. "It means that backer's put their marks and their faith in you. Having a backer means showing everyone they know how to pick a winner. *Having a backer means they trust you to know how to use your magic and not for your magic to use you.*"

The age-old question for all of us casters of full magic. We carry it with us as surely as we carry the magic itself, one never without the other.

"I know how to use my magic," I say.

"I don't doubt that you think that. But if you're going to represent me, I need to know what you represent. What honor means to you. What *dishonor* means."

I blink away the sting of tears. It catches me so off guard that it takes me a second to be able to speak. Ghosts are swirling around me, and I don't know if I want to reach out for them or ask them to leave me alone.

But this might be my best chance to win Piper over.

"My sister, Shire, was the fighter Finch killed last year," I say.

She goes still. Her gaze is nearly soft now as she looks more carefully at me. "You're Shire's sister? Yes, your faces—they're the same, deep down. Shire was very good."

"But I'll have to be better."

"To beat Finch? Yes."

"I have to do what Shire couldn't."

"Finch is a merciless fighter, his hunger for victory boundless. Like Etana the Cruel. We must respect him as a fighter if not as a caster, yes?"

I nod. "What do you know about his backer?"

"His older brother, Oliver. Who often looks like he'd rather be anywhere else than ringside, but I suppose Finch is family, and family can complicate things."

My throat has gone tight. "Family can definitely."

And his name is Oliver. It's nicer than Navy.

So he backs his brother but doesn't fight. He might not even *like* fighting. I wonder if they're brothers in full magic, the way Shire and I were sisters. I'm reminded that I've never seen Oliver cast either way.

"Family might be especially hard for those two," Piper says, interrupting my thoughts. "It's just them on their own, running the Salt Lick over in the Spice Sector."

"What happened to their parents?"

"All I know is that they're gone."

It means Finch fights with ghosts behind him, too. How fresh are they? Do they have anything to do with him being in the tournament in the first place?

"Do you think Finch cheated last year to win?" I ask. "If Shire was the favorite all along?"

Piper taps her lips with a finger. "Cheat? It's hard to cheat in a tournament with so few technical rules. Perhaps you're thinking about bending the rules rather than breaking them. Because there's still honor in doing what must be done to survive, even if such ways are ugly."

"Ugly?"

Her lipsticked mouth curls into a smile. "Survival and ugliness are often one and the same, and as a fighter, you need to remember that."

I try not to shudder. For all her beauty and soft silks, Piper is as barbed as wire.

"Okay, so if it's still honorable to fight ugly when it comes to survival," I say, "then it becomes dishonorable when it's no longer about survival. Ugly versus dirty."

"Very generally speaking, yes."

"So do you think Finch fought dirty last year to win?"

Piper smooths another nail. "I suppose it's possible. A lot of things are made possible with full magic, depending on the caster—their capacity, control, intent—"

"What about gathered spells?"

Her expression stiffens. "Careful, Rudy. The line between honor and dishonor can shift, yes, but never more so than with spells some believe should never have existed in the first place."

I flush. "I just want to know what they are. How they started."

"Back in the days of the Guild of Then, members began to experiment with spells. They wanted to create ones for effects normal full magic wouldn't do. But these man-made spells ended up calling for full magic that was beyond what was found in the earth, and so they ended badly, with casters dying or falling ill and never recovering. So the Guild stopped experimenting and that was that." She lifts an arched brow. "But no full magic is limited by form—once it learns the shape of a spell, it never truly forgets it. So that ghosts of those spells are always just lying around, waiting to be discovered and formed again."

"And these are gathered spells?"

"Gathered spells are what remain of those experiments. Some casters—gatherers are what they're called now—began to view magic as a toy at their disposal, and so re-formed certain man-made spells back into being. And instead of dying as a cost for these gathered spells, casters have to pay a great price in other ways."

I picture it. These spells that are as formless as my magic, but instead of red amorphous clouds, they are invisible vapors, floating around lost in the ether, before someone else's cloud of magic comes and finds them.

"Can you give me an example of a gathered spell?" I ask.

"Bringing the dead back to life. Snuffing out the sun. Time looping. The price is perhaps another caster's life. Their mind. Their *magic*." Piper lifts her other arched brow even higher. "Need I go on?"

"No, it's okay." No wonder the Guild of Then tried to destroy such spells. There's a madness in them that makes the earth slowly falling apart day by day seem almost kind.

Corpses can be made to breathe again, but the intangibles that make up who that person *is* in terms of their mind are gone forever.

Snuffing out the sun is, in general, not a great idea.

Time loops are dangerous because they play with reality.

And to lose your magic . . . It comes dangerously close to losing yourself. A person might not be their magic, but if their magic isn't them, then what is it? What part of you has been lost, sent into that ether, waiting to be found or taken?

"I don't know how you'd find out if Finch used a gathered spell anyway," Piper says. "He would likely never admit outright the price he must have paid for it. You *could* cast a reveal spell, I suppose, though I doubt he would ever give you the chance to try."

Shire, if you could do it all over again, would you use a gathered spell if it meant living? How far would you go to stay alive, to win? Would you let magic use you instead of you using it?

It takes a moment before I notice Piper has stopped talking. She's measuring me up like I'm one of her bolts of silk, and she's deciding the best way to cut me, to hang me up for display.

"You really are determined to succeed where your sister could not. Revenge can be a dangerous motive, but it's also an honorable one." Her gray eyes flash, their lashes coated into tiny feathers. "I will be your backer, Rudy the First, if you'll be my fighter."

Relief, trepidation, a sense of things falling into place—my stomach's churning even as I smile. "My real name is Aza, but I'll stay Rudy for the tournament."

"Aza. All right. I'll save that for after you win, then. Tonight, come find me before the fight, and I'll give you marks to buy your ring starters." She reaches for a bolt of cream silk, the fabric of it shot through with pink and red peony blossoms. "Now, for the armband you'll wear to show that you're fighting on behalf of the Mothery."

She smiles and presses a folded ribbon of silk into my hand. "I'll find you at midnight. Don't be late."

TWENTY-FOUR

I make my way to the Flower Sector in the dark, winding through alleys and taking small detours. It's not likely that Jihen and Cormac are on me this far out of Tea, but I'm still annoyed by having been caught off guard by both. I curse them from beneath my mask. All the other fighters are going to be sneaking around tonight, too, but none of them have to also keep shaking off a gang enforcer and Scout.

Inside my starter bag, the empty glass jar of healing meds clanks softly against stones and twigs. One more thing I still need to get done. Tonight, then, after the fight, and I curse Cormac again for showing up as he did.

Thorn Avenue is on the east end so that I have to navigate through the entirety of the neighborhood to get there. But the night air is sweet with the scent of roses and lavender, and sidewalks are carpeted with fallen blossoms. Baskets of blooms decorate every corner, and if a shop isn't a flower one, it's selling herbs or grasses or small potted trees.

I pass the sector's display cage hanging from a lamppost, and someone's taken the trouble to wind green vines around the metal bars. Scouts wouldn't normally allow the vines—the Ivor inside could turn the vines into whips or another weapon of some kind—but this one is bent nearly in half, too wrecked to want to cast anymore.

The address of the fighting ring turns out to be an apartment building. It's a low-rise, and it's old, the banisters full of rust, the siding warped, moss on the dipped roof. And clearly abandoned, with the weeds that make up the lawn knee-high and the adjacent carport a long and empty stretch of cracked cement.

It's a place at its end, just as the mall was. It must be easier for the Guild to maintain its magic over dead things. To not have to work against the will of something living.

I cross the street and head toward the front entrance. Roses leave my nose as the scent of spent firecrackers takes over. Closer now, the soot stains on the walls show themselves, and some of the windows are shattered inside their buckled frames.

Fire is what chased everyone away. The yellow and blue kinds, not the gentle red of our teahouse.

I find the black coin—the key starter—and cast on the lock. The pain is a minor twinge in my bones as the metal of the bolt retracts.

The lobby is small and smells of age and mildew and rotting wood. Through the broken windows, moonlight leaks in and reveals the blackened floral carpeting, the warped paintings on the walls. The water used to put out the fire lingers as a cool dampness in the air.

But there's the faint echo of voices. The walls and ceiling are full of small tremors, reverberating with the presence of the tournament two floors above.

I cast on the elevator using the black coin. Just as with the mall, the power being already cut here makes no difference, either, and the Guild's tournament magic sets the motor running. I press the button for the third floor and fall back against the side of the elevator.

My nervousness climbs just as the elevator does. It's almost harder walking in to fight now that I know what to expect. Or maybe it's just that I know what's expected of me. I know everything that can be lost now if I screw up.

How can I repeat what still feels like a fluke? What if every spell I've ever cast was never a sure thing, my control over them only perceived? What if seeing Finch makes it hard for me to see that line between honor and dishonor?

I shove my mask away, take a deep breath as the elevator doors open, and step out into the mouths of apartments that no longer exist. Yellow and blue fire were hungriest here, so that the Guild chose it to be the location of tonight's fighting ring—easiest to fill what is no longer there.

The third floor is a cavernous shell, its space full of high, shadowed corners and thick support beams charred along their edges. All its inner walls are gone, with only broken wooden framing and pipes to mark where they were. Its ceiling is missing, too—peering upward is to see a floating darkness, then the hint of the fourth floor's ceiling. Random furniture the fire didn't get to is pushed up against the outer walls, remnants of those who once lived here—a stained couch, mattresses, an old-fashioned console. Light glows down from the dozen or so bulbs that hover in the air. That light wasn't visible from the ground, I remember—the Guild's magic, woven to hide even the smallest parts of the tournament from the outside.

Just as with the food court, the entire space is crowded with casters. There's a table set up on the left side of the room, and someone's scrawled the word REGISTRATION on the wall behind it in thick white letters. The starter counter is at the far wall, while the bets counter is on my right. Here again the casters are the loudest and most anxious, pushing at one another to get their bets in on time.

"Twenty-mark technique on Wilson to cast five bone spells, five-mark status on Nola to survive!"

"Hundred marks on Finch to survive!" An image of Finch flashes, his eyes cold green glass. I've already noticed his face in Oliver's—has he seen Shire's in mine?

"Seventy marks on Pav to request a bow-out!"

"Fifteen marks on Rudy to survive!"

More gamblers betting on me.

A surge of pride leaves my face warm, even as fresh fear is a trickle in my stomach. I want this, and I need the marks collected with each bet. But expectations are also weights, and they're piling up now, breathing down my neck—faith, revenge, escape.

"Rudy."

I turn to see Piper swiftly crossing the floor. She's changed into a green silk dress, her purse a mass of sequins and beads hanging near her hip. Her red hair is coiled into a sleek crown on top of her head.

She takes out marks from her purse and hands them over to me. "Two hundred for your ring starters. Are you ready?"

I slide the wad into my pocket. "I think so?"

She purses her glossed-over lips. "Try again."

"I mean, yes, I'm more than ready. Absolutely. I'll out-flair everyone in this room."

"Well, you'll never out-flair *me*, but the other twenty fighters are fair game."

I take out the folded silk ribbon from my starter bag. "Should I put this on now?"

"As good a time as any. Let me help."

She winds the ribbon around my upper arm, snugly enough so that it doesn't move when I do. Silk peony blossom print shimmers as I move my arm beneath the lights. The weight of expectation grows another degree.

Piper squeezes my arm through the band. "There will be many bets placed on you this match, so don't forget to go by the bets counter afterward to claim your winnings."

I nod, flush a bit. "I already heard a gambler bet on me. To survive."

"Then don't let them down, or me." Her tone isn't unfeeling, but it reminds me how the tournament is a business to her and nothing personal. After all, just this time yesterday it was Luan who was wearing the Mothery's silk band. Has a *backer* ever walked away from their fighter, if another becomes a better investment?

A final squeeze of my arm and Piper heads off.

I go to the registration table first. It's the same clerk as last time, and after he makes a check beside my ring name on the clipboard, he writes RUDY on my cheek. Just as I'm about to turn to leave, he stops me.

"Hold up, you'll need one of these, too." He holds out a small box with a hole in its top for me to draw from.

I pull out a white sticker with the number 15 on it. "What's this?"

"I find out with the rest of you. But for now, you're supposed to put it on your sleeve."

I slap it on and move over to the starter counter. I use the marks Piper gave me and buy twenty ring starters, five of each. The process makes me think of Oliver, and I find myself half searching the crowd for a tall guy with wary eyes and a shirt that fits too perfectly, the brother of the fighter who killed my sister.

But I don't see him, and I stop looking altogether after noticing how many others are watching *me*. Is this a taste of what it's like for Finch? Everyone wanting a bit of you just to feel that much closer to magic the way it once was, without cost and done freely? Most are careful to look elsewhere as soon as I meet their gaze, but one guy—earrings, a strangely rounded beard—can't seem to. His eyes stay on mine, his thirst for magic of old palpable, and because he reminds me of last night's autograph seekers, I quickly move away.

It takes me a few minutes to find the washroom. The original apartment ones were all destroyed in the fire, so the Guild of Now had to cast up another. I follow an arrow through a winding maze of half-broken walls until I get to a barricaded area with two doors. Behind the door to the women's washroom is an exact replica of the washroom from the food court.

I duck into a stall and take out Shire's key holder from my starter bag. I slide on all my new ring starters, combining them with the ones I have left over from last night's fight. The key holder is heavy, reassuring. I attach it to my belt loop, step out of the stall, and crash into the person standing there.

It doesn't surprise me at all that it's Kylin.

She's grinning, back to the confident kid caster I first saw yesterday, her bright chestnut braid swinging over her shoulder.

I should be dismayed that she's clearly ready to fight, but instead I'm relieved she's no longer so nervous. The feeling irritates me, and I stride by roughly.

"What is it with you and washrooms?" I mutter.

"Recognized your shoes," she says as she follows me to the sinks. "From beneath the stall."

"Then I'm changing them for next time."

"I wanted to see if you were okay," she says as she climbs onto the counter. "About your sister. And about Finch, seeing him today."

I stare at my reflection and tell myself I don't see fear there. "I'm fine."

"That's good." Kylin points to her sneakers. They have a sunflower print all over them. "New lucky sneakers."

"No, it's not good that I'm fine." Why does Kylin have to be such a kid? It'd be easier to remember how she almost killed me if she didn't keep talking about lucky sneakers, or asking me if I'm okay. "At least, not to you. You shouldn't want me fine—we're competitors."

"So I've got a new pact for you." She tilts her head as she sees my cheek. "Also, what's your real name if it's not Rudy?"

"I'm Rudy here. And no more pacts—we're not friends."

"But maybe we're not enemies, either. Not really. Not kill-you enemies, just competition enemies, and that's different. We can even enter again next year, if we wanted to."

But I wouldn't, because it'd be too late then.

As for the rest, I glare at her while I wash my hands. "We both tried to kill each other yesterday; what are you talking about?"

"That was *before* our first pact. Which is why I'm asking you to make another one with me."

I say nothing as I dry my hands on my pants. The sticker on her sleeve says 6.

"Let's make a pact that we'll avoid each other in the ring," she says. "We'll just go for everyone else. Maybe it'll even just be us two by the end."

Something flares in me. An ache, when I haven't even cast.

Her words, her wish—I might have said the same thing to Shire. And my stomach hurts because I'm no longer sure what she might have said. Yes, because she always said yes to me. But also no, because the tournament was hers, a secret she'd decided to keep.

"You're forgetting about Finch," I say to Kylin. "Eliminating him won't be so easy."

"I don't think he'll kill in this tournament. The Guild won't vote him in if he keeps doing it, once they have an opening."

"What if he uses another gathered spell?"

"That was just a guess about him using one last year." One of her double-shoulder shrugs. "If he did, he would have had to pay something huge. And also, I guess that means he's still been able to hide it."

A bell rings.

Back outside, spectators have pushed themselves to the outer edges of the room that is now the third floor. Kylin and I walk into the center where the rest of the fighters already are. Twenty-one of us left, standing in a loose circle.

The dimensions of the apartment building are smaller than the food court's were, and the noise level has folded in on itself, waves of sound lapping over one another and growing. Cheers and yells and clapping, a smattering of heckling boos. I make out names: *Pav* and *Rudy* and *Finch.*

I scan the fighters around me and wonder how much better they are tonight than last. Nola has new glasses, and she's wearing the number 4 on her sleeve. Wilson is number 14, his wide grin telling us all how happy he is to be here. Pav is number 13. He looks Chinese, around thirty, with pretty bird tattoos all over his arms and a panicked look in his eyes. Kylin is staring straight ahead, as she did last time, and for a second I regret not agreeing to her pact, if only because it couldn't have hurt. At least, not at first.

And Finch. Number 5 on his T-shirt sleeve, blond hair and celery eyes. There's the shine of a blue-striped ribbon from his arm, showing how Oliver and the family business of the Salt Lick are behind him.

I don't know how long I'm staring at Finch for before he notices and turns. His expression remains unchanged as his gaze meets mine—if he recognizes Shire in me, he doesn't show it. It only makes him colder, how simple his purpose is. He is here only for the challenge of his magic, the weighing and measuring and testing of it, and we are merely the ways he is proving to the Guild that he can be a great.

Shire was better, and in his way.

What are you hiding, Finch? How did you beat her?

I drag my eyes away and there's Oliver in the crowd, just behind Finch. The shape of their bones is an echo of each other's, and they're both tall with wide shoulders. That they're brothers is clear. And if their parents are gone and it's just the two of them, they must be close, too.

I wonder how deep the similarities go, how strong the bond. *Oliver, what kind of magic do you have? Could you ever kill with it?*

A dull, thudding fury grips me—why did it have to be Oliver who I noticed? I *liked* his rusty laugh, his reined-in impatience. I liked the guarded wariness in his eyes that said he cared too much. Why can't someone else back Finch? What is Oliver still helping him hide?

Oliver catches me watching him then, his gaze flickering over, and I know my stare is stony before I pointedly look away.

The sound of the crowd changes, gains an edge of excitement that is as sharp as hunger. I feel it in my own throat, the need for magic. My casting arm twinges as Embry appears and makes his way toward the center of the room.

Then I blink and the burnt-out shell of a building around us is gone.

TWENTY-FIVE

Gone is the singed carpeted floor, and instead we're standing on smooth, sun-beaten pavement. The four outer walls of the old apartment building—soot-stained, broken through with piping and wiring—are now the curved walls of a circular temple. The walls are of a polished green brick, dotted through with bricks of gold and pearl and with cutout windows of painted glass. Fat gold pillars line the courtyard, and covered staircases wind upward toward balconies. Huge potted ginger plants sit on these, full of thick green branches and fat dangling vines. Three tiers of sloped jade tiles make up the temple's roof; massive dragons carved out of pearl perch on their peaks and hang off their edges.

I've only ever seen an ancient Zinaese temple in history books. The ancient land of Zina still stands on the other side of the Pacifik, but is filled now only with the relics of these temples, with ruins of once-great palaces and courtyards. The last one fell more than a thousand years ago.

And yet.

I peer upward, at the sky that is more than vivid with pinks and plums, at the strings of glowing lanterns that crisscross for miles over the length of the temple's inner courtyard. Our shadows are blurs on the pavement, softened by the dusk light. Spectators fill the spaces between the pillars, and their faces are ovals, equally blurred by distance.

The air blows across my skin, as soft as velvet, smelling of ginger; if I stick out my tongue, I know the taste of the plant would stick. How much of that taste is the Guild? Their ethereal magic *is* this world, wrapping around us as it weaves together an existence that no longer is.

I've never felt less like I was dreaming; nothing has ever seemed more real.

"When the first Tournament of Casters took place two thousand years ago," Embry says as he moves closer to us, "it was a test of skill. Three hundred years later came the first battle of caster *families*. It was still a test of skill, but even more so one of teamwork."

His voice is that smooth low rumble again, the one that worms into your brain and makes you question your own magic—*Do I deserve to be here? How do I measure up?* He's in another sleek suit, this one of deepest midnight blue, and his tie is a stark contrasting white with an elegant raised rose print.

He glances around, as though unable to keep from admiring the Guild's work. *His* work.

"This is Jayde Temple," he says, "one of the most revered temples in ancient Zina on account of the royalty who once lived there— emperors and empresses, their families and their servants. It's said the royals were so indulgent with their full magic that the grounds of the temple stayed warm year-round. How even in deep winter, snow would melt feet before it hit the earth. Today only ruins remain, but before it fell, Jayde Temple was also the site of that first battle between families. Two great lineages of casters clashing right here, spilling blood and magic."

His words stir up images in my brain. Standing in the middle of this re-created world, it's easy to picture the royalty that once filled this place, the grand lives they would have led. Back when casting full magic was celebrated, done out in the open. When no one had to hide their power because everyone had the same kind. People in silks and velvets drinking Wu teas while they pulled power from the earth, casting it to do whatever they wanted it to do. How the only challenge they faced were other casters, racing up to the temple walls with fire in their veins and stars drawn on their palms.

"You each wear a number on your sleeve," Embry says, "a number you chose at random. Numbers one, two, and three, please stand here." He gestures to his right.

Three fighters move over: a teenaged boy with the ring name of Hurley, a woman in her twenties named Lia, and a guy in his fifties with a cigarette jammed between his lips whose name is Oscar.

"Numbers four, five, and six, please stand here." Embry gestures to a spot not too far from the first.

This is Nola, Finch, and Kylin. Kylin's expression is just as cool as Finch's as they move to stand together, giving away no sign that she ever mentioned the idea of Finch being a cheater.

Soon we're standing in seven groups of three. We circle Embry like we're numbers around a clock face.

I study the other two people in my group, just as they study me in return.

Number 13 is Pav. Up close the worry in his eyes is underlined by purple bags of sleeplessness, and his hands are shaking. His regret over entering this tournament comes off him in waves. Or maybe it's just pain from fighting last night, or from whatever casting he does outside of here. I don't know if it makes any difference when it comes to needing him to fight.

Number 14 is Wilson. While Pav reeks of terror, Wilson's excitement burns like a fever. He's built smaller than I first thought, is all tightly coiled energy and barely reined-in swagger. But he's bought into that swagger, believes absolutely in his own capacity for magic and control over it. I'll have to make myself believe it, too—that it's better to be on his side for this fight than not.

"Fighters, this is your team for tonight's battle," Embry says. "If one of you falls, all three of you do. So, please take a moment to introduce yourselves to one another."

There's an awkward kind of shuffling among us. We're supposed to knock each other out, not become allies. I think of Kylin and Finch being in the same group and can't deny I'm relieved—I'm not ready for her to be eliminated just yet, and her getting stuck with Finch means her chances of moving on are better than they were.

Wilson just shakes his head as he faces Pav and me. His grin is dismissive. "Let's not bother with the niceties. After this match we move on, and I'll just have to get back to thinking of how I'm going to eliminate you two anyway."

Pav's shoulders slump slightly. "Not the greatest attitude to have for this, kid."

Wilson scowls at the *kid*. "Casting magic is casting magic. Being nice isn't going to help us."

"Doesn't hurt anything, either."

"That's where you're wrong. Everyone knows it's easier to knock out a stranger than a friend."

"I agree with that," I say. "But not for this match. You heard Embry. Tonight's about teamwork if we're going to move on to the next round. And teamwork's easier if we can at least pretend to be friends."

"I *am* pretending," Wilson says. "I haven't complained yet about being stuck on a team with 'Pav the Coward.' I heard the crowd. I know why they call you that. Hiding is boring."

Pav's face goes red. "Casting shield and invisibility spells is a type of strategy. Sorry if it's not one you agree with."

"You're both wrong," I blurt out. "Pav, what you're doing *is* boring. Wilson, that doesn't mean Pav might not be smarter than all of us put together. But we still have to figure out a strategy we can all agree on."

Pav's expression is one of near betrayal. "I can cast other spells, too. I just don't use them as often."

"I'll believe that when I see it," Wilson says, far from impressed. He turns to me. "Fine, I'll be friendly, but none of us are *friends*."

I nod. "We're not, but you better learn fast to care about helping Pav and me stay alive."

"All right, now that everyone's made nice," Embry says as we all turn to face him, "let's move on to the next step."

He flashes a deck of cards so that the cards fan out evenly from his hands.

The gesture's oddly theatrical. It makes me think of pretend casting, the stuff of fake magic shows and staged spells. Which *is* a good trick for Embry, I suppose, considering he's a member of the Guild of Now and the Guild likely knows more about magic than anyone else here.

He walks from group to group, holding out the cards. "One per team, please."

Lia draws for her team.

"What is this?" She flips her team's card over and over again. Its front is blank.

So is the card Finch's team is holding.

More teams draw. Their cards are all blank, too.

Pav's the one who takes our card for us. He flips it over. The front side is completely blank, just like everyone else's.

"Look again," Embry says, the remainder of the deck somehow now gone from his hands.

Pav flips our card again.

The front is no longer blank. Now there's a drawing of a bright silver coin on it.

Silver for breath.

"The card your team holds is the kind of spell your team will be casting tonight." Embry pauses for effect. "The *only* kind of spell."

Wilson's grin turns into a grimace.

And dread fills me at the abrupt dimming of his glee—because it can only mean one thing.

Pav, seeing my face fall or whatever it does to show my sense of doom, turns frantically from me to Wilson and back again. "What is it?"

"It's his weakness," I whisper.

Pav's mouth forms a perfect O of dismay.

Even the strongest casters of full magic can have a weakness, whether it's obvious or hidden. Just having a preference for certain spells can be a weakness, because it leaves you rusty with others. If

Wilson's weak in breath spells, he might not be able to do much more than just protect himself with a shield spell. He won't be able to cast attack spells. No air punches. No heat or fire. Under these circumstances, he might as well have no magic at all.

Now Pav's the one with the scowl, and he turns it on Wilson. "No wonder you're hating on my casting shield and invisibility spells. It's because you're weak in them."

"*Weak* is a strong word."

"You *can* cast a basic shield, right?" I ask, no longer sure. Wilson made fun of Pav for casting his shields, but what if he's been covering up this whole time how he can't cast even that?

"Yeah, of course," he says. "I made sure my shield was good so I could focus on getting great with bone spells."

Pav snorts. "So *that's* why I thought I heard them call you 'Wilson the Boner.'"

Wilson looks toward the ground.

"*Really* useful for this round, all those bone spells you're so great at. Thanks so much."

Wilson flings his arms out wide. "Hey, as if any of us had an idea this was coming. Any other kind of match and *you'd* be the one—"

"We're going to have to deal with it," I snap in a whisper, nearly feeling bad for Wilson except for the very real fact that he might now get me eliminated. But a team, spell restrictions—I didn't expect those tonight, either. "Pav, we'll just have to cover for him."

My brain is frantic. I run down all the breath spells that would be useful in the fighting ring. Rudy would say it's just one more form of sorting, what fits and what doesn't. Shield, air punches, fever, fire, swelling, breathing . . .

"A team is only as strong as its weakest member," Embry says now. He moves closer toward the line of gold pillars, where he means to watch us fight ourselves away. "Just like a fighter is only as strong as their greatest weakness. To be truly great, a caster must know how to balance their magic.

"You'll fight until two teams remain." He scans his teal eyes over us. The weight of his gaze is like static electricity in the air, a storm over a temple from ancient times. "Starting now."

TWENTY-SIX

It is the sliver of space between heartbeats. The seconds between *breath in* and *breath out* within your lungs.

That's how long it is before the entire courtyard is full of cast magic.

"Shield spells!" I yell as I yank free a silver coin. First things first, which means surviving long enough to at least figure out what to do next.

Wilson and Pav cast, and we back into a loose circle, each of us facing outward. Invisible armor turns the lines of the temple blurry, the carved dragons on the roof into unnamable creatures. A twinge of pain from casting passes through me.

Around us in the courtyard, the other six teams are already at it. Figures are barely more than streaks of color and motion. A bright smear of blond is Finch, a swish of a brown braid is Kylin. There are flashes of light—the low sun, glinting off Nola's glasses. There are muffled yells, dull smacks. The crowd roars and cheers from the perimeter of the courtyard.

"What do we do?" Pav asks. His voice wobbles through my shield. "We can't just stay here!"

"Wilson, you do," I say. If he can't help us, then we can't let him hurt us, either. "Stay low and just keep casting shield spells, got it?"

He sputters, indignant. "What, you want me to just stay out of the way the whole time?"

"Ye—"

An explosion sends me sprawling backward. I hit the pavement with a thud. My head pounds like a drum, its beats painful enough that I can't hold together my shield spell. I'm dimly aware of Wilson nearby, calling my name.

I drag my eyes over to the fighter who cast that skin spell on me. It's number 7, a fighter named Bess. She's older, like she works in an office otherwise. She's moving closer, her eyes huge and wild. Her palm is out—she's about to cast again.

My hand's reaching for a starter when a blur of motion crosses in front of me. It's Pav, channeling Wilson at his most exultant. He charges toward Bess as he casts, a sketching of a star, a silver coin dropping from his hand. His long yell is a war cry and it sends a chill along my skin. It bounces off the distant temple walls like the clanging of swords.

Bess drops to her knees, her hands at her throat. Her skin begins to turn blue, the tint spreading outward from her mouth.

So much blue.

It can't just be manipulation of her breathing, then. Pav must have cast magic to change her oxygen, to make it become something else that she's now breathing in. The effect is fast, harsh, telling of both its spell's potency and cost. A twelve- or thirteen-pointed star, at least. And even though we're here in the tournament and the Guild helps lessen our pain from casting, it's still a pretty big hit to put on yourself right at the beginning of a fight, especially when you've already cast for a shield.

Pav, don't get carried away!

Now Bess goes even more frantic. Her fingers scrabble at her neck. Her eyes bulge.

Someone's cast a *second* spell on her, layered on top of Pav's.

I whirl around. Wilson is crouched behind me, pale and trembling as he drops the just-spent silver coin to the pavement. It joins one already there, the starter he used for his shield spell.

"What are you doing?" I shout at him over the roar of the crowd. "Pav's spell is enough!" You can't choke someone when they already can't breathe; any second now Bess would have declared herself a bow-out. Why is Wilson depleting his magic for nothing, especially if he's already weak in breath spells? He's only supposed to be casting shield spells on himself to stay in the fight. To keep Pav and me in the fight with him.

Wilson wheezes, sneers. "You sure about that?"

I spin back around. He's right. Instead of being eliminated and encased in marble, Bess is whooping in huge breaths, palms braced on the pavement. She's managed to outlast *both* breath spells, and now they're wearing off at exactly the same time.

My team has only wasted magic. Wilson is more liability than weapon. And Pav's gone off, charging ahead with his war cry.

I swear under my breath and cast another shield spell. A long shiver of pain as the world shimmers, and my mind's whirling, trying to think, as I toss the spent coin and take in the rest of the courtyard.

On the other side, Kylin, Finch, and Nola are working as a team. They stand shoulder to shoulder as they break up the pavement. Finch is burying a fighter with slabs of stone. It's the teenager, Hurley. A second later, Hurley turns into marble, declared a knockout by the Guild. Two more fighters across the courtyard tip over, also transformed into marble—Hurley's teammates, Lia and Oscar, automatically eliminated in turn.

One team down.

If someone like Finch can figure out teamwork, why can't we? Frustration bites and my thoughts are chaos. How to work *with* Pav and Wilson instead of against? Complement, not clash?

Beside Finch, Nola casts, and rocks fall like rain. Fighters are yelling, dodging. Kylin's using chunks of pavement as huge fists, sending them through the air and knocking fighters to the ground.

Bess, back on her feet, gets hit by one and goes down. She's marble. Behind her, two figures fall over, become marble as well.

A flare of pride—unwanted, dangerous, but here anyway—flashes through me. *Good for you, Kylin.* Five teams left, fifteen fighters.

But then, through the dust and rock, I catch how she's smiling hugely at me, and my heart sinks even as it twists. She knocked out Bess for me. We don't have a pact, but she's acting like we do. Like we're in this together.

"No," I whisper.

I stumble back a step, like she's cast magic to hurt instead of save.

I can't owe Kylin a single thing. Not here, not when I can only care about me. Sure, I would have done the same thing for Shire if she were here, but Shire's gone, and I'm the only one left now. The only one who can avenge her.

A new awareness rolls across the courtyard as the other fighters finally realize what just happened. Kylin's smile was a beam, so that my whispered protest might have been as loud as a scream.

Her coming to help me has marked out my team as the weakest. An easy target.

My vision begins to flicker wildly; black creeps in on its edges. It's the full magic of other fighters, trying to pry apart my shield spell. The smell of fire is everywhere, used-up magic smoldering in the air. The pavement's painted red in swaths, and hunks of stone are flying in every direction. The crowd's a distant wave of cheering and hollering.

Pavement careens into my chest, and my shield of air trembles. Something behind my ribs cracks. My shield trembles harder, goes thin.

Then pain explodes in my head. I can taste it, a wave of copper that stings my tongue. I fall low to the ground in a crouch and my already-weakened shield spell trickles away.

I tear free a silver starter from my holder. Fear swims as blood spurts from my nose, begins to drip from my mouth. My heartbeat roars as the blood in my veins is ordered to stream from me.

The scene takes on a haze of red as I lift my head and look for the fighter out to bleed me dry.

She's hunched down between two pillars. *Freya* is scrawled across her cheek. Her casting arm is out, its palm ready to be drawn on again. Her mouth works as she stares at me with huge eyes. *I'm sorry, I have no choice, I have to—*

I cast.

Wind gathers and spins a loosed ginger tree branch through the air. It pierces Freya's thigh and she topples. She slaps the ground three times and turns to marble. The vague thought comes about whether or not fighters still feel pain after the Guild's changed them, but it disappears as my own pain stabs through me. I fall back, my breathing loud and jagged as I slowly stop bleeding.

One more team down. Twelve fighters left.

A shout. Pav, yelling in my direction, the birds on his arms flying with him. He's no longer exultant, no longer triumphant with his war cry. Instead panic is all over his face, gold-hued skin bleached pale.

"It's Wilson it's Wilson it's—!"

I drag myself to standing, dread cold lumps of ice in my blood.

Wilson's on his feet, staggering and stumbling as he struggles to fend off nearby fighters. They swarm close, six of them, Wilson their choice of prey. They smell weakness the way a gang of vultures will stick close to the nearly dead, knowing it's just a matter of time.

Wilson's shield spell is almost gone as he keeps fighting. He's shaking with the effort, pain in every line of his body as he casts. He is unrecognizable from the Wilson who dared to banter with Embry about winning it all.

My mouth is dry as my hands dig at my starters, as my eyes hurriedly scan the courtyard. Six fighters on Wilson—so where's Kylin's team? Where are Finch and Nola? Kylin might not want to help take down my team, but Finch, who kills, would. Nola, who punched Teller into elimination, would. So where are they?

Pav's helping Wilson already, casting on the six as they approach. One fighter flies backward, a gust pushing him away, but he gets up as soon as he lands. Pav's growing weaker, too.

Panic climbs, is a crescendo in my blood.

There are too many of them. Too many at once for Pav and me to try to fight off and have Wilson still be standing by the end of it. If only there were more of *us*, more of—

My breath catches.

I have seconds to decide. Be reckless or not. Break the rules of only using silver starters or not.

Then Pav's falling, and I choose.

I go to grab at the key holder on my hip. My mind is a storm as Piper's words fill it.

Perhaps you're thinking about simply bending the rules rather than breaking them. Because there's still honor in doing what must be done to survive, even if such ways are ugly.

I draw. Not just a star to fit my palm, but with points that reach my fingertips, that travel to my wrist. So many points, so much magic. An endless red fire in my brain that screams for escape. My body burns, my casting arm and its palm a whole torch.

I yank ring starters from the key holder at my hip. A mess of all four colors, too many to count right now—red for blood, white for bone, silver for breath, gold for skin. My breathing's rough in my throat, my pulse a thrum along my skin.

I drop the coins into my palm.

Magic tumbles from me, a huge bloom of red that I barely just hold back. I stoke it and direct it, begin to shape it with the will of my mind.

I choose a shape I know well.

Azas come to stand around me. Clones of my own skin, bones, breath, and blood. I'm all over the courtyard.

Not more of us, then, but more of me.

There's the roar of the crowd as they shout their approval. The noise is a wall, tumbling across the courtyard. They know I've broken the rules, but they can't help but be entertained at the spectacle.

The pain builds. Splinters of it drive deep into my bones.

With trembling hands I tear a silver coin from my key holder. A dozen other Azas tear one off theirs.

We cast as one.

Air extinguishes itself from the lungs of the fighters zeroing in on Wilson and Pav. Their hands go to their necks, then slam on the ground. *Bow-out.*

The crowd bellows. It's my name—*Ruuudy*—and the noise wants to tear my head apart.

One by one the other Azas begin to disappear as my spell fades. I count the fighters still in the courtyard with eyes that hurt as I move them. Copper fills my mouth again.

Wilson and Pav and me. One team.

Finch and Nola and Kylin reappear from wherever they went— team number two.

The fight's over.

Six of us left.

The last thing I see is Finch, his green eyes narrowed as he finally takes real notice of me.

I black out.

I die.

 TWENTY-SEVEN

I come back to life inside Jayde Temple.

It's a round room, with a sunken center. The walls are covered with white paper that has the sheen of pearls. Stained glass windows are painted with dragons and flowers. The floor is all polished tile—jade, emerald, and gold. Gold lanterns hang from the ceiling.

I'm sitting at a table in the sunken area. There's a bouquet of jasmine flowers on it, so that the whole place smells of them.

Across from me sits Embry.

Being two feet away instead of across a fighting ring makes him no easier to read. His odd teal eyes are like chips of polished glass, reflective instead of revealing. His expression is neutral as he watches me. All traces of whatever charm he once showed are gone while the power remains.

I stare at my hands, at the room, back at Embry again. None of this can be real if I—

"You just *almost* died. The Guild's magic over the tournament was just enough to save you."

My mind goes blank. I say the only thing I can say even though it feels more than inadequate. "Thank you."

"I'm to offer you tea. Would you like some?"

There are no pots or cups in sight, but I nod anyway, understanding. I might not be able to cast marks into existence, but

Embry's a member of the Guild. He could probably do it while half-asleep.

He takes a jasmine flower from the bouquet and places it on the table. It becomes a pot full of hot tea. Two more flowers laid down and they become cups.

I'd expected it, but I'm still stunned. Not at the proof of such magic, but because Embry's hands hadn't moved to cast.

"You didn't do this," I say, growing confused.

"I didn't have to because someone else in the Guild did. We are always here somewhere, in some part of the tournament." He smiles, but it's still not warm. "Without form, like full magic itself."

I have to force myself from glancing around the room, searching for hints of vague, indefinable clouds over our heads.

He pours tea for the both of us. Only after he sets the pot back down does he speak again.

"You broke the rules with the casting of that clone spell. You cast outside your team's assigned starter."

"I did break the rules . . . but only kind of."

"How only 'kind of'?"

"I only used other starters when I cast the clone spell. For spells on the other fighters, I only cast using silver ones."

He narrows his eyes just the slightest bit.

"Even my clones only used silver ones," I press.

"True. Though all those clones would have never been cast in the first place if you hadn't broken the rules."

I take a sip of tea, trying not to wither beneath his stare. "It's okay, I already know you're letting me stay in the tournament."

Now he laughs. "Oh?"

I nod. "You haven't met with any of the other eliminated fighters after a match."

"None of the other eliminated fighters have done what you did." Some of his power peels back, revealing more of his charm. I let myself relax a tiny bit.

"I know I broke the rules." I scrub at dried blood on my arm. There are bruises all over and every single muscle hurts from fighting. I think of doing this again tomorrow, and my mind goes to the empty medicine jar in my starter bag. "But I had to. My team was in trouble."

"Having a reason doesn't change how you still broke the rules. However, given the theme of tonight's match, the Guild eventually voted to allow you and your team to move on to the next round. It was clear you only cast that spell in the name of teamwork, covering for your team's weakness as you did. And as you said, you still only *fought* using silver starters, even each of your clones—the casting of which, I must admit, some of us enjoyed watching very much."

Relief has me slumping slightly. "Thank you."

"But honorable move or not, you'll still have to pay for breaking the rules." His teal eyes stay on mine. "A caveat for the Guild's generosity."

I begin to unwind Piper's silk ribbon from around my arm so I don't have to look at him.

"The tournament has always been about being a show of full magic, a display of skill. It's why the Guild has never banned any specific spell—not when the real world already restricts too much of our magic. But this also means we're responsible for keeping the tournament and its effects under control. Your spell called for too much magic, and our diversion spell was tested. We cannot afford to slip."

I nod, folding up the ribbon with fingers gone cold and stuffing it into my starter bag. The crowd loved the spell, and Piper wanted flair, but I nearly died in casting it. How might the earth now have to pay? My mind skitters away from the thought.

"To keep you from trying anything like it again—and any other caster who might now be considering something similar—the Guild has decided that for the remainder of the tournament, we will no longer use our magic to help you survive the cost of casting."

"You can't do that." Panic unfurls, filling me. "Please." I'll feel everything, while everyone else will feel close to nothing. A punch to them would be an explosion for me. There's no way I can win now.

"It is a punishment that suits the crime," Embry says. "Of course, you don't have to accept our decision. In which case, you can enter again next year. It's up to you."

The panic turns into a fist. My grasp on the tournament—on answers, saving my family, my promise to Rudy—begins to slip. The two hundred thousand marks feel like they're drifting even further out of reach.

But what choice do I have? If I don't agree, the Guild will kick me out of the tournament anyway.

"Fine," I say. "I accept the decision."

"Good. And we want to make clear to you, no more second chances. Another rule broken and you *will* be eliminated from the tournament."

His tone doesn't give away if he cares or not. And I'm not sure why it suddenly matters but it does. Maybe because he and his Guild accept a killer like Finch as their champion, while my saving Wilson has only put me in danger of elimination.

"You said the Guild voted on us moving on or being eliminated," I say. "How many members wanted us out?" I imagine them, a group of seven greats, sitting around and weighing Finch's skill against his cruelty. How many of them might vote in someone like him? How far can Finch go and still be considered?

"It was close—hence the caveat." Embry drinks tea. "As the tie-breaker, I had to come up with something to tip the scales."

"Thank you." My resentment that he decided I would be in pain isn't fair, so I push it away. "Why didn't you vote the other way?"

"As I said, the Tournament of Casters has always been a show. I enjoyed your fist spell from the last match, and then the clones tonight."

"But . . . sometimes fighters die. For a *show*. That doesn't bother you?"

"Not as much as you think it should." His eyes grow sharp. "Leftover magic is for its casters to cast, just as full magic is ours. And while it runs in our veins, death from it does, too, and that is the cost—that is how, whether we like it or not, the world has created us to be now. Those who enter know that death is a possibility, and so we don't prevent it. But it's on us to ensure the tournament stays a secret, and that nobody gets caught. That is why you breaking the rules and calling for too much magic has a penalty—while killing does not."

I blink and the inside of the temple disappears from around us.

Gone are the papered walls and jade brick and dragon-painted windows. Instead of a teapot and cups on a table, dried petals are scattered on the floor at our knees. The scent of jasmine is replaced with ones of smoke and fire, the last traces of a past inferno, of spent magic. We're back inside the burnt-out shell of the apartment building on Thorn Avenue.

"Before I forget." Embry hands over some marks. I count them. There's five hundred, way more than I've ever earned from a job. Way more than a *bunch* of jobs, even. "You weren't able to get to the bets counter after the fight tonight to collect your winnings. You should celebrate—that's a very impressive amount for having only fought twice. You have left an impression."

I tuck the marks into my pocket, wishing I wasn't so pleased that *he* seems pleased. But more than that, this means I can replace the marks I had to take out of the safe for Jihen. My parents can still keep thinking everything is fine when it comes to the teahouse and Saint Willow.

"You also missed my announcement of tomorrow night's location." Embry hands me a small card as he gets to his feet. There's an address scrawled on it. "Midnight, as always."

5040 Helvetica

I tuck the card into my starter bag and get up, too. I hurt all over from fighting, and I think of Rudy's apothecary. More than ever I need to get more healing meds.

"Thank you for the tea," I say, "even if you weren't the one who cast it."

"I didn't cast it because I no longer cast. I fought in five tournaments—they took their toll."

Shock has me gaping. "You're an Ivor?"

He nods. "Bones of glass. I can't cast without shattering apart, even with the Guild's help. The other members cast the magic for the fighting rings, and I am the tournament Speaker. It is the arrangement we came to after I . . . changed."

"But—the playing cards tonight. They were blank and then—"

"The Guild as a whole."

"And tournament magic."

"Yes."

My thoughts run together, threaten to tangle. How many of us might go Ivor over the years because of this tournament? The amount of magic I did tonight alone could have easily tipped me over, because the Guild's magic can only do so much, and Embry is proof of that. For so long I've pushed to the back of my mind the chances of one day ending up an Ivor. Pushed it back so deep that tonight, I was staring the possibility right in the face and didn't even realize it.

I wonder what Embry thinks when he sees a display caster hanging from a lamppost. If he thinks about how it could easily be him up there if not for his damage being hidden, or if he's so busy thinking about his guild's tournament that seeing an Ivor doesn't mean much at all.

I want to ask him about it, but I don't because I think he'll just give me the same answer. The one that somehow disappoints me, even though I don't think it's actually wrong. And I don't have a better one.

That it's just the cost of magic.

Then I nearly tell him I'll keep his secret about being an Ivor, but I also don't do this. Because he already knows I'll keep it. Spilling it would mean having to face the Guild, greats powerful enough to create whole worlds and then take them back apart.

"My name's really Aza," I decide to say instead. An exchange of secrets, I guess. "But I'm Rudy for the tournament."

He nods again. His smile is all charm now. "Good luck, then, Aza."

TWENTY-EIGHT

Once outside, I begin making my way out of the Flower Sector. I head toward Tobacco, moving as fast as I can despite being sore. If not for Cormac, I'd be going home instead of to Rudy's. But there's an upside to his delaying me—now that I know he's staying near the teahouse instead of staking out the apothecary, I'll at least be able to break into Rudy's place in peace.

Salty air blows in off the Pacifik, drifts through my mask, and lingers. It mixes there with the thickening scent of smoke as I enter the Tobacco Sector and get closer to Rudy's shop. The neighborhood is mostly quiet, with a bar and a club a block over still open, and of course the breakfast-all-day diner directly across the street.

There are no new signs or notices posted anywhere outside Shen Apothecary, nothing to let his loyal customers know what happened to him. Rudy would hate that—not only their not knowing, but also that they have to go anywhere else. The blinds remain pulled—briefly I wonder again who discovered Rudy's body, as I couldn't ask Cormac, and he never said—and I peer around their edges to look inside.

The shelves are still full of bottles of tonics and elixirs. Jars and tins fill cabinets. The soaps Rudy was checking are still all over the table, inventory the last thing he did for his shop.

Heat comes to my eyes. I'm not supposed to miss all those days of coming here and being unpaid help while Rudy gritted out bits of advice, but I do. He kept me at a distance because of Shire and the tournament, but I had something to do with that, too, already half-sure when I went to him for help that he was just another enemy. Like Saint Willow and Jihen were. And now there's Cormac. And Finch.

I go around the outside of the shop and get to the back door. I find a rock in my starter bag, brace for the pain, and cast.

Heat travels from my feet and into my hands, forms in my mind as a ball of red haze. I send it to the lock and untwist it. As soon as it's done, my skin cools down and I lean back against the door, waiting, half holding my breath. The pain comes in a wave, hammers on the bones of my arms and legs, and I wait it out, gritting my teeth.

When it finally passes, I stand up again on shaking legs and go inside.

Smells swirl thickly, medicinal, herbal, one of rosemary most of all. I think of the broken bottle when I found Rudy and try not to gag at the scent.

Too tired to even consider leftover magic, I slap at the wall with my hand, searching for the light switch in the dark, finally finding it and flicking it on.

Light fills the room. It looks the same as it always does, stuffed full of boxes and supplies and shelves. I glance down at the floor—it's been cleaned up of Rudy's blood, of the broken and spilled bottles. Everything is so clean and neat—looking at it, you'd never guess someone like Rudy had died here two days ago, a mess of banished magic, secrets, and lies.

I head out to the shop floor, using only the light flowing

out from the supply room to see by. In the dimness, I move slowly around the room, realizing I will likely never see the apothecary again the way it is. How if I ever do come back, the space likely won't be Rudy's anymore—someone else will have moved in, might be selling anything else; all the sights and smells will be different.

The thought fills me with sadness, like I'm finally saying a proper goodbye to the person who connected me to Shire in ways I wouldn't have been otherwise. It also fills me with guilt, because hadn't I kept pushing him for more? To show me the spell Shire had died casting, when such a spell never existed? I try to imagine how he must have felt, keeping that secret, and find that I can't.

I keep working, feeling half-numb. I neaten a basket of dried herbs and straighten a shelf of oils. I find a lone twenty-mark coin on the counter but the till is locked so I slip it into my pocket.

It takes me a bit to find the right healing meds on a shelf, but I eventually do, matching their labels to the one on my empty jar. I debate taking them all, but then I think of how it was bad paperwork that set Cormac toward Rudy—if someone's going to be checking inventory against what's actually on the shelf, a whole bunch of missing meds might set off alarm bells, too.

I take a single bottle, but then duck behind the counter—if I can find Rudy's inventory binder, it'd be easy enough to doctor it so the shop's not missing any healing meds at all. I open drawers and peek into skinny cubbyholes. Before I find his binder, though, I find a notebook, one with dog-eared edges that say he used it a lot. Like me, Rudy never carried around a digital planner, because our magic would kill them each time.

I flip it open. Most of the notebook is a calendar, with some blank pages in the back for notes. The days are filled in with initials and times, which are meaningless to me, so I skip ahead to the back pages. Rudy's writing is messy, but a lot of the notes seem to be about ideas for the shop, things like new formulas and research ideas.

I keep flipping, trying not to feel like Rudy would mind. He probably would. But maybe now that I'm in the tournament and know about his plans and what happened to Shire, he wouldn't mind *so* much. And if there's anything in here that could help me at all over the last two rounds—

Finch's name leaps up at me from a page.

My heart trips inside my chest, and I hurriedly turn the page back. My fingers are clumsy and it takes me longer than it should. And it's dim in here. Maybe I saw wrong.

But then I find the page.

Finch—gath. spell possible?
Oliver?
That was the cost??

Now my pulse is racing. My mouth's gone dry with the shock of what I've found.

Rudy *also* suspected Finch cheated to beat Shire. That Finch maybe used a gathered spell, just as Kylin mentioned.

And that Oliver is somehow involved.

I shouldn't be as surprised as I am. It makes sense that Oliver would be helping his brother hide how he cheated. Just as Piper said, family complicates things, and I of all people know that loyalty sometimes knows no bounds.

Finch longs so badly to be in the Guild of Now, too. If you need to win in the first place to be able to do that, then what does the cost matter *as long as you still win*?

I shut the notebook with trembling fingers, slide it back into its drawer, and turn to leave. All thoughts of doctoring the inventory binder have fled—given the potential of what I've just found, a few missing bottles of medicine really won't matter.

I return to the supply room and exit through the back door, making sure to turn off the light before casting the lock back. Once more pain comes, a slow wave of it that is a knife through my middle.

I yank down my mask, dry swallow a pill, yank the mask back up. I try to walk as steadily as I can down the alley. It's pouring out, the air smelling more of the sea than of smoke, and I'm tired and sore enough to decide to grab a train back to the Tea Sector. I pay for the ticket using the mark I found at Rudy's, saving me from having to use any of the ones I got from the bets counter.

The train's rocking motion and the sound of rain on the roof nearly lull me to sleep. But then the latest news comes on, scrolling across the screen over the doors. No one else on the train seems to pay attention—it's just the most recent addition to a long string of bad news for the earth—but I do because I know so much of it is my fault.

The report is that, as of the last hour, over two hundred fish have washed up on the northern shore of the Flower Sector. The fish are a heavily mutated strain of catfish, warped over the years from adapting to pollution of the Pacifik and Upper Inlet and one of the few kinds of fish still able to survive in local waters. City water authorities have no explanation so far for the sudden mass death of the school of fish, and admit the population might take years to fully recover, if ever.

I'm wide awake the rest of the train ride home.

TWENTY-NINE

My eyes are still bleary from lack of sleep as I head out of the teahouse the next day. The events of last night haven't stopped pulling at me, filling my brain at a low buzz that won't completely quiet.

I didn't think it would be easy advancing to the final of the tournament. I've always considered myself a long shot. That Shire got there is never so much a source of hope as it is one of discouragement—she spent years training to control her magic—she was the reliable and dependable daughter.

But still. As the first rounds passed, I began to believe it was possible. That maybe it wasn't such a wild idea, getting to the final.

And now here I am, fighting for the rest of the tournament without the Guild's protection. They'll cover the cost of my magic when it comes to the earth, but not to me.

I might really die fighting for marks.

Just like Shire did.

For a second, the idea of walking away from the whole thing washes over me. Sure, my parents will lose the teahouse and a family legacy that goes back hundreds of years, but at least not both their daughters. Rudy's dead and can't care about my breaking my promise. Shire's dead, too, and just as Embry said, everyone who enters the tournament enters knowing they could die.

But all those reasons—they're also the same ones why I *can't* quit. My parents and everything they've worked for. Rudy, who might still be alive if not for me. Shire, who didn't know she'd be fighting someone dirty.

Finch, Oliver, the puzzle of Rudy's notebook and what was written inside—I know all of that will keep eating at me. It will never leave me alone until I find out what all of it means.

I cross the street in the direction of the Textile Sector. For the Mothery, and Piper.

I dreamed last night that she had dropped me as her fighter. I'd broken the rules and my chances at winning were slim—why would she continue to back me? The possibility left me shaky enough— on top of fighting vulnerable, the last thing I need is having to go back to worrying about marks for ring starters—that I knew I had to go see her in person and convince her she hasn't made a mistake. So I told my parents I was going to work and slipped out.

My web of lies, still being spun.

And then I stop cold.

Jihen.

He's sitting at one of the sidewalk tables of the café down the street. He's branched out this time with his striped suit, but his sneakers are as glaringly white as ever.

I start to reverse direction before he can see me, but it's too late. He's already getting up, throwing marks down on the table for his bill before he rounds the gate and heads toward me.

Always tempted to use magic to get away from him, my hand nearly goes to my starter bag. The healing meds I took last night worked—though slowly, making me wonder if I'm getting too used to them—and I woke up this morning without pain, despite having barely slept.

But I'm fighting tonight, and now without the Guild's protection. And I've actually got marks on me, a few left over after replacing the rest in the teahouse's safe last night. I might as well pay him and get him off my back again for a bit.

"Aza, good morning, shall we walk?" He takes my arm and guides me along the road.

"I guess so?" I try to throw off his hand, but his grip is irritatingly strong today. The thicker-than-usual undertone of ownership in it makes me uneasy. I glance over at him as we walk. "I have marks for Saint Willow. Let go of my arm and I'll give them to you for him. And then you can leave and do whatever it is that you guys do when you're not robbing or killing people."

His hand squeezes. "You can't rob those who owe you. And we only kill when we have to send a message. Messages are important. They let others know what is expected of them." Another squeeze and I regret not casting magic to get away after all.

We're not too close to the teahouse, but close enough that I'm uncomfortable. I turn a corner in the opposite direction, trying to get Jihen farther away from my parents.

"Here." I pull out the marks from my pocket. "There's more than there was last time—just take it." I brace myself for another round of Jihen making threats because it's still not enough. It *is* more, but never has it been enough.

Instead of counting the marks, though, Jihen stuffs them into a pocket. He gives me his greasy smile that's somehow a little too predatory today. That earlier uneasiness comes back, and I wonder if I've missed something.

He pulls me closer. He whispers into my ear words that turn my blood cold: "*I know you're a caster of full magic.*"

I stumble. His grip tightens and still we walk. I'm only dimly aware of the world that's fading in and out. The rain-damp sidewalk recedes. Shops and other casters go silent. The scents of tea and leaves lingering inside my mask fade. There are only his fingers that dig into my arm, keeping me from running away.

"You're wrong," I finally manage. My voice is thin and thready. "I only know leftover magic. Like everyone else."

"Let me tell you how I found out, Aza. You and I and everyone else in the sector know that Saint Willow sometimes has a . . . hard time keeping any full magic casters on. My boss loves full magic, but maybe a bit too much, and casters get scared off, yes?"

I just shake my head.

"Well, sometimes, being such a distant cousin in the Saint Willow enterprise has its benefits. People stop *seeing* you. They forget who you are. They think *the boss* has forgotten you. So when one of those casters used full magic for a memory wipe on Saint Willow and everyone else important in order to escape, *they forgot me.* And I let them. I let them because one hand washes the other. I let them have their freedom, and they give me a window into your world, Aza. Casters like you will be the end of the earth one day, but I also know there is power in information that others don't have. And so this caster and I—we're still friends, Diego and me. I have full magic right in my back pocket and *Saint Willow has no clue.*"

My heart is beating thickly in my throat, in my ears. Still we walk. I'm only half listening, my mind whirring with different spells to get away. But we're out in the open, in sight of the street, traffic, other people. And Jihen knows this.

"And Diego," he says, "it turns out he's a fan of this underground tournament. All full magic casters, all battling one another for big marks. He tells me about this one fighter with the ring name of Rudy who caught everyone's eye during the opening match."

There's a roar in my ears now. I picture Jihen sitting at the table in the teahouse that night, looking at all the blood still on me, his mild tsk of disapproval.

"So when Diego offers to sneak me in to last night's match, how could I refuse?" Jihen grins. "I missed seeing you up close, but Diego saw you. Do you remember him? Earrings, beard like a bird's nest hanging off his chin?"

I only shake my head again, despite knowing exactly who he's talking about. The guy who couldn't stop staring at me before the round.

"Well, the clones blew me away, beauty. Like a bunch of gorgeous dolls, you were. So many leng goong-doi."

I rear back, desperate for escape. But there is nowhere to go. Jihen pulls me closer.

"Of course, I *should* tell my boss. Then you, Aza Wu, would be Saint Willow's newest full magic caster. And if you didn't work out, there would be a tournament full of others to pick from. For my discovery, I would become the most important cousin in the family. I might even be promoted to something beyond debt squeezer. But then I got to thinking, why share? What if *I* would like a full magic caster? To have such terrible yet fascinating power for my own use?"

It takes a second to process. "You want me to work for you?"

Jihen nods. "You won't have to deal with Saint Willow's tantrums, and I'll have my own personal caster to cast me spells as I need. Do we have a deal?"

My head's spinning. Jihen or Saint Willow—it's like having to choose either getting eaten by a shark or a slow death by drowning. "I can't."

"*Or* the teahouse pays. There are so many ways it could pay. More honor marks. More suppliers cut off. And your parents—they won't want me back on the premises, will they?"

"Stop."

"Or imagine a Scout at the door. How many customers do you think your family's teahouse would get once it's out that their kid is a full magic caster? The despair your parents would feel, losing not only their remaining daughter but also their livelihood, this family legacy they've held on to all this time."

I twist free of his arm, feeling sick, needing to breathe. "Fine, I'll do it."

Another greasy grin slides across his face. "And a cut of the tournament prize, if you win."

Fury explodes at the pettiness of this last demand. How it's just one more thing on top of everything else, when he's already got way too much on me. "Say that again, and I'll go straight to Saint Willow about Diego. He'll drown you in the Sturgeon River the same way Earl Kingston did *his* cousin for keeping secrets."

Jihen's features twist. "You wouldn't dare, you brat."

"I would. So?"

He mutters something in Chinese too quietly for me to catch.

"What's money anyway, when I get a sweet caster of my own, right?"

"Right." I exhale. "I'm leaving now. Don't fol—"

The sight of my parents coming up the street freezes me before I can even take a step.

Why are they here instead of at the teahouse? Panic is a buzz in my head as I scramble for a cover. Where exactly did I say I was going this morning? *Did* I say anything specific? I can't remember.

"Ah, such timing," Jihen says softly. "Should we say hello to your loving fou-mou?"

I rip open my starter bag. "Walk away before they see you, or I'll cast."

"Not so fast. You want to cast something terrible on me, I can tell. But I'd be suffering and so would you. The pain of casting, yes?"

My parents are closer now. They see us. My stomach drops.

"Here's the first of my requests, beauty," Jihen says. "Consider this my test of your agreement, and you can save yourself. And you'll be saving your parents as well—small talk can be dangerous with all these secrets floating around."

Fury claws. *"Tell me."*

"A small accident or distraction right here on the sidewalk. And I'll leave."

I do it before I can think about it. How I'm now casting on orders from *Jihen*. My fingers shake as I pick up a water capsule. I cast, my hands low to my sides. Heat fills me. I stare at the pool of water that's still puddled on a nearby overhead awning and send it flying.

Everyone on the sidewalk gets drenched. There are cries of dismay and the shop owner emerges, confused. Behind it all there are my parents' faces, ovals of surprise as they take in the strange spill.

Through the headache that begins to circle my skull, Jihen's smug voice is at my side: "I'll be sure to give your marks to Saint Willow, Aza. Now don't go disappearing on me. I'll be in touch soon."

I start walking before he can say anything else. My head pounds, and the gray of the sky is too bright. I find my parents and hope my face looks normal. I'm kicking myself for making up a ridiculous lie that's now come true—I'm working for Jihen for real.

"Why aren't you guys at the teahouse?" I glance at the mess on the sidewalk and try not to feel guilty. Nobody got hurt, but soon some part of the earth will pay, however minor.

"Tomorrow is a bank holiday," my mother says from behind her smog mask, "so we're making payments today."

I forgot about the holiday. And tomorrow is Friday, and Friday the teahouse opens late on account of my parents going around the city and paying suppliers and distributors. I only replaced the rest of the missing marks in the safe last night after getting back from the apothecary. The close call sends a shiver through me.

"Aza, did we see Jihen with you?" My father is squinting over the heads of the casters on the sidewalk.

I nearly nod but for the pain. "I had to meet up with him to get instructions for a package I have to deliver." Such bland words—instructions, package, deliver—I use to describe working for a gang. It keeps my parents from remembering Jihen's intimidating tactics when he was squeezing them. It keeps them from wondering if I could be doing the same thing, their reckless daughter who might not understand full magic but who must know to be careful while working for Saint Willow.

"I have to go now," I tell them, "but I'll be home for dinner." I still need to get to the Mothery. To get to Piper and try to convince her she needs to stay as my backer.

"Can you wait for an hour or so, Aza?"

I glance at my mother, curious.

"There's a café down the block—we could all eat some lunch before you have to go?" Her smile is almost surprised. As though she asked before she knew she was going to. And maybe she did. The three of us haven't eaten a lunch together anywhere since before Shire died. Between her ghost and full magic and the teahouse, it's been hard to find room to fit together.

I want to point out that we shouldn't be spending marks on lunch. How the teahouse might be late to open if they don't get back now.

So my answer surprises me just as much. "Lunch would be nice."

THIRTY

It takes until dessert for things to not feel so strange. Without my mother's television to watch or my father's paperwork to read, we only have one another, and there is the awkward shuffling at first that happens when you're eating with strangers.

My headache's gone, at least.

My mother watched as I took the healing meds at the table, her eyes on me the whole time. At first I wondered if she was going to ask me about them, which would have been easy enough to lie about. But then it hit me that she might recognize the bottle or label as being the same as the one Shire had in her room and dread washed over me.

But it was about something else altogether.

"That was Shire's bag," she said, her eyes on it.

I nodded. I ran my hand over the yellow silk. Threads had begun to spring up from it, and there were some thin patches. A tiny hole had opened up near the top corner that leftover magic could probably fix except that I hadn't gotten to it yet.

"It's getting worn," my mother added.

"I know. But it's still usable."

"You should fix that hole before you lose something."

"I will."

Then the waiter came over and we were choosing between pasta and sandwiches and salad, and whether we wanted dessert. I'd been about to protest the price of dessert—the hole of Leafton's contract cancellation was still fresh on everyone's minds—but something on my father's face stopped me. It said we all needed this as much as wanted it.

My mother sniffs her tea now. She makes a face.

"I keep telling you to just order the coffee like I do." My father casts and the spoon in his mug stirs.

"It's research."

He sends me an exasperated look, and I have to smile. My mother has made it a habit over the years to always try the teas of others just to proclaim Wu ones are better. This, at least, has not changed.

The silence that follows isn't wholly uncomfortable. I eat cake and stare out the window and feel nearly half-normal. My mother casts, and the service bell on the wall rings; when the waiter comes, she tells them the tea is off and orders coffee. My father studies the menu like there's some code to decipher, something he could apply to the teahouse's to bring back the customers.

A text comes through on his cell and he frowns.

"It's an office out in the Spice Sector," he tells us. "Some of our statements just got delivered to them by mistake. They can redeliver, but their courier is behind—with the bank holiday tomorrow, we won't get these statements until Monday."

"Can they wait?" My mother nods her thanks as the waiter brings her coffee.

"Well, I'm supposed to meet Yun tonight over them. I've already confirmed the meeting. I'd hate to change it now."

Yun's one of the guys in our distribution system. Trying to fit in a meeting with him is tough because he's always juggling so many different companies.

My mother sighs, tired despite the coffee.

"I can go pick them up for you," I blurt out.

Because Oliver and Finch's family store is in the Spice Sector.

And while I don't think I'll get the chance to cast magic on either Finch or Oliver to get to the truth, maybe just observing their shop for a bit will tell me something. Having a legit reason for being in their neighborhood is too good of a cover to waste. My conversation with Piper will have to wait.

"I'll bring the statements home when I get back for dinner," I tell my parents.

My father's not convinced. He doesn't want me to get in trouble with Jihen or Saint Willow. "Don't you have to get to work?"

I nod and finish my cake in a rush. I *have* to go to Spice now— the need to try to uncover Finch's secret burns as hot as magic does, even if I have no idea yet what I'm actually going to do. "This won't take long. Here, write the address of the office down for me?"

"Well, thanks, Aza." My father writes on the napkin and hands it over. "Much appreciated—you know Yun's schedule."

"I do." I fold it into my starter bag, slip on my smog mask, and start to get up.

"Wait a second," my mother says. "One more thing before you go."

I stop.

She rips off some of her napkin—leftover magic—and casts.

The hole in my bag disappears, the tiny threads around its edge made to knot together.

"Thank you," I say. I can't explain the ache in my throat. Maybe because she still bothered to fix it, when it's just me using it now.

She hands me some marks. "For the train there and back—it's raining again. And don't be late for dinner."

I get to my feet and head for the door. My eye catches on a figure outside the window, standing on the sidewalk, clearly waiting for someone.

Cormac.

THIRTY-ONE

I falter for a second, confused. I'm supposed to get a week. A week where he thinks I'm getting information together to help him bring down casters of full magic, while really I'm just stalling before I can present him to Saint Willow as a cop to be dealt with.

One glance at his face says I don't have a week anymore.

I push open the door and rush out of the café.

"What are you doing here?" I hiss at him, too on edge to be glad that he never went inside looking for me. I *should* have just wiped Shire's file from his memory. Then I wouldn't have to be dealing with him on top of everything else. "You guaranteed you'd stay away from my parents."

He looks almost sheepish. "I'm sorry, I had no choice. I had to find you."

"Just—let's get away from here so they don't see us when they leave."

I head away from the café and the teahouse, but also keep eastward, toward Spice. The rain's coming down steadily, little pins of ice like darts in my skin.

Cormac follows me step for step, as determined as ever. "Listen, I can't get you that week you want. You're going to have to give me something on Saint Willow and his gang before that."

"Why? What happened?"

A flush reddens his face beneath his baseball cap. "This is my first assignment. I'm not getting much leeway."

I almost feel sorry for him, except that he'll lock me up in a second if he ever finds out I'm a full magic caster.

"That's not my problem," I tell him, still walking. "Go back and say you need a week."

He grabs my arm, right where Jihen grabbed it, reminding me he's a *Scout*, not just the inexperienced and overeager cop he comes across as. We do a parody of a casual stroll over toward the mouth of an alley where he drops my arm.

"*Today*, Aza. I already feel foolish that this case rests on unconfirmed informant testimony from a teenager. I need to know what you know." Cormac's mouth is in a hard line. The tone of finality in his voice chills me. "I need something from you *today*, or I'll have to move on and question your parents."

The chill deepens. "Today?"

He nods.

My mind goes blank. I've already told him everything I meant to, the whole part of the plot of *Liar's Lair* that matters. I've got nothing else because he was supposed to give me a goddamn week.

"I can't," I whisper. "I don't have anything concrete. I need more time."

"You said you and Rudy had leads, good ones, ones that will get me full magic casters. You've been working on these leads together since Shire died, right?"

I'm numb. Fear's locked up my throat.

"It's been *a year*, Aza. You've got to be lying about not having anything concrete. My stalling is the only reason why a team of

Scouts aren't talking to your parents right now, do you know that? And I can't give you any more time."

I shudder at the picture that comes. Scouts towering over my parents, who never asked for their daughters to be born with full magic. "You guaranteed you'd leave my parents out of this."

"But I never promised other Scouts would. Just like I never promised you the week, only that I would try. Believe me, I want to leave your parents out of this, too. But you're going to have to give me something."

"You know I want to find out who killed Rudy and Shire as much as you want your casters. Why would I be lying?"

Cormac's blue eyes go all glinty and sharp. It won't be long before he looks like this all the time—a Scout through and through. "Who was that guy you were talking to earlier today? Ugly suit with too-big stripes, even uglier white sneakers."

Jihen.

Panic flutters. Of course he knows about Jihen. When Cormac said he'd be tracking me for show, I knew that still meant the physical act of tracking. He wouldn't be able to help seeing Jihen. It explains how he knew to find me at the café, too.

But maybe if he'd gotten that week, neither of those things would have mattered.

"Aza? Who was that guy? Is he one of your leads?"

My mind leaps on this. "Yes, okay? But I'm still working on things. You can't move in on this yet!"

"Okay, give me a name. Can you at least do that? I'll go back with it and buy you more time."

I look at him. His eagerness to destroy casters like me bakes off him like a fever, the cost of a dream. I want to hate him, but I understand him too much.

I lower my voice. "His name is Milo Kingston."

"Who's that?"

"I was telling you about Saint Willow's gang before, remember?"

"Yes. How Rudy had planted Shire as a mole to figure out who Saint Willow's mole in the police was. And that it was Saint Willow's mole who ended up killing Rudy and Shire."

I nod. "Okay, there's actually a second gang involved. A rival gang of Saint Willow's. Earl Kingston's gang."

Cormac just narrows his eyes. "You're kidding me."

"I'm not. It looks like Saint Willow was contracting out some of his dirty work to the other gangs. That way it becomes nearly untraceable. And Milo Kingston is my access guy to *Earl* Kingston, who I need to bring down Saint Willow."

He sighs. "So the name is Milo Kingston?"

"Yes."

"And all of this will help me get my casters?"

"Yes."

"I just—this is sudden, Aza."

"You just saw Milo Kingston yourself, didn't you?"

If he keeps doubting me, I'll have to figure out some way to cast some belief on him. Except the pain of using a spell like that would be immense. The healing meds work, but only sometimes. And with my new punishment in the tournament, I really can't afford to go in already weakened.

Cormac stares at me for a good long minute. My new lie feels too clumsy, the lie that's now threatening to make all the others spill over. What if he's heard the rumor about Earl Kingston killing his cousin and matches it up with the name Milo Kingston?

Believe me. Just believe this one last lie.

"I'll let you know what comes next," Cormac finally says before walking away.

THIRTY-TWO

I grab a train to get to the Spice Sector, but it breaks down halfway there. I don't mind getting out to walk the rest of the way, though, even with the rain—I still need to think of how I might figure out Finch's secret.

Twenty minutes later, the area greets me with its pungent air, thick with the scent of peppers and herbs and salts that sting my nose through my mask. The first place I go is the office to pick up the Wu Teas statements.

"Here you go." One of the security guards at the front desk hands over an envelope. "The company apologizes for the inconvenience."

"It's okay." I take the envelope and place it in my starter bag. Another security guard at the desk has his cell switched to the local news, and even though I can't hear it, I can see the screen well enough. Across the street from the café where my parents and I ate lunch, a large crevasse opened up on the sidewalk. No one was seriously hurt, though a biker fell in and had to be rescued.

Sorry, random biker.

I speak to the first security guard. "I forgot my cell so I'm wondering—would you be able to look up an address for me?"

The Salt Lick is in the north end of the sector. I make my way over, the High Shore Mountains peeking through buildings and smog like faint smears of gray-green. The Upper Inlet that lines the sector's northern shore isn't visible from here, but it's not hard to picture its dark brown waters where mostly strange things live now. Earl Kingston drowned his mutinous cousin in the Sturgeon River that cuts through the city itself, but Milo Kingston could have easily met his end in the Upper Inlet.

Milo Kingston.

I go from thinking it was a stroke of genius to add him to my story to believing I'm going to pay for being so stupid. I was so lost for what to tell Cormac that when he mentioned seeing Jihen, my mind leapt to it.

But my reasoning is this—things really can't get much worse. Cormac can only buy me so much more time. I'm fighting in a tournament I now have almost no chance of winning. Even winning won't solve everything, now that Jihen knows I can cast full magic. What's one more lie about a dead gangster?

Despite all this, I still have to do everything I can to win those two hundred thousand marks for my parents. If I can just do that, I'll be saving the teahouse. I might still be in Jihen's clutches afterward, but Saint Willow would be off my parents' backs, our family legacy still intact.

Shire must have felt this same way. Must have felt such desperation to save us that it drove her toward the risk of the tournament.

We have more in common than full magic, Shire, I'd say to her now. *We would have understood this part of each other, too.*

We even have Finch in common. He stood in the way of her winning and now he stands in mine. Not just as my biggest obstacle to winning the tournament, but to my getting the truth, and payback. And if he killed Shire to beat her, then who's to say he won't kill again?

I stand on the corner of the block the Salt Lick's on, debating about going inside or not. I almost want to convince myself there's a rule about fighters talking to each other outside the ring. But as Kylin pointed out, if there was, Embry would have said something that first night.

I walk over, my pulse skipping, and peer into the front window of the shop.

There's pale wood shelving everywhere, silver canisters and tins and jars. Barrels sit on bleached wood flooring, little taps jutting out of their sides.

Oliver's helping a customer weigh out something from one of those barrels.

There's no sign of Finch.

I can't deny I'm more relieved than disappointed. It's one thing to face him in the fighting ring, with both of us surrounded by other fighters and the crowd and Embry's watchful gaze. But this is Finch's territory, his place in the city, and to confront him here is like walking into a minefield. That I even thought about trying to break into his mind to search out what he wants to hide now seems beyond foolish.

But Oliver—he's no fighter. Finch's secrets are also his. And nothing's shown me he can cast full magic. Which is what he needs if he wants to fight off a reveal spell.

I fold my mask away, yank the door open, and go inside.

Oliver looks up at the sound and goes absolutely still when he sees me. His hazel eyes go from friendly to wary, even chilly. It takes the customer asking him something to break him from that stillness, but even after he returns to what he was doing, there's a stiffness to him that is clearly from my being here.

I made him laugh when we first met, and he helped me as much as he could being another fighter's backer. But the last time we saw each other, I was glaring at him from the fighting ring. And I broke the rules during last night's fight. He doesn't know if I've been kicked out of the tournament or not. As far as he knows, I'm still his brother's competition.

The last customer leaves, and it's just him and me.

Oliver's expression says I'm wholly unwelcome. He goes over and locks the door by hand. He pulls the shade down over the front window, also by hand.

So far, still no sign of full magic. But nothing that says he's not a caster of it, either.

Should I cast now? Just catch him off guard enough to give me time to find *some* answers in his mind?

He comes back. "You shouldn't be here."

The skin at my neck warms. The leap—from fighting his brother to fighting *him*—feels too big to make. "I, um, want to buy some salt."

He blinks. "You want to buy salt."

"You sell salt, don't you?" My face is warm now, too—I'm *buying salt* instead of casting a skin spell. "This place *is* called the Salt Lick."

"Um, okay." He glances around. "Take your pick."

I point to one of the other barrels, hoping the place isn't just full of overpriced gourmet salt. I only have the marks for the train ride back to the Tea Sector. "Would you recommend that one?"

We both move over. The sign says it's a lemon salt inside the barrel. "Here, hold out your hand," Oliver says. "Right here beneath the tap."

I should just cast. While he's not in protective-older-brother mode but helpful-shop-owner mode, wanting to help *me*. It would be so easy. Just cast and look into his eyes and dive in.

I hold out my open hand, he gives the tap a quarter turn, and a bunch of crystals fall out onto my palm. I try one. "It tastes like salty lemon candy," I say, unable to keep from smiling.

"Sounds about right." He fills a tiny paper sack with it. "On the house."

"Oh. Thanks." I tuck it into my starter bag. My heart's going too fast, and the nerves in my system are all standing at attention. What is supposed to come next when you're about to use magic to invade someone's brain? Make more small talk to throw him off?

If he's stiff with me now when I'm just any other fighter, I can't imagine how he might be if he ever finds out how we're connected through Shire and Finch. He might just snap in half with the awkwardness.

"So are you still in the tournament?"

My skin gets hot again. "Yes. Sorry, I guess? If it means anything, Embry says the vote was close."

Oliver shrugs. "It's the Guild's decision. You don't have to say sorry."

"The other fighters won't be happy about it." Well, Kylin won't mind. And Wilson and Pav won't mind, either. But all the ones

I eliminated will, once they find out. "And I'm sure your brother, Finch, would've been happier to have one less person to battle."

He sweeps salt from his hands. His eyes are still wary. "How do you know Finch is my brother?"

"He's the current champion and you're his backer. Some things just become common tournament knowledge. Even beginners hear most of it after a while."

I pull out the napkin where my father wrote the address for the office and finish wiping salt from my palm. I keep the napkin in my hand.

"I wouldn't have guessed the families of fighters would be very interesting to hear about," Oliver says.

I nearly ask him about his parents, but I stop. So much of Oliver is closed off, and I'm already going to be prying too much. I scan his face, taking in the angles and hollows.

"You and Finch look alike, if no one's ever told you that. The bones beneath. That's another reason why I know you're brothers."

Oliver doesn't move, just lets me keep looking at him. His hazel eyes go to roam my face in turn. Something curls in my stomach, this flicker of heat.

I turn away and slowly glance around the shop, forcing my thoughts back toward the reveal spell. The two of us are still alone—if I'm going to do this, it'd be better to do it before Finch comes back.

"Where is Finch, by the way?" I ask, hoping my voice sounds normal. I drag my gaze from shelf to shelf, thinking fast. My heart's thudding hard, and there's a low rush deep in my ears.

"Out."

I nod, though the answer tells me little about how much time I might have. From Oliver's tone, I'm not going to find out much else, either, no matter how I might prod for details.

I circle closer to where he's still standing, blood racing in my veins. I already feel warm, like my magic is breaking through all on its own. I keep my hands low and draw a spell star.

If he's only got leftover magic, this will be simple.

But if he's got full, then this might get messy.

First, magic to hold him still. Catching him by surprise and hoping for a delayed reaction will only go so far, so I'll have to cast *a lot* of magic to make that hold last. By the time he can break free, I'll already be deep into my reveal spell and uncovering the answers I need. I'll be in pain, but so will Oliver, and that should let me get away.

What did your brother do to my sister?

"Your face—"

I swivel at Oliver's voice, the star already drawn on my palm.

He's pale, shocked, staring at me with eyes gone dark.

"Last year, the fighter Finch beat"—his hand goes up to his own cheek—"you look just like her." The bones beneath.

I rip in two the napkin still in my hand. I drop one half and cast around the other. Heat climbs and there's fire behind my eyes, in my palm.

Oliver goes so still, it's like I've taken his breath as well as his muscles. But there is fear in his eyes as he stares at me, a sharp anger at what I'm doing.

I toss the spent napkin half across the room and bend down,

scrambling for the half I haven't used. My breath coming fast, I grab it and cast.

Seventeen points.

Tonight, in the ring, I'm sure I'll regret this.

In my mind, the red nebulous cloud of my magic dances, waves. I taste salt and smoke and heat; my eyes feel hot. Pain from casting the skin spell comes then, an ache in the form of a wave that rolls throughout me. Heat becomes an inferno. It wraps around my heart and fills it. The world shimmers at its edges, everything I see set to a boil. My pulse is a drum beating wildly in my throat.

I meet Oliver's eyes and will my magic into his brain. Through his skull and then along the coils of his mind, the turns and twists there full of the trees that stand for time, memories, emotions. All of which make Oliver who he is.

And am stunned by what I see. There are memories that stick out from the landscape of Oliver's mind like stars against the night, like scars dug into skin. Not because he's making me see them but because they are still so much of everything *he* can see. I push the red haze of my magic closer to them, dimly aware of how outside my mind—outside Oliver's—we're still in the middle of the shop, unmoving. Out there, time passes in seconds, but in his mind, my magic stretches it long and thin.

Three memories. Each of them is a huge tree, and each has been charred by fire. The landscape around each is blasted fine and bare, like fallout from explosions, from events that still sound. Each tree is still smoking because in Oliver's life, each memory lives on, continuing to haunt. He has nothing but guilt, these memories that have taken over the landscape of who he is. In here, in this world of his mind, guilt is an endless smog.

I will my magic closer, toward the first tree. As I near it, faces form in the smoke it sends out. The magic of my reveal spell knows these are his parents, and so I know. I know his parents died in a car accident when he was a kid, that Oliver was angry and used magic to call them back and it went all wrong, that Finch has never forgiven him for it.

My magic drifts away, moves close to the second memory. As I get closer, my reveal spell makes its tree shape change. It becomes an arm reaching for the sky. The branches are its fingers.

The meaning slams into me like a fist.

Shock tears me away and I fall from his mind. In the shop I crash to the floor, gasping as fresh agony from casting comes. Instead of heat, a cold steely pain fills my chest, the silver lake of it as still as death. Pain takes the form of spears and they jab at my skull from all directions. I lean to the side and retch, but nothing comes up.

"A spell star with seventeen points," Oliver says softly. "All for a reveal spell. I hope it was worth it."

Ever so slowly I turn my head. He's sitting on the floor, his expression more exhausted than anything. There's no pain there because he didn't cast anything to counter my spell. Not because he chose not to but because he *couldn't*.

He has no magic. I wondered if he had real magic like his brother, but Oliver hasn't any magic at all. Not even leftover.

He's lost it.

No. Not lost.

He *gave it away.*

I yank open my starter bag and fumble for the jar of healing meds. I swallow two pills and stagger to my feet. I hope I'm wrong about them being less effective for me, but what can I do about that now?

You gave up magic. You gave up you.

"*Why?*" I ask Oliver.

"You're going to need another reveal spell for that," he says, getting up, too. "And casting again right now will kill you. I don't have to still be a caster of full magic to see that."

That third memory, the one I missed—that's the answer.

But my chance is gone now. Oliver won't let me catch him off guard again.

I *felt* it, while in his mind—the guilt that drove a decision. Guilt that blends into but isn't the same as the guilt he feels over his parents.

The room spins.

"You gave it up for your brother," I whisper. Piper was absolutely right when she said family can complicate things. *Why do you blame yourself for your parents' car accident, Oliver?* "For him to win *a tournament.*"

He goes even paler than before. His eyes are hollow. He looks like he's been gut-punched. "You should go now."

I need to remember that it was Finch who killed Shire, how hundreds of casters saw it happen. How it wasn't Oliver. But being here with him right now, having been in his mind and breathing in that smog of his guilt, the fact feels slippery, thin.

"How did Finch beat Shire last year?" My voice is ragged. "How did you help?"

241

"You shouldn't be here."

He said those same words to me when I came in. Like he knew I was here to take something, and he had so little left to give.

Oliver walks over and slowly unlocks the door. And he does it by hand, just like before. I know now it's because he has to. Just like he had to before, too.

I leave.

THIRTY-THREE

After I dragged myself home from the Salt Lick—I don't really remember much of the trip; a walk to a Spice Sector train station through a white haze of pain, falling into dreamless bits of sleep on the train, then a few more blocks of walking where each step felt like another bone breaking—I crawled into bed and fell asleep.

By the time I wake up, it's nine in the evening. And though my head still hurts, and there's an ache in my bones I don't like, I know I'm not going to die. I'll be able to fight. I eat my warmed-up dinner at the island in our kitchen. My mother sits beside me and watches one of her dramas, while my father and Yun have their meeting out in the dining room of the teahouse.

I know my parents know. How I must have cast full magic to need to heal that way. But my mother only tsked that I'd slept through dinner, and my father cast leftover magic to heat up my tea. So that feels like something. It feels like a lot, actually. It feels like so much that sometimes it even blots out what I wasn't able to sleep away.

Helvetica Street is in the Paper Sector, east of Tea, and at eleven I head out of the teahouse.

I watch for signs of Jihen and Cormac to see if they're following me, but there's nothing. Still, I'm careful to keep checking, and only after I leave the Tea Sector and am well within Textile do I let myself stop taking roundabouts. As I walk, every once in a while I'll shake my starter bag just to hear the rattling of the healing meds inside their glass jar. I'll need them tonight if I have any chance of making it home after getting through this next battle. My magic can once again hurt me for real.

My thoughts come back to Oliver and the gaping hole that is his magic. The absence of the thing that is so much *him*. He paid such a terrible price, and for what? To somehow help his brother destroy us?

But . . . what if *Oliver* didn't know, either? What if all that guilt I sensed is because of something he wishes he could have stopped? I know guilt, too. Wanting fire to dance and Shire's scar, hounding Rudy until he died—even if I didn't mean either of those to happen, I'll never stop feeling bad about them. Just like however Oliver came to give up his magic, it would change him forever. His parents' dying would have also altered his path.

My thoughts chase me forward, and soon I reach Paper. The sector is just east of Textile, and the changeover is like going from an oil painting to a watercolor. Bright hues turn into cream and grays. Bookstores replace fabric ones, and print shops replace tailor houses. Kiosks are on every corner, selling newspapers and magazines.

The location of tonight's fighting ring is the sector's—and therefore Lotusland's—oldest library. It's been shut down for years, a shadow of the past.

Whoever built the library was an admirer of ancient Xulaian architecture, and so the structure is a replica of the famous Vigo Baths halfway across the world in Xulai. It's been scaled down a lot, but the library still takes up a whole city block. It's a huge circular building with a roof that's made up of a series of connected glass domes and painted archways. The ceilings inside are thirty feet high, and dozens of rooms all flow into one another. The original baths were sorted by water temperature, from sweltering to icy.

At a quarter to midnight, I cross the street to get to the main entrance. At the door, shoving my mask into my back pocket, I glance around to make sure I'm alone, and I am—this part of Paper is quiet at night anyway, made even more so with this whole block being dead for so long. No longer protected by the Guild's magic, I brace myself as I cast with my key starter.

Heat stings, becomes an ache wrung into my bones just as water is wrung out of rags. The lock twists open with a *click*. Pain still swirling beneath my skin, I pull at the door and step inside.

A small foyer that is dark and empty, marble floors stretching out in front of me and leading to a pair of large inner doors.

I open them, and the sight I see is fast becoming a familiar one.

It's the library's main room, and a crowd fills it, all the way to the corners and spilling out into side corridors. Everyone is walking in all directions and talking in loud voices and yelling out to one another. Oversized bulbs bob in midair and fill the room with light.

All the books are gone now and all the shelves are thick with dust. The huge stone pillars inside that held up the roof are still there, though the roof's glass domes shattered a long time ago. Signs of the quakes that have hit the area over the years show in the deep cracks across the frescoes that cover the walls, in the marble floor that lifts and dips.

The registration area's set up on the left side of the room, and the starter counter is on the right. The library's checkout area in the middle is now the bets counter. Hugo and Jack are calling for bets, both raising their voices to be heard over the noise of the crowd.

I can't help but look for Oliver. To see his face and figure out what comes next. I can't tell if he's my enemy, or if I even want him to be my enemy. His height makes him hard to miss, though, so I know he's not here yet. Or if he is, he's somewhere else in the building, likely reliving this afternoon just like I am. Reliving losing his magic, too. The memory has never died out for him, but I'm pretty sure I just gave it new life, something that leaves me torn between guilt and satisfaction.

I also look for signs of Piper. I still haven't seen her since I broke the rules last night, my plans to find her earlier today interrupted by my decision to go to the Salt Lick instead. Oliver ended up answering a lot of the questions I might have asked her, but I still need to find out if she means to keep backing me. If she does, then I need marks to buy starters. And if she doesn't—well, then that's *two* disadvantages I'll have to fight with.

But I can't see her yet, so I head over to the registration area. As I weave through the mass of casters, my ears pick out my name— pick out *Rudy's*—and I get snippets of what it might be like to be in the audience instead of in the fighting ring:

I've got five hundred marks on Rudy to survive, no way she'll top the clone spell.

I still think Finch will win.

I still think she and her team should have been eliminated since she broke the rules.

I like how Rudy's done something unique each time.

She doesn't cast enough blood or bone spells and I bet it's because she's weak that way, less control over those—

I frown as I keep walking, trying not to be irritated and to remember that the spectators don't know me outside of the tournament. They don't know anything about what's happened this past week, this past year, my entire lifetime.

Still, the word *weak* digs in like a splinter. The words *less control.* I don't want to be that caster anymore, when once I wondered if I'd ever be anything but.

At the registration area, I get my name written on my face, and then make my way over to the starter counter. A headache threatens, the last of the pain from the spell I cast to get inside. I'm beginning to worry about not finding Piper in time when I finally spot her in the crowd. She's also looking for me, and we both head toward each other.

Right before I reach her, my stomach drops. This really could be it for me. As far as I'll ever get in the tournament. Without Piper's support, I'll have nothing working for me, only too much against.

But I want to show everyone she knows how to pick a winner.

"Piper, I'm really sorry about the clone stunt," I blurt out before she can say anything. "Embry's already given me hell for it, if that makes a difference. And even though I'm stuck having to fight without the Guild's protection, I promise I'll fight through the pain."

Piper sighs. "Are you done?" She's in a cream silk tuxedo, her purse a slip of black velvet. Her hair is a pile of red amassed on top of her head.

"Yes?"

"Good. I'm not dropping you as my fighter. You broke the rules, but for a good reason. Just don't do it again."

I release a deep breath, wholly relieved. "I won't. I can't, or I'm definitely out for good."

She smiles. "You broke the rules with flair, at least."

"I was lucky."

"Luck is a part of a lot of things, some more than others." She opens up her purse and gives me two hundred marks. She helps me tie on my silk armband, smoothing it out with enough care that for a second I want to tell her about Oliver's magic. I want to ask her about the loss of such magic and if she could ever imagine it.

But the discovery feels too raw still. It's not even my memory, but the sight of it lingers in my own mind, like I touched someone else's wound and am now also stained with its blood. And I can't explain why it feels nearly like a betrayal, telling anyone about Oliver without knowing the whole story. Maybe because it makes him look worse and that doesn't feel right. Why couldn't it have been Finch alone?

Then Piper is wishing me luck and leaving, saving me from having to think any more about Oliver at all.

I go over to the starters table and buy my ring starters, rashly deciding on a few extra red and white because I can't stop hearing *weak*.

I follow dusty plaques bolted to the walls of one of the corridors leading out of the main room and find the washroom. Inside one of the stalls, I take out the key holder from my starter bag, slip on my new ring starters, and attach the whole thing to my belt loop.

Someone comes into the washroom. They go into the stall next to me.

I sigh and peek down.

Sunflower-printed sneakers.

THIRTY-FOUR

I sigh again, get up, flush, and leave the stall. I pause outside Kylin's stall, then knock.

"Okay," I say to the door, "why are you following me?"

She flushes and emerges. The letters of her name on her cheek seem exceptionally big tonight, as though she's smaller than I remember or she asked for the guy to write it that way. I'm betting on the latter.

"It's a public washroom," she says, washing her hands in the sink beside me, then sitting up on the counter the way she always does. "But, yeah, I was following you. I didn't see you after the second round. Are you okay?"

"Still in the tournament, no thanks to you."

Her mouth drops open. "I *helped* you."

"You *drew* attention to us is what you did. You made us look weak by helping. We never made a pact, Kylin. You have to stop imagining we're in this together because we're not, at all."

She snaps her mouth shut, but she can't hide how upset she is with what I said. It shows in the sheen in her eyes, the way she tugs at her braid the way a little kid does.

"Actually, I wanted to ask you again about making one," she says. "We really should, now that there's just six of us and we both have a good chance of making it to the final. It really could be me and you tomorrow, fighting for the championship."

I dry my hands on my pants, almost envious of her ability to dare to believe so easily. To simply want and not worry about paying for that want. Or, at least, to not worry so much it keeps you from wanting at all.

I give her a look. "I can kill you tonight, you know, and you're asking me to be in a pact with you?"

"Except you wouldn't, because you're not Finch. And with two fighters moving on, I say we have a better chance if we stick up for each other."

"Kylin, even if we make a pact and it works and we do move on, it'll just make fighting each other tomorrow harder. There's only ever going to be one winner." To be honest, I already think it's too late for us to stay strangers. Having to fight Kylin would no longer be as easy as it once might have been. I shut the door on her, but somehow she snuck in anyhow. Or maybe I let her in and just told myself I didn't. But I can't tell her this. It'd be just like her to use it against me, to say since it's already too late, we might as well make that pact. I know this because I would have said the same thing to Shire.

She scowls, then grins. "How about a pact to gang up on Finch together? That might be a good idea, too."

Oh. Now I'm hesitating.

She leaps. "C'mon, how could it hurt? And he's the champion—he's going to be the hardest out of everyone. We might as well try. We cast invisibility spells last round to wait out the fighters teaming up on you. I didn't want to see you eliminated with all the teams ganging up on you because it seemed unfair, and I told Finch that. So his idea was that we sit back by hiding to let the other teams cancel each other out. It worked really well!"

A chill runs along my arms. Kylin showed Finch a weakness and it's me. "You can't trust Finch. You can't trust me. You can't trust anyone but yourself, Kylin."

She frowns. "I don't trust him. And I do trust myself."

Nothing about not trusting me, and I glare at the back of her head in the mirror. She's nothing but a distraction, really. I look at her and see how I can fail out there in a fighting ring because I have to think of someone other than myself. Shire was thinking of our parents and me and everything the teahouse stands for, but all of that was in her head only, and still she died. I've already got revenge and ghosts and the weight of Saint Willow in mine—I don't need a real live Kylin right in the fighting ring with me as something else to worry about.

"So what do you think?" she asks. "About a pact?"

"This tournament isn't for pacts." I stare at my reflection, at the letters on my cheek, and tell myself that's all I can be right now. The ring name of a fighter.

Kylin sighs. "Okay, but maybe we can be friends after the tournament. I can come visit you, wherever you are in the city."

I try to smile at her. "Okay, sure."

Though I'm not certain at all. I think this tournament will never leave me entirely once it's over, whether I win it or not. I think maybe seeing Kylin outside of a fighting ring will only make me think of Shire and how much I miss having a sister. Or of Rudy and what happened, of Oliver and Finch and secrets of lost magic and gathered spells.

Or . . . maybe seeing Kylin will help me *stop* missing having a sister so much.

A bell clangs.

Kylin hops off the counter. "Good luck, Rudy—but only until we have to fight each other."

I have to laugh. "Now you're learning."

She's nearly out the door before I call her back.

"My real name's Aza, okay? Since you asked last time."

"Cool." She smiles like we made some kind of pact after all, and I follow her out of the washroom, down the corridor, and back into the main room of the library.

Spectators have pushed themselves out toward the walls. Kylin and I go to stand in the center where it's clear. Wilson, Pav, and Nola are here, too.

And Finch, who's already watching me by the time my eyes get to him. The blue-striped ribbon representing the Salt Lick is wrapped around his upper arm. His gaze is flat and direct and tells me I made a mistake in making him notice me. For a second, I think it's because Oliver told him what happened, what I know. But then I remember his glare at the end of the last match, when I cast the clone spell.

Whichever the reason, he makes sure to let me know I'm the fighter he'll be going after tonight. Whether I'm the sister of the fighter he killed who now wants revenge, or the fighter who put on a bigger display than he did last round, it makes no difference to him. I'm the fighter standing in his way of the championship, of the Guild. Of being a great.

A cold vise that's shaped like a fist squeezes my heart and I look away. For all that Finch is a killer, he's also a winner, and I long for my head and heart to be as clear as his. That they not be so crowded with faces and questions.

I keep myself from looking for Oliver, knowing he's here.

Then Embry strolls in from one of the corridors. He's in a suit of dark maroon silk this time, the shade so dark it's nearly black. He's paired it with a shirt and tie of the brightest poppy red, his tie a print of orchids. There's little sign of the caster who talked to me about his glass bones and not being able to cast anymore. Again I think of Oliver and just wish tonight's fight would start already.

Embry's teal eyes are back to being more watchful than welcoming. The crowd shuffles and falls quiet.

He walks up to us in the middle of the room. Six of us left. It seems like so few, and at the same time, too many.

He flashes out six playing cards, front side down. "Pick a card, please." His low rumble of a voice echoes off stone and marble.

I'm beginning to think I wouldn't mind too much never seeing a deck of cards again.

Finch is first. He holds his card up. It has a single number on it. Number 1.

Nola's next. Her card's a 3.

Wilson chooses. It's a 2.

I choose. 3.

Pav chooses. 1.

Kylin's last. She's a 2.

Embry walks over to one side so that he's standing with the spectators.

"In ancient Xulai," he says, "the most powerful didn't go to pubs or bars to hang out, they went to the Vigo Baths. The greats were known to stay for days at a time, drinking and bathing and *frolicking*."

Someone hollers, "Even the greats had to do it!"

Laughter is a ripple through the crowd.

Embry smiles. "Sometimes it's easy to forget how the original seven greats were human, just like everyone else. They loved, they fought, and they hated. Eighteen hundred years ago, Max the Deceiver cast a love spell on Otta the Swift to win her from Valery the Bleeder. And so Valery challenged Max to a duel. Right here, in the famous Vigo Baths."

The Guild of Now—wherever and whatever they are in here, as specks of dust in the air, as winks of light in their bulbs—casts.

A millennium and a half winds back in time.

And we're in baths across the sea.

THIRTY-FIVE

The lower half of my body is on fire, and I peer down, terrified of what I'm going to see.

Steaming-hot water comes up to my chest. I'm standing in a sunken stone bath that's bigger than any of the city public pools. And it's much bigger than the main room of the library in the Paper Sector. I hadn't realized just *how* much it'd been scaled down as a replica.

Only the fighters are in the water, and we're all spaced out from one another, twenty feet apart. The spectators are crowded onto the marble platform that wraps around the entire rectangular bath. They're already cheering, a reverberation of noise that bounces off ancient stone and washes back over us.

For a second, I think of Jihen, of Diego. Whether they're watching me from the crowd right now, parts of another world bleeding into this one. But it's impossible to try to make them out, and maybe it's better that I can't tell. I wasn't bluffing about going to Saint Willow to blow Jihen's secret if he didn't leave me alone about the tournament, but it doesn't mean I want to do it, either. The idea of purposely seeking out Saint Willow chills me.

I peer up at the glass dome that is this part of the ceiling. It's the biggest one of the baths, and through it, the night sky is beautiful. The moon is full and silver, the kind of moon Lotusland will never see again. There are stars, too, a spill of diamonds onto velvet—the city will never see these, either. Pearly light floods down and into the bath and mixes with the flickering amber glow coming from the torches sticking out of the walls.

"So can we get out of this oversized hot tub already?"

It's Wilson, way over on my right, kicking at the water. He looks oddly uncertain, dark skin flushed and without a sign of his typical swagger. His voice is a hollow echo as it rolls across the vastness of the bath. Behind him is Kylin. She's staring up at the sky just as I had, her expression dreamy and distracted, and I want to yell at her to wake up.

"What's the matter, can't swim?"

I turn my head at the taunt. It's Nola, standing behind me and at the opposite end of the bath.

"Did I say that?" Wilson's voice is churlish. "I highly doubt we're here to swim, genius."

But I hear it in his voice. The heat's already getting to him. The water seems to get even hotter as the thought crosses my mind. I take a step along the stone bottom. My legs are sluggish. My *brain* feels sluggish.

"'Nek' means *hot* in ancient Xulaese," Embry says. He's standing on the thick stone edge of the bath so that he's looming over us. "'Sui' means *water* and 'fwong' means *room*. Nek sui fwong. This is the hot water bath, right here. It's built to fit up to five hundred bathers at a time. The water temperature is a consistent one hundred and nine degrees Fahrenheit. The average bather will begin overheating within five minutes."

"And you want us to battle in *this*?" Nola frowns and wipes sweat from her forehead. She takes off her eyeglasses and shoves them into the back pocket of her jeans. "What if we get heatstroke before the fight's done?"

Embry's teal eyes are the same shade of the water but without the warmth. "Then make sure the other fighter gets it first."

Finch is off to my left. His laugh is low, a dark and dry and somehow *knowing* chuckle that slips into my ear. Despite the heat—it's an envelope around me, already pressing too close, nearly smothering—I shiver. The laugh is the first sound I've ever heard Finch make during the tournament.

Pav is behind him. Caught between silver and golden light, his complexion is nearly green. His panic spills from him, a kind of fever on its own to mix with the heat of the water. Invisibility spells are virtually useless if there's any kind of liquid or rain involved, since it shapes around your form and gives away where you are. Which means he's mostly left with just shield spells, his other go-to. And every single fighter here—and likely most of the audience as well—knows it.

Who will it be tonight, Pav? Pav the Coward or Pav the Brave?

And I'm Rudy the First. The audience wants me to be like that again, expects me to entertain and surprise them—I sense their demand like a pull from all sides of the room.

I'm hot. Dizziness creeps close, circles me like predator to prey. My pulse thuds hard enough that I *feel* the great drum of it, deep in my ears. It pounds at my wrists, along my neck. The strain of dread pulls at me just as the audience does, and I am thin from it, about to snap. I long for winter and ice and the luxury of casting a chill spell through the water.

Embry hops down from the edge of the bath to stand on the marble floor of the room. "There are six of you. Three duels, three winners, and your direct opponent is the fighter who's drawn the same number as you. *Go.*"

For an entire heartbeat my mind goes blank.

Number?

Then it comes to me, a headlight behind my eyelids:

3.

Another heartbeat.

Your direct opponent is the fighter who's drawn the same number as you.

Who, though? I can't remem—

Another heartbeat.

Nola drew the other 3.

She's behind me in the water.

Another heartbeat.

I take a deep breath and duck beneath the water's surface.

The bath is liquid fire. It engulfs me in clouds of seething, swirling jets of bubbles. The world in my ears dials down—to the thump of my own pulse, low muffled shouts, the churning of the water all around me.

Everyone else is now thrashing around, too. They're digging through wet clothes for their starters, fighting the weight of the water as they move because it's become another enemy in the ring.

I twist around in the water so that I'm facing the back of the bath. So I'm coming at Nola and she's coming at me. Only her jean-clad legs are visible from down here—she's still standing up, ten feet ahead and getting closer. Through the frenzy of churning liquid, her hand turns into a light brown blur at her side. She's reaching for a starter.

Staying beneath the water's surface, I yank a silver coin from the key holder on my belt loop. The skin of my face burns; my *eyeballs* burn. My chest is starting to tighten, lungs getting heavier and heavier with the instinct to breathe.

Did Shire's eyes feel like this when she died? Did she see fire from the outside as well as the inside, more of it than she'd ever seen before? Was fire the last thing she saw, felt?

A wave of nausea hits me, the same kind that comes when I've been in the sun for too long. If I don't stand up soon and cool off, I'll pass out. I'll drown.

But I stay beneath the surface. I draw and cast. Shield. I'm already hot enough that I barely feel the fresh heat of magic climb through the stone bottom of the pool and into my veins. The water against my skin *morphs*, forms a kind of skin on its own.

Then the pain of casting comes. And it's pain the way casting magic always hurts outside the tournament—whole and deep, alive with its own pulse. It jolts through me, an ache that travels from head to toe.

Dread goes off in my mind like an alarm. I've gotten too used to the Guild's protection. This fight—I'm going to suffer.

I tear off another silver starter and cast again. Air.

Fresh oxygen propels into my bloodstream. The pressure in my chest goes from explosive to bearable, the urge to take another breath beaten back. A hard ache clangs through my skull at the casting, and it lingers, deep claws sinking in. I am nearly compelled to cast again right away, just to get a bit more breath, a bit more fighting time. But I need to save magic for attacking, to think about the cost of casting that's going to pile up fast without the Guild's protection.

Nola's already down in the water with me. She's dunked herself beneath the surface, too. I see a silver coin drop through the water as she turns to face me—has she just cast a shield on herself? A second passes, and when I feel nothing, I know she must have.

I drag my hand to my hip, reaching for a new starter.

But Nola's already got one in hand. She casts first, faster than me.

A punch.

She's good with them. I should have remembered Teller, being driven into the sand. But I didn't, so when the giant invisible fist crashes into my stomach, the impact catches me flat out. My shield spell falls apart. I'm driven backward through the hot water, my legs a numb blur of darkness through pale blue. There's a single wild second where I can't figure out who the legs belong to.

I'm still moving backward through the baths as I fumble a white starter from my key holder. My hands are slow, clumsy—the word *heatstroke* flashes across my brain. Across from me Nola's going for another starter, too, her hands moving just as sluggishly through the water.

I'm faster this time. I draw, I cast. A thick, undulating ripple of pain spreads outward from my spine like thorns along a branch.

Her hand falls from her pocket. Her entire body goes limp, as limp as I've cast her bones to go. Her eyes are flashes of panic.

My lungs are burning again. There's a high-pitched ringing in my ears. I need to breathe.

I yank off another starter, gold this time. There's a body on the bottom of the bath, gone to marble in the chaos of the water. The world wavers, flickers gray, and my chest has become a tightly wound bundle of agony—*I need air.*

I draw. I cast.

The panic in Nola's eyes becomes a flood as her airway tightens. Her arms give a single useless twitch at her sides, their bones still too soft for her to move.

Pain floods me, a storm inside my body the way the pool is one outside. It's the cost of casting, building faster and higher, threatening to break. I push back, imagine I'm a dam. My lungs are spilling fire. I'm about to black out.

Nola has already begun to drown, unconscious and sinking.

Knockout.

I grab her by the arm—she's deadweight, and terror that I'm too late stabs me like a dagger—and stumble to my feet on the bottom of the bath. I drag her face free of the water.

Cool air comes and I'm drinking in huge gulps of it. Nola's draped over my arm, still out. I draw another spell star and tear at another gold starter. I cast, despite knowing how it's going to hurt.

Nola coughs as her airway opens back up and air rushes in. Between gasps, she asks, "Why are you saving me?"

"Because." I'm still gasping, too. Agony is a swollen, knotted fist in my skull. "I've already beaten you."

THIRTY-SIX

Finch, Kylin, and me.

We're the last.

The three of us are still standing in the bath. The crowd around us is on their feet, cheering and clapping. The sounds of our names come at me as shouts and yells, and the ring of noise encircles me, presses close, makes me feel like I'm drowning again. My heart is loud in my ears, beating in a wild rhythm that matches my still-hungry breathing, the jagged pain that fills my head.

Shut up.

I want to beg. How all their noise *hurts*. But the crowd keeps cheering.

Shut up!

My eyes scan faces, desperate to see Piper, Embry, even Oliver. Anyone I know who's talked to me and can remind me I'm still someone else, someone outside this fighting ring. To remind me I'm Aza Wu and how I exist outside these terrible ancient baths.

But I see only strangers. Just those who came to see magic, and if that magic has a cost, then they will accept that, too. Because we're casters of a banished magic and this is our world now.

I drop my eyes to the side of the room, hating everyone here.

Pav is out of his marble state, sitting stunned on the stone floor. It was him at the bottom of the pool. Eliminated by Finch. No surprise there.

Wilson and Nola sit near Pav, equally hunched in defeat. They're still soaked and water drips off them back onto the floor.

I begin walking out, needing to get out, to get away. Water has never been heavier as it drags at my legs. The pain of casting that final breath spell to save Nola is still alive inside my head, has become one with my bones and muscles. Bruises form all over my body. I long for sleep, for recovery time.

Behind me, the water stirs again as Finch and Kylin follow.

Then Embry's at the front of the crowd again, and everyone falls silent, confused. He's supposed to have left by now, already back with the rest of the Guild somewhere. His disappearing at the end of a fight marks the end of that round.

I stop moving. So do Finch and Kylin.

What now?

My brain's like taffy in the sun as it struggles to recall the ending of the story of Valery the Bleeder, Max the Deceiver, and Otta the Swift. Did I ever learn it in school? Who won between Valery and Max? What happened to Otta? How did those three greats declare their battle done?

"You see, Valery thought he'd defeated Max," Embry says. "But Max was known as the Deceiver for a reason. He'd cast magic within magic—if Valery ever broke the spell that made Otta love Max, Otta would turn on Valery. And so the battle continued, this time with three."

The water in the bath turns icy. The bath shrinks, becomes half the size it was, turns into a rough oval.

"Here in the lungh sui fwong is where they fought," Embry continues. "The *cold* baths."

The glass dome disappears. A massive painted arch takes its place. I get a glimpse of painted figures before the last of the silver moon fades from my eyes and only dim torchlight flickers from the walls.

Embry says, "Only two casters will be moving on tonight."

Kylin moves first. She draws and grabs at the surface of the bath. Casts.

Freezing water climbs in a wave and slams down. Again. The waves fill the air with their roar. It's the sound of the world's coldest beach.

I'm knocked from my feet. Knives of ice pierce me all over as my side skids along the bottom of the bath. Stone scrapes and pulls at the silk tied around my arm. I hurl my weight to one side, trying to grab hold. Water dives into my nose and mouth.

The waves keep coming. I can't see anything past them. I cough out ice water. I'm still scrambling for a starter with nearly frozen fingers when I slam into the side of the tub.

Stone tears my knuckles open and the water around my hand streams red. There's no pain, though, since my hands are so cold. The crowd's shouting, loving the full magic that has turned the baths into a storm at sea. *Kyyylin*, they scream.

But she's made a mistake in her rush to cast first, in casting for repeated waves. It's too wide of a spell with not enough of a focus. She should have cast only with enough magic to affect Finch and me. Now her magic will be slow to recharge, on top of her already hurting. More than anyone else, I could have reminded her to cast with caution.

The waves build beyond her control—higher, faster. A second

later, and all three of us are dragged under, and the world is nothing but blue and ice and struggling to breathe.

Oh, Kylin.

A wave crests, breaks, crests again. Through the water still rushing at my ears, I hear the crowd, cheering.

Finally, I surface all the way, and I look over for Kylin and Finch.

They're across the bath. She's in retreat, one arm bent at an unnatural angle—Finch must have cast a spell to break it. And she's too pale, the icy cold working its way through her.

He looms over her, about to cast again. Kylin's on the verge of elimination and he knows it. One more spell, a final dose of magic, and he'll be in the final round.

Dread comes in a flood. It makes me as cold on the inside as I am on the outside. The water's a roar and the crowd is shouting and I'm trying to get to my feet.

Is this what it was like for Shire? Had she already been backing away, and still Finch had come?

A new wave of water builds.

I yank off a gold starter. My fingers are icicles, thick and unbending as I force them to draw. I cast.

Against the icy water, the heat that climbs my legs is excruciating. It burns upward and into my veins, a red fire billowing in my mind.

Finch flies backward. My magic drives him through the water. He hits the edge of the stone tub with a deep thud.

The crowd erupts. *Rudy, Rudy, Rudy—*

Pain is a sheet of lightning behind my eyes.

The icy wave crashes down.

I claw at my starters from beneath the water. I tear off another gold coin. The wave flattens and Finch is still in the water, trying to stand up. I cast again, unable to care about the lightning still shooting across my brain, how there will be more now.

He falls back into the water as his muscles seize, exactly as I meant them to.

The coldness that had been dread filling me now feels darker, sharper, *sweeter*. Control has never felt so close, my magic never so touchable. When more lightning flashes behind my eyes, I barely blink. I can only think about destroying Finch.

Because that fine line between honor and dishonor—I can't stop it from shifting.

I toss away the gold coin and grab a white one. I cast.

Finch has dragged himself up to lean against the edge of the bath, and he screams as his bones shatter.

I stagger my way through the water. Kylin's waves are fading, her spell run out. She hasn't moved, is still standing in the bath. She's shivering even harder than I am, still cradling her crooked arm. Just behind her, Finch is still slumped against the stone tub, frozen by pain as much as he is by the water. His eyes are wide and stunned—he's never looked more vulnerable.

When I reach them both, I loom over Finch the same way he loomed over Kylin. One more spell and he's out. New pain of my own comes, as pointed as knives in my guts.

I'd meant for it to go full circle, for me to beat him in the final. I'd meant to poke around in his brain and find out answers for all my questions. But what does it matter, if I still beat him? If he still dies for killing Shire, for nearly killing Kylin?

The audience is one huge roar, amplified by all the marble and stone. I can't tell if they're cheering more for me or for Finch. A part of me wishes I could tell. That maybe if I could hear chants of Rudy the First and nothing else, then I wouldn't need to do this. But everything's happening so fast, and magic is just a different kind of roar in my blood, urging me on.

I draw, then tear free a silver coin.

The line shifts and shifts and shifts.

I cast.

Finch becomes an inferno. I burn him from the inside out—for all the water around him, it can't stop what it can't touch. I watch him burn and wonder why my heart stays frozen. Why I don't feel satisfied when this is supposed to be payback.

The sound of the crowd changes, turns slightly uneasy. I'm not supposed to be like Finch, who can live with the cost of magic. I'm supposed to be all about the show, here to entertain.

"You've surprised them."

Kylin says this. But her voice is Finch's. She grins, and it's with Finch's green eyes.

My mouth goes dry, and I blink.

Because it's Finch standing where Kylin was. Or where I was *made* to think Kylin was.

It's not Finch in the water, burning away. It's Kylin.

"A disguise spell," Finch says softly. There's venom in his voice, stinging my skin.

The crowd realizes what's happened and their cheers are thunderous. The swell of the noise rolls through me, and I want to be sick for all the longing I hear in the audience.

Shire, did they cheer like this when it was you? And there I was at home, furious with you for leaving me behind.

I'm numb. Ice is everywhere and everything. Kylin's body slips beneath the surface of the water and a sob wrenches free from my throat. She was about to eliminate Finch and I stopped her. Because of his spell. And now—

No. No. I'm sorry, Kylin.

"I knew who you were as soon as I saw you."

I turn to face Finch, his broken arm still at an angle. "How?"

"I never forget a fighter I beat. Each of you, just helping me get where I want to go. And you look like her, especially when you're casting."

The bones beneath.

I shudder. "Why the trick?"

"The Guild's watching—they like a show, too." Now he smiles, and it chills me the way all the ancient cold baths in the world never could. "And Kylin was weak. She didn't want to fight you— she thought you were *friends*. She showed me that herself last round, and that was her mistake. Now it's just me and you, tomorrow night. Let the best caster win."

THIRTY-SEVEN

I run while the crowd's still loud.

The Guild's magic unweaves even as I crash my way toward the entrance. The cold baths and arched ceiling and fat stone pillars disappear as I shove my way through casters. Contact hurts, each part of me bruised and aching, but I keep going. Eighteen hundred years pass as the library's main room comes back with its empty bookshelves and cracked-open frescoed walls. People turn and stare and I can't meet anyone's eye. Blood trickles from my nose, and a low roar fills my ears.

Maybe we can be friends after the tournament. I can come visit you, wherever you are in the city.

I push open the doors and rush outside into the night. Sunflower-print sneakers chase me down the street, the swish of a braid. I'm crying, my chest burning, the fire there nothing but a weak echo of the one I lit up inside Kylin.

Why didn't I agree to that pact? Why couldn't I have just done that for her? Kylin might be alive then, and Finch eliminated, and none of this would be happening.

I'm sorry, Kylin, I never meant to leave you behind!

There's no full silver moon to be seen out here. No stars because they never stop hiding. I run beneath a smog-covered sky as the last remnants of an older time fall away, left in my wake like lint picked from my clothing. Goodbye, all you dueling greats, all of you who made magic a game, you who created the Tournament of Casters in the first place. Dropped newsprint lies silently across pavement and murky light billows from the streetlamps.

If a Scout found me now, one look and they would know me for the caster that I am. I feel stained all over with full magic, with the terrible things it can do.

I keep running, then slow to an awkward limp, out of breath, my tears and drying blood thin smears on my cheeks. Casting has cost me tonight, and I feel all its claws still inside me, still scratching and digging. I lift my hand toward my starter bag, but then drop it. Hurt, Aza. You deserve to.

"Rudy."

I swivel at the voice.

It's Oliver, coming up behind me. He's breathing fast, too, running to catch up. In my need to get away from the library, I didn't think to check if anyone would follow me. I guess killing Kylin has distracted me from the basics. The faces of Jihen and Cormac and my parents swarm me and my eyes get teary again.

I turn around and start walking fast. A confused kind of anger fills me. I want to hate him but I can't forget those burned-out memories of his, the absence of his magic that's so gaping its edges have touched me, too.

"Go away, Oliver," I call back. "Go congratulate your brother."

"Wait—"

"I can't."

He runs faster and then he's at my shoulder. "One minute, okay? Here, I collected your winnings from the bets counter."

I stop and take the marks. There are a lot, even more than what

I got last time. It feels like blood money with Kylin dying tonight, and a queasiness in my stomach rolls and rolls.

"You should put those away before you lose them," Oliver says, watching my expression. I can tell *he* can tell that I've been crying.

I stuff the marks into my pocket and start walking again. I drag on my smog mask, wanting to hide as much as I can. He follows me. "I just tried to kill your brother. Why do you want to talk to me?"

He doesn't say anything right away. Then a soft: "I'm still working on that."

"You can go do that on your own, you know."

"What he did in there, tricking you like that—I'm sorry."

My heart pinches and pulls. "He killed her. He didn't have to." I'm no longer sure if I'm talking about Kylin or Shire.

"I'm sorry," he says again.

The simple apology hurts more than if he'd defended Finch, and I can't tell if he means Kylin or Shire, either.

I push back because fighting with him is easier than hurting. "I'm not going to say I'm sorry about that reveal spell I did on you."

"I know."

"Why don't you just tell me how he cheated? There's nothing I can do about it now anyway. But I need to know."

He ignores me. "Why didn't your reveal spell show you?"

"Because. It ended too early." *Because I was too shocked about your magic to keep it going any longer.* It would have told me. Why didn't I hold on?

"So how do you know he cheated?" Oliver's tone is careful, like he doesn't want to set me off any more than he already has.

"I didn't. Not at first. But then pieces started coming together.

And then tonight, finding out about your magic—" I glare pointedly at him. Or *lack* of magic. Even the lack of leftover magic, when everyone has that.

"And I'm his brother, so my lack of magic has something to do with it."

A catch in his voice finally lets me stop walking and face him.

He stops, too.

That earlier hollowness is still in his eyes. He looks haunted and uncomfortable and like he's wishing he could be anywhere else. Chasing me down this way—I had thought maybe he was doing it because he wanted to, not because he felt he had to. It makes me feel stupid, not seeing this until now.

"What else did your magic see in my mind?" His eyes have gone dark, more brown than hazel.

"Your parents," I say. "The car accident. How you blame yourself. You cast magic and something happened. Finch has never forgiven you."

A muscle works in his throat. "I was twelve. I'd been arguing with my parents, and then they had to leave for a party. But I . . . wasn't done arguing. So I cast myself into their heads as they were driving. I distracted them. They died listening to me yell at them."

A new pinch forms in my heart. "I'm sorry. I—the last time I talked to Shire, we argued, too."

He nods. His eyes say he's sorry in return. "And it changed Finch. I went from being a big brother to the person who took away his family because I couldn't control my magic. So we used to be friends and now we're not. It made him hate full magic just like it made him hate me. In his own twisted way, winning this tournament, getting into the Guild, I think it's him proving he's stronger than magic, if that makes sense. Becoming a great is his ultimate way of beating magic at its own game."

Against my will, a small twinge of understanding *does* come. The things you hate the most are the things that are loudest in your head, so that you can't hear anything else. Because they are also the things you fear the most. I'm still scared of having no control, and so I hate the idea of being that way.

But as much as I can get this aspect of why Finch is so messed up, I'll also never forget what he's done. Shire never coming home again, his smile tonight as he revealed himself as Kylin—I'll never forgive him.

Oliver exhales. "Okay, so there's a reason why I'm out here. Why I came looking for you. I want to make a deal with you."

My chest goes hollow. *So can we make a pact?* "What kind of deal?"

"If I tell you how Finch cheated, will you promise not to fight him tomorrow night?"

I blink. "You mean just . . . walk away from the tournament?"

He nods.

All the reasons why that's impossible—from the marks to my promise to Rudy—push close, wrapping around me so I can barely breathe through them. I was always going to fight if I could, whether I found out the truth about last year or not.

"I can't walk away now," I say to Oliver. "I need to win this as much as your brother wants in on the Guild."

His expression turns grim. "And if he kills you? Like he killed your sister and Kylin?"

I try not to shiver. "I have to think I won't let him. It's a contest and I've made it this far. And his arm is broken, which works in my favor." I can't decide if I'm more insulted that Oliver thinks I'm going to lose or happy that he's trying to save me.

"You and I both know he'll have it healed by morning," Oliver says, "if he hasn't already."

Then I'm staring at him, realizing something, and almost hate myself for having to say it. "But now you *have* to tell me. Because if you don't, and it could have helped me beat him, and he kills me anyway . . ."

He's beyond grim now. "Then how could I live with myself?"

"Well, *could* you?"

Oliver swears. His expression clouds over. "You have to promise you won't kill him, then. Beat him, but that'll have to be enough."

Enough as payback for Shire, he means. Can any payback ever be enough? She's gone and I'll never get her back. I could have all the full magic in the world and I could cast until I died, but it'd still never be enough. While Finch lives on, killing other casters, trying to become a great.

"I could just cast another reveal spell on you, you know," I say.

Oliver shakes his head. "No way. You caught me by surprise last time. And even if you *could* cast without me catching you, you're way too wiped out from tonight's fight to handle casting another seventeen-pointer now. So either promise or you'll never know."

He's got me and he knows it. I haven't even told him about how the Guild's punishing me for the rest of the tournament and he's got me. Frustration is a knot in my stomach, pulling tighter and tighter.

If I agree . . . I'll still beat Finch. I'll still win. I'll still be taking away what he wants the most, and that'll have to be enough. I think Shire would want it to be. Would want her reckless sister being sensible in this.

"Okay, I promise," I finally say.

THIRTY-EIGHT

Oliver holds up his casting arm.

"I owed him," he says quietly. "That's what he said after I killed our parents with my magic. For years, he shut me out, never letting me be his brother again. But last year, for the tournament, he asked if the Salt Lick would sponsor him—if I would sponsor him. So I said yes. I thought it would bring us closer together, help fix us. But after he began to doubt he could beat your sister, he came to me, again. And he said he'd forgive me, if I gave him one thing."

"Your magic." In the thickening night smog, his face is full of shadows. I can barely see the shapes of shops and outlines of roofs behind its haze. Tendrils of it curl through the streetlamps' patches of light, and the city seems covered with a layer of gauze. I taste it on my tongue—exhaust, metal, dirt.

"He went to meet a gatherer," Oliver says. "And the gatherer had a spell Finch wanted. Time loop. But for a price."

My stomach curls just like the smog does. "The price of magic for a time loop? That's hardly equal. It makes no sense."

"It does when it's not his magic he's offering up." He gives me an empty smile.

"And so you did it," I say. "Because you owed him." *And Finch is your brother. And maybe . . . I would have done the same for my sister, too.* There are probably a million different ways family can complicate things.

Oliver nods. His expression is bleak, as pale as it was in his shop when he realized who I was. "All the winnings I get as his backer, I put right back into the Salt Lick. And since my parents, I've barely used magic anyway. If this got me my brother back, it would be more than worth the price. I didn't find out until it was too late how Finch really meant to use it. I never thought he'd kill your sister. Just that he'd use it to win."

I make myself ask. "What did he do?"

"He used the time loop on himself to see how the final round between him and Shire would go. He saw exactly how she would beat him."

The world sways and I think I'm going to throw up. "So Finch would have known all of Shire's spells ahead of time. He could have had all his counterspells ready. He could have beat her easily and let her walk away. *But he still decided to kill her.*"

Oliver nods, looking about as sick as I feel. "I'm sorry, Rudy. If I'd known, I would have never given him my magic."

Rage floods me. It's too late for all of that now. *Sorry* doesn't matter. All that matters is tomorrow's fight. "Where can I find a gatherer, Oliver?"

"Only Finch knows. I didn't go with him."

Something crosses his face and I know he's holding back.

"The deal is you tell me how he cheated," I say. "This is still part of it. Tell me the rest."

"You promised," he says.

"I never said what I would or wouldn't do with whatever you told me. I said I wouldn't kill Finch."

"Rudy, I—"

"My name is Aza, Oliver. Now tell me."

I watch him explore the name in his mind, see him wonder why I told him.

"I don't know where you can find a gatherer, and that's the truth," he says finally. "But I can tell you how you can find out. I can tell you who this one worked for."

I wait. The city's smog drifts between us, and for a second, he disappears on me before appearing again.

"Saint Willow," he says. "Tea Sector's gang leader."

THIRTY-NINE

I stumble back a step, like Oliver's just cast a huge spell on me.

Saint Willow, who obsesses over full magic because he can't cast it. Who has to settle for a semblance of it because he'll never truly know the real thing, has to accept that he'll only ever control ugly man-made spells and nothing more.

"Where's the fight tomorrow?" I ask Oliver. I left the library too soon, trying to escape from what I'd done.

"979 Discord Road."

I commit the address to memory, turn, and begin to run. I'm still hurting all over from fighting, but the ache is buried beneath the ache in my chest about Kylin. There's a buzz in my head, a low thrum in my veins.

"Where are you going? Ru—Aza, *wait*."

"I have to go!" I call back over my shoulder. I need to think about what comes next, and it can't be with Oliver. He clouds up my feelings and it's all too easy to forget why I'm here. What I want. What needs to be done. "Tomorrow, the fight—I'll see you then!"

"You promised, remember?" His voice comes through smog, turns smoky-sounding. I already can't see him. "You can't kill him!"

I call back again. "I know!"

I mean that as assurance, even as a tiny dark pit deep inside my chest says otherwise. To know that Finch could have let Shire go and didn't. That he used Kylin and me to put on a show for the

Guild. Fury stokes that pit into a blaze of hate. And it's hate that I don't want to control. To just be reckless and let it explode. Because then Finch would get what he deserves, while I'd still win everything.

But for a promise. For a *pact*. I made it with Oliver, but it's Kylin I keep hearing in my head, and how I said no, how she helped me anyway, and now she's gone.

Well, there are spells for things worse than death.

Soon, the smog is so thick that I can no longer see far in front of me, and I have to slow to a careful walk. My hand disappears into the gray, so dense that I can't see the bruises marking my skin in this huge bloom of pollution. I glance around, and the light from streetlamps has dimmed down to almost nothing. Sector streets are nearly pitch-black. Fear is like tendrils of the fog, weaving their way into my brain.

It hits me that this is because of the tournament. This blanket of dirt and exhaust is because of our fight tonight in the ancient baths. We did this.

By the time I limp to the edge of Tea—my joints on fire—the smog has only gotten thicker, just inches of visibility all around. Until it clears, there's no way Jihen and Cormac will be able to tail me.

My mind is still circling over everything that's happened in the last few hours—the last few days—as I turn into the alley that lines the back of the teahouse. I feel for branches of the snowball bushes that make up our fence and pull them to the side, preparing to squeeze through. Petals shake free, disappear into the smog as they fall.

The blade emerges from the dark and presses against my throat.

Shock is like a blow to the head, and I'm frozen with it. My mouth goes dry, and whatever I was thinking about instantly vanishes.

"You're one of the Wus, aren't you."

The voice is thick and rough and comes from right beside me. I don't recognize it. My heart is lodged inside my throat, a drum stuck pounding.

He nudges the blade against my neck. In the smog, he's nothing but a voice and disembodied weapon. "Yes or no," he grunts.

"Who's asking?" I let my hand drift toward my starter bag. In the smog, he won't even see. I can cast and—

"Hands up, don't even think about casting." I wince as he slowly tilts the blade back and forth against my skin. "I've got metal right here in my hand as a starter if I want, so who do you think is going to cast faster?"

I don't know if he means leftover magic, but it doesn't matter because he's likely right. He probably would be faster. And the knife isn't making me want to test him.

I raise both arms.

"I've been assigned the whole night to get answers, girly," the guy says. "Maybe we can go inside the teahouse and wait there."

The memory of Jihen inside while I dreaded the possibility of my parents walking in—I shudder and say, "Yes, I'm a Wu."

"Of Wu Teas?"

"Who wants to know?"

"Earl Kingston sent me. You know Earl Kingston?"

My mind spins. *Cormac.* He's talked.

"Yes, Earl Kingston from the Tobacco Sector," I say.

"Here's the deal. We're getting whispers of a city cop asking about one of our own, a guy named Milo Kingston. And the whispers are that the girl whose family runs this teahouse here is the one who's talking to the cop about Milo."

Anger slithers in and leaves me cold. The scents of smog and snowball bush petals swirl together and make my stomach clench. *Cormac, you fool.*

"I never talked to the cop about anyone named Milo Kingston." I grasp for words and hope they're believable. "I was on shift at the teahouse when he came in and met up with another guy. I was their server, I overheard the name Milo Kingston."

"So why are the whispers that you were the one talking to the cop?"

"I don't know." My voice shakes. From the knife at my neck, from having to make up another workable lie when I want to be all lied out. "Maybe it came from the other guy. Maybe he got scared that someone would remember him talking to a cop about Milo Kingston."

"Who's the other guy?" His voice comes from within the smog. He pushes the knife even harder against my neck. The skin there stings, and I know I'm bleeding.

I almost answer with *I don't know* again. But then I realize a name would have the benefit of keeping Earl Kingston and his men busier sniffing around a dead end.

"The cop called the other guy Diego." It's the first name that comes to mind, and now his face, his earrings and wild nest of a beard. The full magic caster who stays far away from the Tea Sector because of Saint Willow, a friend to Jihen and someone Earl

283

Kingston and his guys will likely never circle back to because he has no connection to anything at all. "He was doing most of the talking, if that means anything."

"Maybe, maybe. I'll pass it on. We'll ask the cop about it."

Trepidation dances on my skin. "You guys are going to talk to the cop?"

The knife lifts from my neck. "Girly, we've had Cormac for hours. Lucky for you, we've doubted every single word out of his mouth. Now we'll go see what this Diego has to say."

He disappears into the smog.

I squeeze my way through the snowball bushes and climb into my bedroom window. My pulse skids around in my veins, a loosed animal running scared, even as everything else shuts down, beyond exhausted. I tear off my mask and fall into bed. I'm asleep within a minute.

Faces chase me in dreams. Oliver's, Finch's, Kylin's, Cormac's.

And a face that stays veiled, like the earth with its smog. I know it's Saint Willow's even if I've never seen him before. His power over the Tea Sector comes as much from the mystery as it does from the long legacy of his family name.

If you need him, you're out of luck unless he also needs you.

FORTY

It's breakfast and the smog still hasn't lifted.

On the news they're calling it the Summer Souper, and it's the main thing everyone in the city is talking about. While it's thickest over Lotusland proper, it extends out over the Pacifik in the west, past the High Shore Mountains in the north, over the blighted lands in the east where nothing grows anymore, and spreads south into the last of the pink woods. No trains are running, and not much is open. We're all supposed to stay inside for as long as the smog lasts. Having so few customers in the teahouse finally feels acceptable.

Environmentalists can't pinpoint a single reason for it, so they're saying it's a whole bunch of things—factories, cars, the combination of years' worth of buildup of pollutants running into perfectly windless conditions. None come close to the truth.

My father is out on the teahouse floor, doing inventory. My mother casts at the stove to start eggs and toast. I sit at the island in the kitchen with her, now only half watching the news because no one can predict when the smog is going to end, my heart tightening like a turning screw with each passing moment that I can't go outside.

I need to find Jihen. Only through him can I get close to finding a gatherer of magic. My promise to Oliver to not kill Finch tonight is only that—to not kill him. Anything else, though . . .

That tiny dark pit deep inside my chest stings and grows.

Around it, the rest of my body continues to hurt. Last night's fight is still with me. All my bones and muscles are wound up tight, a taut fist of pain. I opened my starter bag this morning only to find that the jar of healing meds wasn't waterproof. As I fought in the baths with my bag submerged, the healing meds dissolved. I found nothing but a dried white film.

Whatever pain I'm still in when it comes to the final round of the tournament, I'll also be fighting with.

But . . . maybe this is the way it should be. Because daring to think about Kylin hurts even more, makes even the worst bruises and aches seem almost easy. There's a question that keeps circling my brain, too, relentless and awful, and it's this: If not for my need for revenge, would have I been able to see through Finch's trick?

Not that it matters, in the end. Because tricked or not, I'm still the one who cast the spell that killed her. So for Kylin as much as anyone, I can't let Finch win.

My mother brings over breakfast. I'm trying to make room for the food around this new physical agony, around that tiny dark pit of rage nestled within it, when she passes me a slim package.

Inside is a new starter bag.

It's made out of rich red silk, with a vivid floral print. I recognize all the different blossoms—jasmine, wisteria, rhododendrons, chrysanthemums. I'm transported to all the mornings I spent in the workroom with Shire, building gentle red fires together over the fireplace.

I run my hand over the bag. The softness of the silk is a balm against the skin of my fingers, against the knuckles that now wear scabs from having been dragged across ancient stone of ancient baths last night.

"What's this for?" I ask as I glance up at my mother. "It's pretty." And it is. Not as plain as I might have picked, but not as fancy as Shire would have. Something in between.

"Your sister's old bag is getting so worn. Your father and I thought you could use a new one."

I look down at Shire's bag. I have it close by as always, at my elbow on the island—my connection to her magic.

"You didn't have to do that," I say to my mother. My throat's gone tight. My parents do not shop outside of buying things for the teahouse. "I can just start being better about fixing Shire's bag."

"You can do that and save this for later, then. I think Shire would say the print suits you." Her smile says the worry she has carried for me since I was eight and made magic explode is starting to change.

I pick up the bag. Red silk flows. "I think she'd say that, too."

The smog finally begins to lift at noon, and I leave the teahouse, telling my parents I'm late for work. Through my mask, the air still tastes too strongly of exhaust, and there's an odd yellow light to the sky, but otherwise the earth has righted itself once more from us casting banished magic. I finish adjusting my new starter bag over my shoulder and start walking, making sure I'm easily seen.

I'm careful to stay within the sector, and especially within the blocks closest to the teahouse. It's where Jihen has always found me, and where he most expects me to be. But I have never *wanted* to be tracked down by him before. And today, he has something I need instead of the other way around. I need him to find me.

I don't think about Cormac tailing me because he's gone—unless I find a way to free him from Earl Kingston of the Tobacco Sector, I might never see him again. His higher-ups know what case he's been working on, so his disappearance will eventually lead them to me.

Jihen finds me in thirty minutes. I glimpse his black suit and white sneakers out of the corner of my eye and pretend I don't see him. I turn into an alley that cuts a block in half, both of its sides lined with back doorways, knowing he'll follow. I duck into one of them and wait for him to pass. Nerves turn my pulse fast and my hands are clenched into fists.

He walks past, his sneakers the whitest things in the world against the damp gray stones of the alley. He's glancing around as he moves, wondering where I've gone.

"Jihen," I call out.

He turns to face me, and approaches. His expression is annoyed. "I've been looking for you. I have another request, a casting one." His fingers reach out to grab my upper arm.

I cast around the small rock I'm already holding in my palm, the starter that sits in the center of the spell star I drew as he walked by.

A nine-pointed star and a bone spell.

Jihen's body locks up mid-step. My magic, holding still his legs and arms.

His face contorts. Amazement comes first—*Aza, have we not*

worked together so well until now?—then fury—*you'll be answering to Saint Willow for this!*

Good.

"What are you doing?" Jihen's voice is a slither of a hiss.

"I need you to bring me to a gatherer of magic."

His surprise is real. Real enough that he forgets to try to hide it. "What are you talking about?"

Pressure that is the headache from casting the bone spell begins to grow behind my eyes. I swallow thickly and force myself to look through it. "Gatherers, the ones who put together old man-made spells. They work for Saint Willow, for your gang."

His muscles work in his neck as he strains to move. "I have no idea—"

"I have a lot more rock starters in my bag, Jihen. I can break every bone in your body right here, one by one." It's more a bluff than not—I don't want to use more magic because I don't want more pain. And I can't forget that I no longer have healing meds. "So take me there, now."

He sneers, but it doesn't hide the confusion in his eyes. "*Now* your family's teahouse will suffer. *Now* you can be scared for your parents."

It clicks. He really doesn't know. Saint Willow has kept this from him. Jihen might be blood, but distant blood, and only good enough to squeeze marks from small family-run businesses. No wonder Jihen keeps Diego and his discovery of the tournament for his own secrets—they are his way of rising up past his current situation.

Family, always complicating things.

"Then bring me to Saint Willow," I say.

More surprise, and just as real. Casters know to stay out of the gang's way, and that means following the rules and lying low. "Why would I do that?"

I take another rock from my bag. I don't want to do it—already there are unsheathed knives clashing around inside my skull, and I have to fight tonight—but I'm too close now.

I draw, cast.

Jihen's baby finger snaps.

There's a gurgle of a scream low in his throat.

"Because he'll be able to tell me how to find it. So will you take me to him, or do we need to keep doing this?" Daggers are swinging around with the knives now, and I feel each and every one of their points.

"Stop," he says. "I'll take you. But you're going to see—whatever you've been hearing about these gatherers is wrong. There's no such thing. And now I'll be paying a visit to your family's teahouse."

"Do that and I'll tell your boss not just about your secret of Diego but about the entire tournament." Jihen's already told me he's keeping its existence from Saint Willow. And obviously Finch never said what he was using his gathered spell for, or Saint Willow would already know about the tournament through him. "What do you think is going to happen once Saint Willow knows? He'll take it away from you. It'll be his, just like the Tea Sector is his."

Jihen's lips work. Like he's reasoning silently to himself and still can't keep from mouthing the words. How Saint Willow would react learning that Jihen has kept something from him.

"Fine." Jihen flexes his arms, my bone spell now wearing off, and cradles his broken pinky. His glare is resentful and touched with still-stunned betrayal. "Let's go."

We turn out of the alley and walk down the street. Two minutes later, a fire truck blasts by, its sirens wailing. Jihen doesn't make the connection. But *I* do. As the sound of the siren fades, I try not to think about what part of the world my magic just broke, killed, destroyed.

FORTY-ONE

Saint Willow's headquarters are on the south side of the sector, right at the edge of the city. As Jihen drives, I get the occasional glimpse of the pink woods beyond, land cast hundreds of years ago to always grow trees that pretty shade.

The south part of the sector is heavy in supply shops and corporate offices. But just when I think I'm going to have to cast again to make Jihen turn back—which I really don't want to do with no healing meds—he pulls up to a tiny building and cuts the engine.

The place looks closed, a run-down, thin rectangle of dusty brick and dirty glass. The front window has its blinds pulled, and the door is just solid wood. Only the small sign with faded red block printing that's nailed above the door tells me what this place is: DIM SUM.

"Don't talk to anyone in there until I say you can," Jihen says. "You wouldn't be the first caster who thinks they're special enough to approach us only to not walk away again."

He gets out of the car.

I do the same, pretending that fear hasn't collected into a lump of ice that's sitting in my stomach. I follow him to the door, slipping off my mask and tucking it into my back pocket. "You're telling me a dim sum restaurant is Saint Willow's headquarters."

"It is today. Maybe it won't be this time next year, or maybe it won't be tomorrow."

He pulls open the door. Dim amber lighting, the tinkling of an old piano, and fragrant smoke waft out, symbols of a family legacy even older than that of Wu Teas. I step in behind Jihen.

The walls are papered over in gold, and the carpet is deep red with yellow lotus flowers. Five round black wooden tables with matching chairs are crowded into the room. Someone's playing the piano at the far end of the restaurant, their shoulders arched over the keys as notes are plunked into existence. The air is thick enough with smoke that I think of last night's smog, and a thin gray haze turns the already low lighting even lower. Different scents come: perfume, cigarettes, tea, smoked meat.

A woman and two men are seated at the table in the middle.

Jihen heads over and I stay near. My heart is pumping too close to the surface of my chest, wanting to leap out. I stare at the two guys and try to guess which one is Saint Willow. The one with the sleeves of his white business shirt casually rolled up as he drinks tea around the cigarette hanging from his mouth? Or the one still in his jacket and tie, tea and a bowl of rice at his elbow as he lays down a card on the pile on the table. They're playing War. The woman sits between them, dressed in green silk and reading a book, tea also in front of her.

All three glance up to watch as we approach.

It's the woman Jihen speaks to.

"Saint, this is Aza Wu. Her family runs Wu Teas. They're one of the families I've been collecting honor marks from on your behalf."

This is Saint Willow. A woman. My mind spins back to past conversations, trying to see how I missed this, why I assumed the leader of a gang would have to be a man. Jihen himself contributed to it, never correcting me. I guess even Jihen knows about mystery adding power.

Saint Willow slowly sets her book down on the table and her eyes lock on mine. They are darker than mine, and even harder to read than Embry's. Reflex makes me want to look away, but I sense that would be a mistake, so I just stare back.

"And why is she here?" Her voice is as soft as the silk of her blouse, hiding how she's made of steel. Her glossy black hair tumbles down to her waist.

"She . . . needs to know how to find a gatherer of magic."

I watch her eyes as Jihen says this—they don't change at all. Her gaze still on mine, she says, "Luna and Seb, mind going to the kitchen and seeing if they need any help?"

The two guys get up and walk away.

"Sit down, Jihen," she says as soon as they are gone from the room. Her tone is light but Jihen being in trouble is obvious. I slowly exhale as he pulls out a chair and Saint Willow turns her eyes on her cousin. "*Why* again have you brought her here?"

"She needs a gatherer," Jihen says. "I told her there's no such thing."

"So she just asked nicely?"

His mouth flaps. He doesn't want to admit I gave him no choice. More, he doesn't want to reveal I'm a caster of full magic. It would mean the loss of a toy.

"I cast full magic on him and made him bring me," I say to Saint Willow. In the background, piano notes rise into the air, heavy and somber.

Jihen glares at me, and I remember I wasn't supposed to talk until he said it was okay.

"It doesn't matter anyway because there's no such person," he says. "Or I would have known about them."

But Saint Willow isn't listening. Her eyes have come back to me. Now I *can* read them, and I shiver at the gleam of hunger there for my magic. It reminds me of the hunger Finch has for the Guild, something stoked by his *hate* of magic.

She gestures to a chair. *Sit.*

I do.

"Aza Wu," she says, "of *the* Wu Teas, your family's name once recognized by royals. Did you know at one point, more people in the world drank Wu Teas than every other brand combined? Incredible."

I can't tell if she meant for me to feel the barbs in that. "That was a long time ago."

"My ancestors once helped *your* ancestors settle here, hundreds of years ago. And now here we are, meeting each other, descendants of those ancestors. I'm the one who's had to assign a squeezer to get your family to pay what is owed mine, yet *you're* the one who's a caster of full magic."

"I'm here to make a deal with you," I say before she can get another dig in. "Bring me to a gatherer, wipe my family's debt, and I'll work for you as a caster."

Jihen sits up. He shoots me an indignant look and his mouth flaps open again. But then he snaps it shut. He can't reveal I already promised to be his caster because that would be admitting he's kept me a secret. And he's probably heard the story about Milo

Kingston and the Sturgeon River, about how it was family who put him in there.

Saint Willow's gleam of hunger sharpens. "Why do you want to find a gatherer?"

Now Jihen gives her a hurt look. "So they're really a thing? Why didn't you tell me, Saint?"

Irritation crosses the gang leader's face as she looks at her cousin. "You know what you need to know to do your job for this family."

The piano notes change, become lively and quick.

Saint Willow turns back to me. Her smile is elegant. "Cast full magic right now and we can talk."

"What do you want me to do?" I ask.

"Something to convince me you're not wasting my time."

I draw, grab one of the chopsticks still laid over the bowl of rice, and cast.

Heat flows through the lotus-printed carpet and into my shoes, up into my hands, and into my mind. I gather the red cloud that forms in there and direct it toward Jihen. I make the muscles of his legs move so that he's forced to stand.

He glares at me, scowls. "Stop it, Aza."

I push my magic and he jerks backward. His chair crashes to the ground. I make Jihen's legs start walking toward the kitchen. He's fighting me—his motions are awkward, uneven, his steps more shuffles—but still I push.

"Aza!" He starts swearing in Chinese. His face is red, sweating. "Don't think you won't pay—!"

He disappears into the kitchen, I let the magic slip away, and pain swamps. It's a massive punch to the middle, a wave of invisible gnashing teeth that I feel everywhere.

Saint Willow sits back and watches me grimace.

"Tell me," she says, "why a gatherer?"

"I want to buy a gathered spell," I say, my jaw clenched.

"What for?"

"It has nothing to do with you."

She frowns. "How did you know to come find me to ask?"

"You don't need to know that, either." The piano is still playing. I don't recognize the melody. Back to somber notes anyway. "So do we have a deal?"

"It's not that simple. The caster who finds these spells has developed the ability to pull together lost magic. It's no easy task, and these spells are not for just anyone to buy. Not even casters of full magic."

There's a note of dismissal in her voice—of near boredom—and whether she means it or not, desperation still chills me. What if she decides she's heard enough and forces me to leave? Then what?

"I guess you're right," I say, making sure to sigh a bit. "If you have access to those kinds of casters—to actual gatherers—why would you even need just a caster of full magic like me working for you?"

It's a huge risk, my pretending to not care if I leave empty-handed. But knowing what I know of Saint Willow, I think there's something she hates even more than suspecting her time is being wasted. And that's letting an easy opportunity slip away.

The elegant smile returns. That predatory gleam to own. "Ah, but gatherers can only do that—gather together the magic needed to re-create gathered spells. I still need a caster of full magic to cast those spells, as well as to cast more common ones."

"So maybe I'm the one here with something to offer, and not you." I widen my eyes just the slightest. "Not that I blame you for wanting to feel close to full magic by spelling gathered spells. Not if it's the only way."

Her smile tightens. "And yet, who has come to who, and why?"

She has me there. The pianist is still playing, though more quietly now. It's the only way I can tell the minutes are passing. With the covered windows, low lamplight, and curls of smoke that hang suspended in the air, late evening never leaves this room.

"Do we have a deal, then?" I ask again. Oliver pops into my head, but I push him away—simply considering a gathered spell isn't breaking my promise. But then it's Embry, wishing me luck, and Piper, telling me to prove she's picked a winner, and Kylin, making a face as she talks about cheating, and their faces are harder to push away.

Saint Willow nods, as authoritative as Embry can be. "We have a deal *except* for erasing your family's debt of honor marks. That is family business that goes much deeper than either one of us. You and your magic are just for me. You cast as I request, and I'll get you to a gatherer."

I nod back. "But no more visits to the teahouse. Leave my parents out of this." Disappointment claws, but I'm also not surprised. "So where is a gatherer?"

"Nima," she calls out, "will you come over here, please?"

The piano falls silent. The pianist stands up and heads over. It's a girl about the same age as me, and as soon as our gazes meet, I know she's an Ivor.

The color of her eyes is orange.

I rub mine, wondering if I'm seeing wrong.

"No, Nima really does have orange eyes," Saint Willow says, sounding amused. "She wears contacts when necessary, otherwise Scouts would have found her by now. Also, she is mine, which is another reason why she hasn't been found yet."

Mine. Like Nima is her pet. Like the way some Scouts keep Ivors as pets. Doesn't she own me just the same now?

"Aza, this is Nima," she says. "My gatherer of magic. Nima, this is Aza, and she would like to buy a spell from us."

Nima frowns as she comes to stand by the table. She's wearing a necklace of midnight-blue beads. Her orange eyes scan my face. "I don't know if you can handle a gathered spell."

I bristle. "Can you get me what I need?"

"That depends, what kind of spell do you—?"

Not here, I make my eyes flash.

Her orange ones slide just the slightest bit in the direction of Saint Willow before sliding back, and I can tell she understands I have secrets. But how could she not, considering what she does?

"Nine p.m.," she says, "the lounge at the Tea Chest Hotel."

FORTY-TWO

I head home, my walk stiff and careful.

Luna and Seb said Jihen had stalked off somewhere from the restaurant kitchen to sulk, and so after I was done with Nima, I left the dim sum restaurant by foot. I didn't mind not having Jihen drive me back. I was spared from him yelling at me for deserting him and bringing my magic over to Saint Willow, his whining about his broken finger and about his cousin keeping secrets from him. It left me time to wonder how I could escape Saint Willow just like Diego did, without leaving my parents in danger. I pictured all the ways Earl Kingston and his men were likely promising careless Cormac pain if he didn't give them information he didn't have.

I think about gathered spells and the match tonight and how I might fight.

I think of the ways I want Finch punished and how I might be willing to pay.

Can you ever be sure you're using magic and it's not using you?

I'm about to cross the street when I see a group of Scouts on the far corner. There are three of them, and they're preparing to rehang a display cage from a nearby lamppost. It's the changing of the Ivors, that time of the week when display casters are switched up.

Not wanting to get close, I stay on my side of the street to pass. I tug my mask up higher over my nose. Fear is the cold sweat that pops up all over me as I keep walking, not wanting to look at the Scouts but having to all the same, the way prey does as it's slipping past a predator. Only the most experienced and strongest of Scouts get to do the changing of the Ivors. Cormac is a Scout, but he's a Scout in the way a flower's thorns start out soft, still to be hardened with time.

Two of the Scouts climb up on stepladders to lift the cage up to the lamppost, while the third stays on the sidewalk, keeping watch over the milling crowd of curious people. His face tilts upward as he says something to one of the other Scouts and shock makes me stumble.

Embry.

The sight of his teal eyes is unmistakable.

What? How? *Why?*

The crowd jostling its way past makes me realize I'm just standing and staring. So I start walking again, still trying to understand. The world is back to being off-kilter.

What does it mean when a caster of full magic is also an undercover Scout? More, when he's a member of the most powerful group of casters *and* a Scout? I made up that story for Cormac about cops going undercover and how full magic casters were involved because I never thought anything like it could be true.

But I should have known better, because secrets—they surround me.

Rudy and Shire. Oliver and Finch. The tournament and how it only half exists, its own secrets of gatherers and gathered spells held within it. Full magic *itself* is a secret, buried away even as we keep casting. I can touch my casting arm and know it's real, but what is real when you're always having to hide?

Soon enough I'm nearly back home. Last night I didn't worry about Jihen and Cormac because of the smog. This time, I don't worry because Jihen's still off licking his wounds, and Cormac's probably being threatened with a burial in the empty vastness of the blighted lands right this minute.

Back in the teahouse, I set my alarm to wake up in time for dinner and go to sleep, wanting to heal.

The Tea Chest is in the central area of the Tea Sector, so not that far from the teahouse. It's one of the city's oldest boutique hotels, its concrete frame surviving quake after quake and somehow staying mostly intact. People flock to experience its themed rooms—the decor of each inspired by a kind of tea—the Marquess Blue room is gray and cream velvets, the Sparrow satins in shades of cinnamon and apples. There's even a Wu Teas room, which is as yellow as ever, the color of royalty.

I forgot there was a piano in the lounge of the Tea Chest. Or maybe I just never noticed. But now, walking through the lobby, there is the plunking of keys and I follow them.

Nima's there, playing. It's another song that I don't know. There are about a dozen people scattered around the sunken couches, a couple more at the bar. We're on the ground floor, and the window reflects back the lamps of the lounge. There's no view to miss anyway, just the side of the building next door, the smoggy gray night sky.

She looks up as soon as I walk in—she's been expecting me. She's wearing blue contacts. I cross the room, wondering if she has different colors, depending on the occasion.

She slides over on the bench even as her fingers never leave the keys. *Sit.*

I sit down beside her, stiff.

"So tell me," she says, "what spell do you want?" The melody is slow and liquid, hiding our conversation from the others in the lounge.

I only hesitate for a second.

"I want to take someone's magic away," I say.

"That's a pricey spell."

"What will it cost me?"

She keeps playing. "*Your* magic."

A chill rolls throughout me. Instinctively I pull my casting arm close. "Magic for magic."

She nods. "Is that acceptable to you?"

Yes. No. Both words stick in my throat. Shire wouldn't want me to, but she's gone and I'm still here, hating how Finch took her away. Is this how Oliver felt when he was told the price of being a brother? Love but also hate?

Finally I nod, and that tiny dark pit that's in my chest stirs.

"Then listen," she says softly. "Not a star, but a spiral, twenty revolutions, no more, no less. And the appropriate starter, of course, there on the music rack."

A midnight-blue bead sits on the piano where sheet music might sit. Nima wore a necklace of them just hours ago.

I pick up the gathered spell starter. "It's plastic."

"It's *essence*. Ether. Or the most tangible forms of such intangibles anyway, collected and re-formed."

Ghosts of spells lying around, waiting to be picked up again, spells that need twisted magic.

I close my fist around the bead.

"But I've already told Saint Willow I'll be her caster," I say, suddenly realizing. The relief of an escape would be bigger, but my mind is too full of the immediate—this ugly magic now in my hand, the tournament tonight.

"The price of the spell is the price of the spell." Nima switches up the song, picks a more fast-tempo one. "I'll tell her myself."

There's a note of satisfaction in her voice, but her profile remains unchanging.

"You don't want me working for her," I say, confused. "Why?"

"Do you think you're the first full magic caster she's found and had work for her? While she runs them into the ground, who do you think is there, trying to keep her under control?" Nima's fingers fly over the keys. "So that the world doesn't explode?"

I think of Saint Willow's face when I told her I was a caster of full magic. The gleam of hunger in her eyes, equal to Finch's for the Guild. Finch, who terrifies me.

"I'm doing you a favor." Nima turns her concealed eyes my way. "I wasn't always an Ivor, you know."

I grab a train out to the Electronics Sector. It's east of Tea, on the opposite end of Lotusland. The ride takes thirty minutes and I spend each and every one of them full of doubt. My casting arm twinges—phantom pain, as though my magic is already gone. How much will my arm hurt when my magic is gone for real? Does Oliver's still?

Neon lights are shining in through the train windows, and I get off at the stop closest to the address. But Discord Road is still blocks away, and so I walk down streets lit up with electronic signs and ads. Night is when the sector comes to life—a lot of its shops and arcades don't even open until after dusk—and the sidewalks are crowded. Everyone's loud. The blue bead hangs from the key holder at my hip, ether at its heaviest.

When I arrive at the abandoned warehouse, I cast open the lock using my key starter. There's a thrum in my bones, the echo of it a deep ache. Slipping off my mask, I pull open the door and step inside.

The warehouse is vast, the size of a ball field, one with a concrete floor, concrete walls, and a soaring ceiling instead of a sky. The front half of the space is still and quiet, while the second half is full of spectators and light and noise.

I walk toward this second half, and it's like walking into the surf and still trying to breathe. The tournament reaches for me and pulls me in and then I'm in the light.

Noise crashes into and rings off the warehouse walls; there's the sound of my name, of Finch's, of applause and anticipation and a hunger for a world that is long dead. The overhead orbs glow, cast into life by the Guild one more time for the year. I hear Hugo and Jack yelling for final bets, either Finch or me, because there can only be one winner.

Can a heart pound so hard that it bursts? My veins feel too full, magic threatening to spill over. Fear is the taste of silver in my mouth.

And yet, that tiny dark pit in my chest begins to bloom.

I weave my way to the starter counter—there is no registration area now that it's the final—and wait there for Piper. I know she's probably looking for me, too, the fighter she's put her faith in and shouldn't have.

She's here the next minute. Her silk gown tonight is gold, her purse a wisp of brighter yellow.

"Rudy." Her voice is brusque even as her expression stays soft. "I'm sorry about what happened." *Finch is a merciless fighter, his hunger for victory boundless.* "How are you feeling about tonight?"

I take a deep breath. "I'm ready." *I'm sorry.*

She helps me tie on my ribbon, gives me my marks, wishes me luck. Her words are a blur, but I smell her perfume, and in there she is my mother, she is my father, she is Shire and Rudy and Kylin.

The bell rings, the crowd rushes out like the tide, and then it's just Finch and me in the middle of the light.

His eyes are as cold as the Pacifik in winter. His arm is no longer broken, healed by magic. Another spell, some other cost, a pattern that can never be broken.

Chants of our names fill the air and I shiver. I'm half looking for Oliver in the crowd when the world changes.

FORTY-THREE

I'm standing on the slope of a long, jagged embankment. It's angled steeply enough that I have to brace my feet against the ground to keep from slipping backward. The sky's a dome of blue-gray clouds and it's pouring rain, sheets of it hard on my skin, turning the ground into mud.

The mud's blue.

It smells of flowers.

I look down.

A hundred feet below, there's a line of shrub, then a wide rushing river. Its surface churns and foams as rain crashes inward.

Dread is trickling into my stomach and there's Finch, twenty feet away from me, also standing with his feet braced in the embankment. I adjust mine even as I notice him because I'm already starting to slip.

That river down below . . .

"These are the Painter's Cliffs of ancient Rinra."

Embry's voice comes from the top of the embankment. I peer upward as rain streams into my eyes.

He stands there, the crowd a thick mass of color behind him, their cheers drowned out by the rain. His suit is black tonight, the shoulders gone even darker with wet, his tie the green of jade. The world is so overly blue that it tints his eyes, changes them from teal to cerulean.

Nima's orange Ivored eyes flash across my mind. I think of Embry telling me about his bones of glass. And then of Embry out there in the sector, his teal eyes as bright as gems as he helped keep an Ivor entrapped.

Who are you, Embry of the Guild of Now?

"The blue of the ground comes from a form of lichen that grows just beneath the surface," he says. Once more, his low voice shouldn't be heard above the rain, but it is. He crouches down and picks up blue mud, examines it in his palm. "These cliffs are gone now, and this lichen extinct. But when both existed fifteen hundred years ago, painters would travel here and try to capture the sensation of the sky melting into the ground, of the ground climbing into the sky. Some succeeded, and some failed, but each painted with passion.

"Just as it was when the greats fought here. And many greats did, because to win in this place was to conquer another world. Where natural phenomena stopped making sense. Where the sky was the ground and vice versa."

The Guild, their *essence* all around, casts.

A creaking sound comes from deep inside the earth.

The blue-gray sky shifts, begins to tilt over. As if the horizon has become some kind of stationary axis and the outer surface of the world wants to spin around it.

My stomach spins with it, and I clench my teeth against a wave of dizziness.

The *ground* shifts now, right along with the sky. It follows the same tilt, so now the sphere of the earth is spinning around the axis of the horizon.

I fall to a crouch as the ground keeps curving around. Some of it's instinct, getting low—if you're going to fall, you won't have as far to go—and some of it's because I'm still dizzy.

But getting low to the ground is useless here. If the earth is going to be completely upended, I'm going to fall no matter what.

Everyone's going to fall.

The entire river's going to spill out.

And then we're all upside down.

But my shoes stay planted in the mud. Only the heaviness of my blood slowly collecting in my head tells me I'm upside down. *Or that somehow I'm still standing up even as I'm hanging from my feet from the top of the world, an impossible that is now somehow possible.* The scents of wet soil and flowers—*lichen*—waft up my nose.

"Let me guess," I call out over the creaking of the earth, over the thunder of the rain, "the sky's the ground and the ground's the sky?"

Embry nods. "Gravity still applies, of course." He gestures upward toward the blue ground. "Mostly."

Finch points down at how the blue mud is making him slip. "It's 'mostly' no help with the rain."

The rain that is now coming from below us, landing at our feet above our heads.

Still crouched, I slip another inch. My mouth goes dry as I glance at the river. I look at the thin line of trees that's keeping the embankment from sliding into the water.

There's that, at least.

It might have to be everything.

All my thoughts have become snarled. Everything I know to be true is now half a lie. There's gravity, but I can still stand upside down. The sky's moving and it's not the clouds making it look that way.

Embry's smile is wry as the world spins back to upright again. "Do you think the greats ever said, let's wait for better weather before we fight?"

"Maybe." I flick mud off one of my shoes with my hand. "If they didn't want to end up in the river."

"And if they embraced the river as part of the fight?"

I glare up at him. I can't shake the dizziness from this world he's built. And I'm still tired of water from yesterday's ancient baths.

"So here we are," he says. "There are two of you left, but only one will win. You can choose how you fight, or you can let your magic choose for you, but either way, only one fighter will remain standing. Good luck."

Embry gets up, turns around, and disappears behind the lip of the embankment.

FORTY-FOUR

There's still mud in my palm from cleaning off my shoe.

It's a head start, two seconds.

I flick my eyes toward Finch. My heart's a knot in my chest. Head start or not, I should cast a shield spell. That's always first.

But.

I draw, close my palm, and cast.

Heat blasts upward from the mud at my feet and drives itself into my veins.

The red cloud of my magic blooms wide in my mind. I make it tear the mud thin beneath his feet. His green eyes flash and then his feet plunge through and he disappears into the hole in the ground.

The crowd roars. It's the sound of my name. The noise is rapturous, washing over me just as the rain does. *Rudy.*

My bones are on fire from the casting, like magic's spilled over and is burning them up. I ignore the pain. I claw at more mud. I draw and cast again, and my magic piles mud on top of Finch. I flick blue from my fingers, draw on my palm, and yank a gold starter from the key holder. I cast again, and my magic directs Finch's blood to thin. My head is starting to pound; the pain in my bones is now agony.

The crowd bellows. My pulse flies, and magic is red and hot and seething through my veins. Agony sharpens, goes as pointed as knives.

I drop the used-up gold coin into the mud. My fingers are trembling, wet with rain. I lift them to the blue bead starter.

I have just seconds. He's bleeding and hurt, buried down there beneath the mud. But I know he's also already fumbling for his starters, preparing to cast on me. But still, I can take his magic right now, and it'll all be over.

Or, I *don't* take his magic.

I can just eliminate him. Just cast a simple spell to close his airway, or one to change his oxygen into something else. Either way, he'll be knocked out and I win.

I could even kill him, except for a pact. That damn pact.

But ... this is my chance to hurt him beyond anything else. Without magic he'll never fight again, just like he'll never be voted into the Guild. Embry can no longer cast, but he Ivored after he was already in.

And the price is only *me*.

Indecision is a roar in my mind. I don't know, but I need to *be sure*—

An invisible kick knocks me backward. I hit the ground with a thud, and the pounding that's still in my head soars.

I look over. Finch is free. Through the rain and mud there are flashes of his face, of his green eyes as he pushes at mud. There's the sound of the crowd—bellows of his name, heightened cheering, *Fiiiiinch!*—and applause for his magic strokes the land of the Painter's Cliffs, just the way a brush does over canvas.

Dizziness swarms. Desperation to get away is suddenly

everything—*I can't think!*—and panic licks as hot as fire. My hand shakes as I rip off a silver starter. I draw and cast—shield.

The air around me bends, shapes over me as a protective cocoon. When the cost of the spell comes, it's a series of internal punches that leaves me out of breath, even more panicked.

Not good. I have to slow down. The effects of casting are piling up fast.

I begin to struggle up the embankment, the blood pooling in my face as the world keeps spinning. The ground up there can't be sloped, right? There the mud would only be messy instead of dangerous. If I can just get on even ground, the Guild can wheel the earth around as much as they want and I won't be so dizzy. If I can just get up there, I'll know if I'm ready to cast my magic away. My shoes slide in blue mud and the river below (above?) foams. Rain lashes downward.

I twist, looking for Finch, reaching for a starter, when every muscle in my body freezes. My shield shatters. Pain slaps at me all over, and I utter a single useless gasp as I fall face-first into the mud.

Blue liquid stings my nose, gets shoved into my mouth. A vise cranks tight around my chest and breathing becomes impossible.

The vise cranks harder.

Then I'm flung sideways across the ground, an invisible force reverberating along my ribs as I skid along. Blue mud curls over me in a wave and splashes back down, coating me. To one side, the river flashes, a wild stream of yet more blue.

For a second, nothing makes sense. Finch can kill me right here. But instead he just casts his magic as an impact spell. A strong one, but that's it. Not even enough to knock me out.

Suddenly I get it.

He's going for show tonight. He wants to win the Guild over completely, the Guild who loves style and skill most of all.

I'm whooping for breath, coughing mud and rain from my mouth. I drag myself to my knees. Finch approaches, a figure against all the blue that has become the world. The ground shifts, and my stomach swims.

Is this it, then? The end?

"You almost killed me," he says. His voice is stunned, almost betrayed. But he's also short of breath, holding his side. Casting is costing him, too.

I turn my head and look him in the eye. He's a sight, covered in blood where he's not blue.

"You should have never asked Oliver to give up his magic for you," I say.

Another impact spell, and I'm blasted along the embankment. No, *down* the embankment—toward the rushing river. Pain explodes in my head. I try to grab for some kind of hold as mud grinds into my teeth, but my hands only flail at the ground. The thin line of shrub is ten feet away, maybe even less.

I get to my knees again. There's mud in my palm. I draw, I cast. No reaction. Finch didn't feel it all. He's cast a shield spell.

"He owed me," he says. "And he didn't deserve to keep it. He let it ruin everything."

The cost of casting skewers through me anyway, a thin line of agony that makes me utter a low scream even as I scrabble for mud and cast again. Fresh heat fills my legs, chest, hands, mind. I form the red cloud of my magic into a knife and push it into Finch's head.

He stumbles, shield spell shattered.

"How's the headache?" My words are thick and clotted with mud, strained with fatigue and pain. My own headache blooms, and I nearly retch. A wild buzzing grows in my ears, promising me the end is so close, that I'm nearly there. I grab at more mud and cast again, suddenly unable to care how much it hurts, I just want him done.

Finch grabs the sides of his head even as agony slams into mine. Through tearing eyes, I watch him bend over and gag. His fingers clutch at the ground.

I stagger to my feet. The earth turns and turns, past the halfway mark now. Blood begins to leave my face and head—we're no longer standing upside down. The sky twirls and nausea rises. I smell soil and flowers and fire, the scent of cast magic. Rain pelts.

An invisible fist meets the side of my face. I rocket back. My shoes skid through mud as I struggle for balance, my arms out. My hands smash into branches, leaves—I'm at the line of scrub. The river just behind it roars for me.

I reach for the key holder at my hip. I grab the blue bead and tear it free. Magic pounds in my veins, is a red fire in my mind, and I see Shire in there, helping me build it. Rudy and Kylin are in there, too, stoking the flames.

My eyes fill.

Am I really doing this?

Magic for revenge?

Finch is gasping. His gaze is all ice. "I could have let her live, you know that? But magic isn't fair. It never will be."

Then he casts around the mud in his hand.

A blow. It sends me slamming back into the trees. I scream as a branch pierces my shoulder from behind. Fire lights up my casting arm, turns into a white ball of agony to spear my brain.

The roar of the crowd swells.

I keep my arm across my chest, pinned there because to hold it any other way hurts even worse. The tip of the branch sticks out of my front like a giant thorn. The world and the sky and my stomach all spin.

Finch is bent over, struggling to stand up.

"She begged," he says. "She knew what I meant to do and she *begged.*"

Rage floods, as hot as pain, as hot as magic.

I drag my other arm up. Still clutching the blue bead in my fist, I begin to draw on the palm of my casting arm with a shaking finger.

He staggers close now, his face pale with pain, still half-bent with it. He grins at me and reaches down for a final scoop of blue. The rain pours down.

"I just laughed," he says.

The tiny dark pit in my chest explodes.

I drop the blue bead into the middle of my spell spiral.

I cast.

FORTY-FIVE

Magic is never lost.

Lost is too gentle a word.

We never lose it the way we might lose a mark, or a shirt, or a word that stays forever on the edge of our lips.

Magic, it turns out, is *taken*.

It is ripped from us like the removal of an organ, the cutting out of a tongue. It is the excising of the part of our brains that stands for language, one of the ways we communicate. In Oliver's mind I saw it as a burned-down tree, because magic is fire, alive and vital and hot. All that's left afterward is ruin.

I watch Finch change, a part of who he is extinguished like the snuffing out of a candle. A shadow crosses him the way a cloud would have once crossed the hidden sun, and for a long second, every part of him *dims*. When he comes back, the only thing he has left of his magic is the memory of it, a smoking tree in the landscape of his life.

I'll never see it for myself, because my magic is also gone. As I watched it be taken from Finch, he watched it be taken from me, and now his eyes are dull with disbelief. The pain I see in them now is phantom pain, the pain of absence.

"No." He backs away from me. He falls into the mud. "No."

I nod. But I can't talk because I'm crying. I clutch my torn shoulder and drop the used-up blue bead into the mud. I'm standing in the middle of a woven world, but the absence of my magic is as fresh as a new wound, raw and stinging and undeniable.

And magic is as real as blood, but is as formless as a dream—where is mine now? Taken, but to where? A burst nebulous cloud now in invisible pieces, lying around waiting to be collected, re-formed, *reused*?

I shudder. To have someone else take my magic, to take it for their own—

The noise of the crowd begins to break through the shock of what I've done. The earth and sky continue to spin, the river to foam—so much blue, forever in motion. There's no sign of Embry to signal the end of a round.

Because the tournament isn't over, I realize. The Guild still needs a clear-cut winner. One of us has to be knocked out by the other, or one of us has to bow out on our own. Or one of us can die.

Except neither of us are full magic casters anymore. Or casters at all. We are without magic, and neither of us belongs here. The crowd has no idea they are cheering for no ones.

Before I can do anything, Finch—he's still sitting in the mud—slams his hand three times into the blue mud.

Bow-out.

From his expression, he's as stunned by his surrender as I am. And there's delusion there, too. As though he won't believe his magic is really gone. That if the round will just end, he will feel his power again. That this tournament might be over for him, but he'll fight again in the next.

The crowd is yelling, shouting. The sound of it is like thunder rolling across the Painter's Cliffs. I hear my name, the word *champion* added to it.

Embry emerges from among all the casters. He stands in front and peers down at us from the top of the embankment. Everyone falls quiet until there's only the sound of the rain, of the rushing river. Finch is still sitting and staring down at the ground; I'm standing near him, my hand cradling my bad arm. Both of us are blue, soaking wet, miserable. The idea of pretending to celebrate makes me even dizzier.

"Everyone—the champion of this year's Tournament of Casters." Embry's smile is reserved, which it usually is anyway. But his eyes are too aware as they go from me to Finch, and I wonder if he knows. Then his gaze meets mine and I know he does. "Thank you for fighting as legends do, Rudy."

I am no legend.

I've won, but I am empty.

I shut my eyes and around me the world changes back.

From within the dark, the spinning of the earth and sky comes to a halt. The rain stops and the river goes still. The scents of wet soil and blue lichen fade away. And when I open my eyes again, the Painter's Cliffs of ancient Rinra are gone, and once more it's just the abandoned warehouse in the Electronics Sector.

Everyone's moving again. Casters start making their way toward the bets counter, wanting to pick up their winnings. I'm half-aware of Finch getting to his feet and slinking away. For a second I wonder if I should call him back—but to say what? Everything I could ever think to say—about Shire, about Kylin and Oliver—was all wrapped up in what I took from him, and the price I paid to make him listen. There's nothing left.

I follow him for two steps anyway, thinking about Oliver, wondering if there's anything left for me to say to *him*. How maybe I need to see him once more to know.

There shouldn't be. We only ever had Finch between us. And I think for the next little while, Finch is going to need his brother again. More than he's wanted to for years.

It's Piper who I see first. She's grinning as she walks over, so pleased with me for what I've done. *There's still honor in doing what must be done to survive, even if such ways are ugly.*

She shakes her head at seeing my shoulder. The branch is gone now, a part of the Guild's fighting ring. But the hole it left remains.

She takes a small swatch of silk from her purse, draws, and casts. Her leftover magic works on my shoulder, turns the throb that's deep inside into something closer to a thrum.

My eyes sting from the gesture. "Thanks. It feels better."

"Oh, we both know it's nothing, but it'll help a bit until you recover enough to cast again."

She doesn't know how that's impossible. Some wounds never close, never get filled back up. This is just the new tiny dark pit that's replaced the first.

"I'll go pick up your winnings from the bets counter now," she says, "and after the Guild gets you your two hundred thousand marks, we'll meet again for *my* cut of those winnings, Aza." Then she's gone in a swirl of gold silk.

The Guild.

Embry.

I search the crowd for signs of him, needing him for something that has nothing to do with collecting my marks. Dizziness creeps back as my eyes scan the room for bright teal ones. I shouldn't have waited this long, but—

"Rudy."

It's Oliver, headed toward me, coming out of the milling crowd.

It shouldn't matter that I'm seeing him again—that he cares enough to not blow my cover by calling me Rudy still, even though the tournament is officially over—but it does, and my pulse skips.

One look at him and I know he knows. Finch must have already found him and told him, then. Or maybe Oliver only had to glance at Finch to know. To recognize the touching down of that second of *dim* across his brother's face and know what it means.

"Why?" His voice is low, shattered. "You don't know what it's like . . ."

"Because." I take a shaky breath and push back my wet hair. "I wanted Finch to hurt for what he did, and I knew this would hurt him the most. He could never be in the Guild, Oliver."

"Okay, but . . . *your* magic—"

"It was the cost. I paid it because I was willing to. And that's not really the same thing as wanting to, is it?"

His gaze burns and then he nods. I know his parents are now on his mind, and it's not what I meant, but I can't change how he thinks about that. I don't think it's for me to change.

"You know where to find me," he says, "if you ever need me." *To ask what it's been like. To be able to hold the world in your hand and then have it all be gone.* "I won't mind."

"Thanks. Maybe. I'm—do you know Wu Teas? It's in the Tea Sector. So that's where I'll be. Aza Wu. If you need."

He nods and turns away to find his brother. And my heart is still pounding as I go to search for Embry again.

Only because he's been looking for me as well does he let himself be found. He might never be able to cast again, but it's undeniable that he still has some kind of power. Beneath all the damage, some of that magic still remains in his veins, forever a part of him.

He crosses the warehouse, an envelope in his hand. He hands it over when we meet.

"Is it still Rudy, or is it Aza now?"

I take the envelope. It's thick with marks, both paper and coin. After Piper gets her cut, the rest will pay off our standing debt of honor marks to Saint Willow's family. I stuff the envelope into my starter bag that will no longer need to hold starters. "It's Aza."

"I'm unsure if I should congratulate you on winning the tournament, given the cost."

The back of my neck gets hot. "It's okay, I really don't want you to."

"You really didn't need a gathered spell to win." He sounds almost disappointed in me. As though how I fought in the first three rounds made him think I was capable of more. Something different, something better. And maybe I was. But now I'll never know.

"It wasn't about winning the tournament as much as it was about taking something from Finch."

"Because of your sister and what happened last year."

I stare at him, startled. "You remember Shire?"

"Yes. You look a lot like her, so I suspected. And I'm sorry she lost the way she did, just as I'm sorry Finch won the way *he* did.

We discouraged him from using a gathered spell during this tournament, after what happened last year. If that was the only way he could win, there would be no place for him in the Guild."

So Embry knew about Finch using a gathered spell.

I want to be mad about his being okay with this, about how the tournament runs on cruelty as much as it does on magic—and maybe cruelty and magic are two sides of the same coin anyway, just like magic and pain are. He would just say the same thing—how full magic has always had its cost.

"I would have voted against him becoming a member, Aza," Embry continues, "if and when a spot opened up. Most of the Guild would have."

I don't know what to say, or what he might want to hear from me. But I'm too tired to be mad, and I can't care anymore. I no longer have anything to do with the Guild or with the tournament or anything like that, now that I have no more magic. But Embry's power—for that I can't leave just yet.

So I only nod. And given what I need to ask, maybe it's for the best that Embry is now hoping for my understanding.

"I need your help." I speak quietly enough so none of the casters still close by will hear me. "I know you're a Scout. I saw you today, helping hang up a display cage."

For a second he's shocked enough that he can't speak. Then he simply says, "Oh?"

"I'm not—I don't want to ask *why* you're one—"

I take a half step back as his teal eyes go sharp enough to cut. I no longer have reason to be scared of any Scout, but a lifetime of built-in fear is hard to get over so fast.

"You mean why would a caster who helps runs a tournament based on full magic also be hunting down its casters and locking up his own kind?"

The back of my neck gets hot again. "Yes."

"For every Ivor I keep locked away and every caster I chase down, there are many more I'm able to overlook. We pay in many different ways for our magic, Aza."

I nod. He's right. We've always been paying. And I might not be a caster anymore, but that's just another way I paid for magic.

"What do you need my help for?" he asks.

"It's about another Scout, actually. He's new."

"Who?"

"His name is Cormac. He's been watching me."

"You've no more magic, Aza." Embry's tone is almost gentle. "He'll be assigned elsewhere soon enough."

I shake my head. "It's not that—not anymore anyway. But I had to get him in trouble with one of the city's gangs in order to escape."

"And?"

"Do you think you can go rescue him?"

I walk home, shoulder singing, all my bones and muscles throbbing and bruised. There's mud in my hair that's already smeared my smog mask, and the noise of the crowd lingers in my ears just as the scent of fifteen-hundred-year-old blue lichen won't fully leave my nose. The streets stay sleeping and dark as I head west, from the Electronics Sector through to Government and then on to Tea. It's not raining but the air still feels damp because it's Lotusland.

My mind is on none of these. It's too busy wrapped up around itself, around the memory of magic, when magic had been who I was and how I'm no longer that. So where does that leave me? Who can I be now, if not a caster?

When I get to the block of the teahouse, I don't bother turning the corner to get to the back alley. Now that Jihen no longer has any hold over me and Cormac is stuck with Earl Kingston until Embry finds him tomorrow, there's no reason to have to worry about being seen.

But I didn't know someone else was still looking.

Waiting at the front entrance of the teahouse are Saint Willow and Nima.

Fear prickles along my entire body.

Nima must have told Saint Willow about my magic. I knew she would, but not when. And now the gang leader is here to make me pay.

"What are you doing here?" My voice is thin in the night. It's starting to rain again, a fine drizzle that sits on my hair.

Saint Willow smiles her elegant smile. "I just wanted to make sure you haven't forgotten about our deal, Aza. I lead you to a gatherer and you cast magic for me."

I glance at Nima, confused. But her eyes don't meet mine, and she's pale around her mask.

"The price of the spell," I say to Saint Willow, "was my magic. I can't cast for you even if I wanted to."

She opens her hand.

In her palm is a blue bead.

More fear comes, full lashes of it.

"I don't need another spell," I say. "Spells are useless to me without magic."

"Nima, explain, please," Saint Willow says.

"This starter is for full magic," Nima says. "You'll have magic again."

My stomach lurches. "That's impossible. You can't get your magic back once it's been taken. It . . . *scatters*. Like—"

Ether. *Essence.*

"It's true, it's likely not *your* magic," Nima says. "But it's still *full* magic, collected and re-formed. It'll be nearly the same thing."

"Consider yourself lucky, Aza." Saint Willow's smile gains a bitter edge. "Full magic can only be given to those who once held it."

I stare at them both, at the bead in Saint Willow's palm that lets her pretend. She longs so badly for full magic of her own, but having access to someone else's must do.

"I can't." I feel sick. To have *someone else* in your veins, in your *mind*—

Except I'd be a caster again. Under someone else's control, and with a stranger's magic, but . . .

"You can because we have a deal," Saint Willow says. "Don't make your parents pay for a cost that you agreed to."

We pay in many different ways for our magic, Aza.

I nod, numb inside now as cold rain falls.

The price, always to be paid.

"Okay," I say.

ACKNOWLEDGMENTS

All my thanks to these amazing and wonderful people:

My agent, Victoria Marini, who is a constant inspiration and forever encouraging. I'm so very fortunate to have you in my corner.

My editor, Matt Ringler, for trusting me with this story about a girl and underground magic. Your enthusiasm and sharp eye have been everything. Plus, you're pretty cool.

The fantastic team at Scholastic who helped make *Caster* into a real book—Shelly Romero, Maeve Norton, David Levithan, Josh Berlowitz, Rachel Feld, Shannon Pender, Tracy van Straaten, Amy Goppert, Alexis Lassiter, Yesenia Corporan, Celia Lee, the Scholastic Emerging Leaders, the IreadYA team, and the book clubs and book fairs.

For always being just an email or text away, great writer friends Ellen Oh, Gail Villanueva, Jess Huang, and Sangu Mandanna.

And, of course, family. Especially Jesse, Matthew, Gillian, Wendy, Mom, and Dad. Lots of love to all of you.

Aza's story continues in
Spell Starter: A Caster Novel.
Turn the page for a sneak peek!

ONE

The inside of the bar is dim. Shapes of black-painted furniture form within the gloom, and there's the dull glow of unpolished fixtures. A thick gray haze fills the air, and through my mask comes the bitter hint of tobacco. I smell more, something sweeter—the scent of tea, floral and grasslike.

Chang's is inside the Tea Sector but located close enough to Tobacco that people come to the tea bar also looking to smoke. Customers hover around bar tables crowded with ceramic teacups and metal ashtrays. Classical music plays over the speakers, strains of violin strings mixing with the low rumbles of conversation.

A headache teases, and unease blooms, even though I haven't cast yet.

I know I'll have to. The inevitability hangs over me, as dense and suffocating as the smoke in the bar. It's how I'm paying for what I've done.

Old Chang knows of my parents, just like they know of him. Both his bar and Wu Teas are longtime establishments, though each place started out differently. My family's legacy traces back to the days of serving the finest teas to empresses and emperors, while the Chang business goes back to the pubs and taverns of old, to being barkeep to the staff of that same royalty.

When tea slowly fell out of favor, the entire sector fell into decline—it didn't matter who your clients once were. Wu Teas would still be just one more struggling business if I hadn't paid off all we owed.

On the surface, it's easy to see how finally being freed of debt gave us the chance to prosper again.

But Chang's fallen behind on his payments owed to my boss.

Saint Willow is why I'm here.

I let the front door of the tea bar fall shut. The sliver of pale sunlight disappears, returning the place to near darkness. The few faces that turn to look at Jihen and me glance away, already bored. In the back corner of the room is a shadowed pocket of an entrance—the owner's office.

Guilt comes at having to do this, anger at being cornered. Shame, too. It wasn't long ago that my parents were in the same position as old Chang is now.

Beside me, Jihen slicks back his waxed black hair and tries to look cool. "Shall we?"

I shake my head. "I can do Chang alone. Just wait for me over by the bar."

He gives me his greasy smile. "Now, Aza, you know the rules. Saint wants me to keep a close eye on you. Make sure you do what you need to do."

"I'm the caster, not you. And I know business owners. You don't."

My tone is rude and I don't care, just as Jihen's is smug and he doesn't care. We still hate each other, even though we both work for Saint Willow. We're stuck here together.

Jihen is the gang leader's cousin, and while family goes deep when it comes to gang membership in Lotusland, she hasn't been happy with him lately. I'm not here by choice, either, and he knows it. Right now, his only enjoyment comes from my being a prisoner who is forced to cast magic on demand.

"Doesn't matter what you know," he says, "if you don't do as ordered."

"Getting the marks is the order."

"Getting the marks *using magic* is the order. Saint wants you back to casting the way you always have, and that's it." A snort of derision. "Ai-ya, squeezing without magic—anyone can do that. Even little beebees—screaming brats that they are—can find a way to do that. Even *I* can do that."

I nearly laugh at his clumsy attempt to insult me. Still, my pulse starts to race, dread growing along with it.

"I need more time." I'm still trying to get used to casting again. I'm beginning to doubt it'll ever happen.

"Yeah? Well, you're not getting more time. This is your third squeeze, and while I might be your babysitter, Saint says no more hand-holding. I've got my orders, same as you." With a leer, Jihen slides his eyes over my face. "So go in there and cast. And do it right."

Not wrong like my first squeeze job, when I refused to use magic at all. Facing Saint Willow's fury afterward left me cold for hours.

Or the second, when I *did* use magic, and half the roof fell in on us. At least the place was nearly empty, as most businesses in Tea tend to be nowadays.

Getting full magic back—magic that's not mine—hasn't been easy. In the month that I've been living with this strange and ugly new power in my blood, casting's become unpredictable. Every spell feels different. All the control I've ever learned is gone. Nothing but chaos remains, like I'm at war with myself.

Casting pain starts early. Sometimes while I'm still casting, making it harder to focus.

Recovery takes longer—bruises that stay until morning, headaches that follow me into dreams.

And then there's the planet. I'm destroying it more than ever.

The consequences are adding up, and I can't help but wonder about payment. The same way I can't ever forget how I got magic back, no matter how much I try to avoid the memory. I do my best to keep those thoughts away, but I still keep tripping over them. Falling in. Getting stuck in the past until I can crawl back out.

I'm silent for too long, and Jihen gives an impatient tsk. "Listen, beauty—"

"You really need to stop calling me that."

"Then cast." He clucks his tongue. The complaint takes shape on his lips: mah-fung. *High maintenance.*

I make myself nod. He's right—I *will* have to cast. What I did was terrible, but it's also in the past. Unchangeable and useless to me. Saint Willow is my now, wholly in my face and with the power to make everything even worse.

Still, it doesn't mean Jihen gets to watch again.

"I'll use magic," I say, "just like I'm supposed to. But I'm going in alone. It'll be easier for Chang to accept my coming here with less witnesses."

Jihen knows I'm talking about saving face. He might be a gang member, but he's also Chinese, same as me, same as Chang. Some concepts can't be shaken. They run deeper and longer than any gang rule.

He grunts, considering, and lets his gaze drift toward the bowls of free nuts on the bar. He takes out a shred of tree bark from the chest pocket of his suit jacket and casts. Just leftover magic, the only kind he—and most people of the world—can cast. The kind where there's no pain as a cost, no damage to the earth.

The shoulders of his black suit lift and neaten themselves, the lapels pressing smooth. His pinkie curls as he flicks away the depleted starter of the bark. It's the finger I broke last month, now completely better.

I had to cast with the new magic to heal it. There was a brief second when I hoped it would all go wrong—more pain for Jihen. It ended up hurting me more than him, but it was still worth it, since it finally got Jihen to stop whining about how I broke it in the first place.

"Make it fast," he says now as he heads toward the food. "We can't return to headquarters empty-handed."

I turn away, too, annoyed at his use of the word *we*. It's his way of telling himself he's still necessary and more than just my babysitter. I even go along with it when Jihen reports back the overblown version of his effectiveness. What do I care? Saint Willow is never going to let me go. Having me at her disposal is how she gets to control full magic.

It's why she forced this unknown magic inside me.

Why I'm no longer sure who I am.

TWO

I weave my way around tables until I get to the shadowed corridor in the back. A long drape of dark red silk is the door.

A guy—tall, run-of-the-mill face, arms too thick for the size of the rest of his body—steps out from the side to block my way. "Sorry, staff only."

"Saint Willow business," I say, meeting his suspicious gaze.

He hesitates.

Don't make me cast to get through, I think. My starter bag lies across my chest, messenger style, and I place a hand on it. *Please. It'll hurt me, but it will also hurt you, and this place. More than you can imagine.*

His eyes move to my starter bag. There's another beat of hesitation, and then he steps back.

I shove the silk drape to the side and walk inside.

It's a closet of an office. The walls are covered in faded blue paper where they aren't obscured by wooden shelving stuffed with yellowing file folders. The air is just as hazy in here, but the smoke comes from the burning of cheap incense and nothing else. Its scent is heavy enough that I know my smog mask will carry it all day. I'd have taken it off by now since I'm indoors, but this is a squeeze job—staying undercover helps keep this version of myself separate. She's a version of Aza I don't really want to know.

The song from out in the bar is also playing in here—straining violins.

Chang is seated at a tiny table at the other end of the room. His expression is grim, a blend of terror and resignation. He must be expecting this—he can't have lived in Lotusland this long to not know the price for holding out. The question, then, isn't why Chang is late—no reason has ever mattered—but what I'm going to have to do to make him pay.

He's older than I thought.

Cold sweat rises on my skin. Elderly people are frail, particularly vulnerable. They make my current level of control over magic—magic that won't listen to how I want to cast—especially dangerous.

"Who are you?" Chang's voice is a creak through the haze, snapping my mind free.

I take three steps until I'm standing in front of him. The incense burner is right on the desk, and the smell rising off it makes my head swim. "Your honor marks for the bar. I'm here to remind you that this month's payment is now overdue. Do you have them for me right here, today, to bring back to Saint Willow?"

He looks me up and down. Scorn dawns. It forms a shine in his eyes, sharp and cunning. "*You* work for Saint Willow? How old are you?"

"I don't want to hurt you, but I will if I have to. Do you understand? If you don't have the marks right now, we'll have no choice but to look into stronger . . . techniques of encouraging you to pay. Trust me, you don't want that—"

Chang laughs. "Trust you? *You?*" He makes a show of trying to peer around me. "Bring me someone who is important, and then I'll negotiate."

I sigh through my teeth, wishing I had some way of avoiding this and knowing I don't. I take out a slip of paper from my starter bag. I draw a six-pointed star on my palm and place the paper in its middle.

"What are you doing?" Chang is sputtering. "Stop wasting my time and leave before I call the police."

A flesh spell, I decide; a relatively small one to suit his aged heart, and hopefully it won't leave the gang with a body to bury.

"Saint Willow doesn't negotiate," I say quietly, "and neither do I."

I take a deep breath and imagine the red cloud of magic in my brain into a shape. A fist around a ripe peach.

I cast.

The floor trembles. Heat spears its way from my feet to my chest. From my arms to my hands. It builds in my one palm. Loose papers drift from the shelves as the incense burner clatters and jumps along the top of the desk.

A deep whooshing sound fills my ears. The taste of the incense smoke in my mouth intensifies, is acrid on the back of my tongue.

I imagine the pictured fist clenching just the slightest bit. The ripe fruit denting from the pressure.

And Chang's throat denting the same way.

The shop owner grabs at his neck, trying to breathe. His gaze is full of panic and disbelief. Shock at what I can do. *Full magic, here? Cast on me, and by you?*

My own shock is nearly as great. The correct spells aren't guaranteed anymore when I cast. Relief swirls in.

"I told you I didn't want to hurt you," I say even as casting pain finds me, thin whispers of it ebbing from behind my eyes, swallowing up any relief that had just been there. I let the depleted starter—the paper gone lacy and ash-like—fall to the floor. "Are you ready to talk about your late honor marks now?"

He nods so vigorously I'm worried about his old heart again.

I wait for the spell to run out. Six points—it should be any second now, and then he'll be fine.

Except the spell keeps going. My palm starts *burning*, the sensation so hot it's nearly icy. The pain behind my eyes bursts into a wide web of agony. Invisible fingers wrap around my skull and dig in.

Chang shoves his chair back—it leaves a gouge in the wall—and staggers to his feet. He begins clawing at his throat. The skin of his face goes mottled, the red parts as dark as the silk drape door to this office. His panic is frenzied. He knows he is dying.

No. No! Not again!

I lean across the desk, hands out. I want to shake him, like such a gesture is anything but useless.

The magic inside me, this terrible power I've accepted—I hate it the way I hate Saint Willow. I hate myself for ever thinking I deserved to have full magic again just because I once did. When I gave it away in the first place just to keep from ever having to use it to serve her.

Chang's eyes are wild and searching, full of his desperation to breathe. His fingers dig in harder.

Then he begins to cough, finally drawing in huge, hoarse gulps of air. I stumble back, the pain behind my eyes thickening even as the pounding of my pulse deep in my ears begins to let up. Over the sound system, the violins have morphed into flutes. I can't place the song, only that it's cheery and light and the very opposite of this moment.

"You"—he's gasping—"*you*—"

He stares at me like any second I might choose to cast once more. His terror is back, all signs of resignation and scorn gone.

"I do not have the honor marks," he wheezes. "Business has not been very good. But I'll get them soon, I promise."

"Promises of soon aren't enough." I struggle to speak above a whisper, pain coming in slaps. "Until you find a way to pay, the bar's going to start failing health inspections, your suppliers will cancel contracts, loyal customers will stop coming. Do you understand?"

Chang nods, still pale in his cheeks. At least he's not dying anymore.

"This place has a safe." I hold out my hand. The stink of incense turns my stomach and makes the room tilt again. "Empty it of marks. And if there's nothing inside, then empty your wallet."

"My wallet? But—" Everything about him seems to shrink. "There's nothing else."

"And still it's Saint Willow's," I say. Then I make myself shrug, as though I don't care at all about his situation. But really, I understand everything about his despair. Saint Willow has me trapped by my family's legacy, too.

Wu Teas, always within her reach if I don't obey.

THREE

I shove marks into my jacket pocket as I leave the office. It's nowhere near what he owes, even though I left his safe and wallet bare.

Jihen's at the bar, his ugly white sneakers so bright they practically glow against the beaten wood floor. He swigs back the last of his drink as I approach through the haze of tobacco smoke.

"Tea's not bad at this place," he says. "No Wu blend, of course"—he winks, and my stomach rolls again—"but good enough. Ho-goh mo yeh."

Better than nothing.

"Let's go," I say. Everything is louder out here because of my headache. Laughter is the pounding of drums. Flutes turn into chain saws. I long to sleep off the effect of casting, but that's going to have to wait until after we're done reporting back to headquarters.

Jihen burps. "Got the marks?"

"Everything he could give me."

"You going to throw up in my car?" His smirk spreads across his face, oily and wide. "Ha-mai beng? Feeling sick? Maybe you should walk."

I wonder just how bad I appear and how much of my pain shows. Jihen looks for my weaknesses the way treasure hunters collect clues.

"I'm fine." I push down the pain, hiding it out of sight. Away from him. "Never been better."

"Well, beauty, one thing's for sure—you cast magic after all, just the way you were supposed to. So I won't have to rat you out, at least." He gestures across the bar, where workers are sweeping up glass and ceramic. A huge crack has split the back wall, tearing a shelf loose and sending cups and dishes crashing to the floor. It was only luck that no one was sitting close enough to get hit.

I leave the bar first.

It's a ten-minute drive from just past the midway mark of the sector down to headquarters on its south side.

I sleep for all of it, burying my headache beneath oblivion. I wake up only when Jihen's already out of the car and slamming the driver's door shut.

I slowly sit up, blinking. The pain is better, I tell myself.

Sunlight is thin and bright, the smog that's layered into it a long-time staple of the world. Beneath it, Lotusland is as wet and gray as ever, the city's dampness one more thing no one living here ever escapes for long. It's summer, but it'll probably be raining by tonight.

We're parked outside a dim sum restaurant. It looks as vacant as it did the first time I saw it—covered windows, dusty and dingy brick, a faded sign above the front door.

No one would ever guess that the sector's powerful gang leader schemed and worked from within. Which I guess is probably the whole point.

Across the street are the pink woods. The scarlet trees lie along the bottom of Lotusland like the frill on a skirt. It's the part of Tea that forms the city's southern border.

The pink woods have been this way for over two hundred years. A permanent reminder of magic that was too powerful to harness, the scar of demanding too much.

A group of casters—full of magic but inexperienced, thinking of dares and of showing off—wished to make a mark of some kind. To bring beauty to a world that was falling apart all around them. They cast in unison, believing danger spread thin was nearly no danger at all. That they would be safe and live to tell a tale. Instead, none of them were, and the acres of trees have grown pink ever since. Their tale, told by trees.

That was also the year that a typhoon hit Ena Island and hundreds of people drowned.

One more way full magic made its mark.

I get out of the car and walk toward the restaurant. I don't bother knocking before I pull open the door. For better or worse, I'm part of Saint Willow's gang now, and who knocks before entering their workplace?

Only a month, and already everything inside is too familiar. The amber lighting, the gold-papered walls, the red-and-yellow lotus-print carpeting. The round black tables and matching chairs. Scents of tea and perfume and cooked rice. And live music—Nima, bent over the piano at the back of the restaurant.

The two of us don't speak. Not since the powerful gatherer of dark spells helped Saint Willow put magic back into me. Not since that night, a night I'll never be able to shake myself free from. Or deserve to.

Nima lifts her head as I step inside. Her orange eyes are a bright flash in the dim. They're the only visible proof she's an Ivor, her full magic turned useless because casting again would break her apart. This fact matters little to Saint Willow. Nima is still her gatherer, a tool for her to use as she likes. What does she care if Nima can't cast as long as she still has the ability to collect the world's most dangerous spells?

Nima drops her gaze and goes back to playing the piano.

The gang leader is seated at the center table.

Saint Willow is elegant and striking the way cats are elegant and striking right before they attack, all liquid lines and sleek muscles. Her clothing is the same, always silks and satins, each piece perfectly draped over her body. She's flipping through a glossy magazine, appearing bored.

Sitting on either side of her are her two most trusted men, Luna and Seb. I tell them apart by how Luna hates jackets and wears his white sleeves rolled up, while Seb is never without a full suit and tie. They're playing cards, their favored hobby between jobs.

I'm sure they know Jihen would kill to take over for them, just as I'm sure they aren't worried about it. Jihen isn't clever enough to figure out how to do it without Saint Willow knowing who's behind it. And Jihen would hardly be her first choice to replace them, anyway.

She flips a page in the magazine and asks coolly, "Any problems with Chang?"

Meaning, did I squeeze using magic? It's her only concern, making sure I'm at my most powerful so she will be.

I stay by the front door and wait for Jihen to begin the report. He loves every chance to prove his importance to his powerful cousin.

He pulls out a chair and sits himself down across the table from her. "No problems at all. Ho hoong-yee. Simple as anything. And Aza squeezed just as you asked."

Saint Willow nods. "I'd like to speak to Aza, please."

She still hasn't looked up from her magazine. But the order is more than clear, so I head over, slowly tugging my mask down over my chin. Fresh trepidation tingles along my spine—what might she want to hear from me that Jihen can't tell her?

My headache from Chang's bar comes roaring back. The slow song Nima's playing isn't helping, every single note heavy and thunderous, pounding away just as my head does.

Jihen settles into his chair, seeming unconcerned. "Sure, and she can tell you how before she cast, it was me who—"

"I want to speak to her alone."

Still yet to say a word, Luna and Seb simply lay down their cards, get to their feet, and leave for the kitchen.

Jihen stares as they go, his mouth flapping in surprise. "But we still have to give you our full report. About Chang."

"Aza can give it to me." Saint Willow's long black hair is wound into a bun, and it sits on the top of her head like a crown. "And on your way out, go ask Xu in the kitchen to bring out some tea."

Another flap of Jihen's mouth, and he pushes back his chair. He gives me an ominous glare as he gets up, as though I have any say over the sector's gang leader.

As soon as he's gone, Saint Willow shuts the magazine, lays it down on the table, and watches me.

Piano notes continue to sound, breaking up the silence. Saint Willow never asks Nima to leave, the way pet owners will keep their pets alongside them regardless of who else is around.

"Sit down."

I slip into the seat Jihen just left and place Chang's marks on the table in front of her. Unease stirs—from the headache that's a fist inside my skull, from the taste of the words I have to say next. My report on Chang will be nothing but an echo of Jihen's own report on *my* family. Back when he was squeezing *us* for marks we didn't have, staking out the teahouse, and threatening all of us. That person is me now.

Saint Willow's eyes pin me into place. "Did you *cast* on Chang?"

I give her a harsh smile. "Did I have a choice?"

Her expression stays elegant, her eyes unmoving. "Good."

"I still don't see why I have to do it every time. When it's not necessary."

"It's always necessary."

The memory of old Chang clawing for breath. I push it away.

"The shop owner was old," I say. "I could have found another way to get the marks." One without pain. "You're wasting my casting."

A single crease appears between Saint Willow's brows before being entirely smoothed away an instant later. She leans back in her seat, as casually observant as before.

I was meant to miss it. This extra careful shuffling of her thoughts, like caution slipping through.

But it's also like she's holding something back, and I shudder.

Whatever she wants to talk to me about, it's not some routine squeeze job. And she knows I won't like it.